WHEN
STARS
GO OUT

RANSOM GREY

When Stars Go Out

DEFIANCE PRESS
& PUBLISHING

Printed in the United States

ISBN-13: 978-0-9987704-3-7 (Hard Cover)
ISBN-13: 978-0-9987704-7-5 (Paper Back)
ISBN-13: 978-0-9987704-5-1 (eBook)

Library of Congress Control Number: 2017963495

Published by Defiance Press & Publishing, LLC

Editing by Janet Musick
Cover design by Nathaniel Dasco
Interior designed by Deborah Stocco

Distributed by Midpoint Trade Books

WHEN
STARS
GO OUT

RANSOM GREY

DEFIANCE PRESS
& PUBLISHING

With deepest gratitude to my family for helping me all along the way, and especially to Jennifer who taught me the love of writing.

Chapter I

February. The drab mantel of winter buried the Virginia terrain in snowless folds of gray and brown. Leafless forests huddled beneath the frozen skies, and a heavy layer of dead sod smothered the hills, frowning up at the sullen clouds. The bleak landscape below did nothing to improve Reed's spirits. He hated coming to the East Coast. He'd fought hard to stay in southern California, where he'd been born and raised. But what could he do against national laws? There were hundreds of thousands of other teens in the same plight, deported from their homes and shipped all over the country.

Shipped, Reed thought bitterly, *like cattle for market.*

He stared out the small window as the plane circled down toward the airfield. The government had declared America's youth should experience the world for themselves—get out on their own and gain some life experience. "Re-education" and "conditioning" were the terms they used. Their solution: seizing anyone between fourteen and twenty and relocating them across the country. "The Great Reorganization Operation," or GRO, they called it—the greatest federal program of the century.

As the plane taxied into position at the gate, Reed prepared to disembark. He jammed his flat brim down further over his jet-black hair and felt under the seat for his carry-on. Thanks to his sudden departure, he hadn't been able to bring much luggage with him; the light windbreaker lying on the seat was his only jacket. One glance out the window told him it would not be enough. He shouldered his bag and joined the other passengers exiting the plane. A handful were deportees like him, with the same red tag pinned on their shirts. None of them seemed any older than him. All were silent, many with their eyes fixed on the navy carpet as they moved up the aisle.

As they filed out of the jet way into the terminal, they were met by a group of men waiting on either side of the gate. Clad in black suits and long black overcoats, they did not look like typical airport staff. Their clean-shaven faces were expressionless as they scanned each passing traveler. One of them spotted Reed and motioned him out of the crowd with a jerk of his thumb. Reed's jaw tightened, and he narrowed his blue eyes. He obeyed but stood with his arms crossed among the growing group of teens behind the men, scowling.

When the last passenger filed past, the agents turned without a word and, motioning the group of perhaps twenty young people to follow, strode through the airport. They reached the lobby before one of the men, tall with a shaved head and a bundle of papers under his arm, held up his hand to stop.

"Welcome to Virginia, your new place of residence," he said curtly. "You have the privilege of being part of a great program for your country. You are here to further your education and ensure the quality of your development with the help of the governing authorities. Here you will be able to think clearly for yourselves and re-start your lives under careful guidance and watchful supervision."

It was a canned speech and, though his words sounded nice enough, something in the man's tone and the way he studied them sent a shiver down Reed's spine. The rest of the group was silent.

"A bus is waiting outside to convey you to your accommodations. You have been assigned work positions in the city; an official will give you further information later tonight." With that, he stepped aside and waved them out the door.

Outside, the cold and damp hit them in full force. Reed shivered and zipped his jacket up to his throat. As the man had said, a large blue bus waited at the curb, hissing and rumbling in the drizzle. The officer had not mentioned the uniformed guards posted on either side of its door. One by one, the deportees slipped between the motionless figures and found seats along the narrow aisle. Once they were all aboard, the guards and officers climbed in, and the door slid shut. The bus jerked into motion, pulling away from the curb and onto the street. As it gained speed, the passengers settled back in the gray cloth seats; no one had mentioned how long the drive might be.

Reed ignored the boy next to him and stared out the window as his new home whizzed by. The view from the ground was even less inviting than from the air—a dull cityscape of dead landscaping and dripping buildings huddled under a leaden sky. He eyed the uninspiring strip centers, empty malls, and cheap restaurants, comparing them to the modern, bustling city he left behind. A mere handful of people scurried along the sidewalks, collars turned up against the wind.

The bus turned into a residential area where darkened neighborhoods and cheerless apartments replaced the stores and parking lots. The few people disappeared altogether. The Colonial brick buildings stared blankly at the passing bus with shade-drawn windows and dark doors. Reed thought of very different houses far away, bathed in balmy, Pacific breezes and sunshine. Home. He turned away from the window.

Out of the corner of his eye, Reed studied the young man next to him. He looked about eighteen, Reed's age, with close-cut blond hair and a thin, alert face. He stared straight ahead, arms folded across his chest. Reed eyed him for a minute before venturing in a low tone, "Hey, where're you from?"

"Missouri." The other boy spoke in a whisper without turning his face. "When you talk, don't look at me. The guards are watching. How 'bout you?"

"California. The name's Reed."

"I'm Hunter."

Silence. Reed counted the red diamonds in the carpet for a moment. "Do you know what they're going to do with us?"

Hunter shrugged slightly. "Give us a new start in life, supposedly. From what I've heard, we'll live in barracks and work in the city."

"Work?" Reed glanced toward the nearest guards. "What kind of work?"

Hunter shrugged again. "Depends on your grades in school, I think. Higher GPAs get jobs in offices and stores; the rest get the factories. 'Vocational education,' they call it. At least we get paid."

7

Reed felt a twinge of remorse for his own grades. But, before he could say anything else, the bus downshifted with a rocking shudder and began to slow. It had been climbing steeply and now crested a low hill. Glancing out the window, he saw the city spread below them in a large, flat valley. On his right, a group of buildings crowned the high ground. The bus stopped directly in front of them.

They were long, narrow buildings, red brick and three stories high. More than a dozen of them marched in straight lines that ran back from the road. Trees dotted the spaces between them, and a large bricked area was just visible in the center of the group. In the light of a summer's day, with leaves shading the green grass between the cement walkways, it would have been lovely, but the winter dusk was dismal as the weak light faded from the sky.

Reed eyed the buildings suspiciously. Though a few windows were lit, most were dark and empty, and not a soul could be seen. But then a man stepped out of the closest building and approached the transport. The tall agent from the airport got out to meet him and, after a brief conversation, handed him a packet of papers. The man leaned in through the open door, muttering to one of the guards.

"Unload!" bellowed the guard.

The passengers gathered their luggage and obeyed hurriedly. As Reed stumbled out of the warm bus, the chill struck him in the face again, cutting through his jacket and t-shirt. He clenched his teeth to keep them from chattering and tried to draw deeper into his jacket.

After the last teen climbed out, the agents reentered the bus, and the door slid shut. With a final hiss, the bus swayed into motion and roared out of sight. The huddle of teenagers stared after it. The man who remained drew himself up and cleared his throat.

"Welcome to the Dorms."

Here we go, thought Reed.

"I am Director Connors, superintendent over all the dorms and the residential director for Dorm One." He spoke in a deep, measured voice that snapped each word like a whip. "I will be assigning you to rooms; you will each have two roommates who are already here. Each dorm has its own residential director who lives in the building to maintain order and enforce rules. Those RDs answer to me, and you will answer to them."

He paced in front of them as he spoke, hands clasped behind him. "I am going to make a few things clear. First, Dorms One, Three, Four, Seven, Nine, Eleven, Fourteen, Sixteen, Nineteen, Twenty-One, Twenty-Three, and Twenty-Four are men's; Dorms Two, Five, Six, Eight, Ten, Twelve, Thirteen, Fifteen, Seventeen, Eighteen, Twenty, and Twenty-Two are women's. No one will *ever* enter a dorm of the opposite gender without permission. Ever. Is that clear?"

The man glared at the group as if to pound his words into their memories with his stare. They all nodded quickly.

"Second, a ten o'clock curfew is strictly enforced. If, for any reason, you must be out later, you will apply to your RDs for permission. They will explain further rules to you. Line up—two lines!—and I will give you your room assignments."

While Director Connors worked his way down the first row, Reed sized him up out of the corner of his eye. He appeared to be in his early forties and wore black-rimmed glasses that he peered over when scrutinizing one of the teens. He was tall and shaved bald, and his large hands dwarfed the pencil he held. He worked his way down the line, demanding each teen's name, checking their tags, and assigning room numbers. He reached Reed. "Name."

It was not a request. Reed felt his chin go up instinctively. "Reed." Venom packed the word. "That's two e's and a capital R, *sir*."

The eyes fixed on him over the glasses, piercing and ominous. Reed hadn't realized before how broad the director's shoulders were. For a dreadful second, the superintendent said nothing. Then he grabbed Reed's tag from his outstretched hand and checked his name off the list.

"Dorm Four, third floor, room 316. And I suggest you watch yourself *very carefully*." Raising his voice, he added, "That goes for all of you! We have our methods of discipline here." He threw the tag back at Reed with a parting glare and continued down the line. It was only then that Reed realized he was shaking all over, and it wasn't because of the cold.

When Director Connors reached the end of the second line, he snapped the file under his arm and wheeled on the group once more. "Proceed immediately to your assigned dorms. Your RDs are waiting for you." With that, he turned on his heel and stalked toward Dorm

One, the few unfortunates who had been assigned there following timidly behind. The rest scattered, looking at the painted numbers above the glass doors on each building for their assignments.

After trying two wrong dorms, Reed stopped in front of a building directly to the left of the bricked area, its long side running almost the full length of the paved yard. The door was on the front side, and on the glass panel above it was printed a large, white "4" with the word "Male" directly under it.

Suddenly, Reed felt very small and very cold. The gathering gloom of the strange place pressed down on him until the brick walls seemed to tower over him. This was to be his new home. He didn't know anyone, and he would be living with two strangers and an RD as terrifying as Director Connors. He swallowed and glanced back quickly over his shoulder. Several other boys had turned and were walking in his direction. Reed took a deep breath, opened the door, and entered Dorm Four.

Chapter 2

In front of him, a closed wooden door led to the first floor hall. To his left, two flights of metal staircase crisscrossed upward. Reed climbed them to the third floor. The wooden door at the top was propped open, and he peered through.

Before him, a hallway stretched for perhaps a hundred yards of white tile floor and beige concrete walls before ending in another door. Dozens more doors lined both walls. Down this hall, a man was walking, swinging a bunch of keys in one hand and a clipboard in the other. Reed liked him immediately. He looked to be in his mid-twenties, shorter than Reed, with coppery hair and a short, well-trimmed beard. He wore a navy hoodie and khaki cargo shorts. His face was friendly and his walk quick and confident as he whistled his way down the hall. When he saw Reed, he waved. "Hello!" he called. "Are you the new one?"

Reed shrugged. "I guess so."

The man reached the doorway and flipped back a few pages on his clipboard, scanning the pages. "Ah, here we go. Reed, from California? Pleasure to meet you. I'm Michael, your RD." He stuck out his hand. Reed shook it tentatively.

"It's not 'mister' or 'director' something?"

Michael chuckled. "Well, it's Mr. Ryan around Connors, but the rest of the time, just make it Michael." He winked. "I was just getting your bed ready. Come on, I'll show you your room."

Reed picked up his bag and followed Michael down the hall. The RD chatted all the way. "Everything's kinda empty right now since all the guys are still at work. They'll be back in half an hour, and you can meet your roommates."

Reed felt a surge of anxiety. "Um, who *are* my roommates?"

Michael pursed his lips in thought. "One is Reagan from Florida; the other's Riley from New Jersey. Reagan's kinda awesome, and Riley's pretty quiet, but I think you'll get along fantastically."

Reed hoped he was right. "So how many guys are on this hall?"

"Seventy-two now. You filled our last opening. You'll get to meet most of them during free time in the evenings."

"Will there be much free time?"

Michael didn't seem to notice the bitterness that crept into Reed's voice. "A fair amount. Most of the guys have to leave by seven-thirty in the morning and get back around five-thirty. Until ten is free time. Dinner's served in the cafeteria from six to eight."

"Oh. So what do they do with it?"

"Dinner? They eat it." Michael flashed a grin. "But if you mean the free time, it depends. When it's nice outside, they play games on the Square or go into town if they like walking. A few have laptops or game consoles, but most just hang out."

They reached room 316. Michael unlocked the door and threw it open. "Here it is!"

The room was large for a dorm room, perhaps twenty feet square. Like the hall, it was white tile and beige-painted concrete. A single window was opposite the door. There were three beds: a double bunk along the right wall and a loft with a desk underneath on the left. Two desks and chairs stood in the middle of the room. There was a nightstand by the window and a sink against the wall at the foot of the double bunk. Shelves on either side of the door reached three or four feet shy of the tall ceiling.

Reed entered and set his bag on the floor. Judging by the unmade covers, one of his roommates slept on the bunk over the desk and one on the bottom of the double bunk. The desks were cluttered with items, and a clock blinked on top of the nightstand.

Reed took off his cap and tossed it onto the top bunk. "I guess this is mine." He walked over to the window and looked out. Though it was beginning to grow dark, he could tell his window overlooked the bricked area, or the Square, as Michael called it. A leafless tree directly outside partially blocked his view, but he could make out a few people on the sidewalks. He turned back toward Michael, who stood watching him from the doorway.

"Come on," the RD said, "I'll show you around."

The tour was short. Michael showed him the bathroom, the fire exits (the same as the regular exits, but regulations are regulations), and the custodial closet where he could get soap, toothpaste, and other supplies. "Have to come get me, though," Michael said, jingling his keys. "It's locked. My door's outside on the right at the front of the dorm."

He took Reed back to the room and pointed out the general direction of the cafeteria from the window, down a slope on the opposite side of the dorm, invisible from their point of view. "We call it 'The Mushroom,' like the fungus," Michael informed him. "You'll see why in the morning. Breakfast is served from seven to eight. It's not home cooking, but be there early or the best stuff's all gone."

The door at the head of the stairs slammed, and footsteps echoed up the hall. "Ah! The guys are back. Stay here and get settled in; Reagan and Riley'll be here soon, and they can take you to supper and give you the extra room key." He shook Reed's hand again. "Nice to meet you. I hope you'll be comfortable here, but feel free to come see me if you need anything."

He turned to leave. Halfway through the door, he turned back. "Just remember, Director Connors is always watching. Try to behave." With a quick wink, he disappeared.

Reed stared at the closed door for a moment. Then, with a sigh, he turned and kicked his bag toward the closest dresser. "I guess I can start unpacking."

That was depressing. He was done in less than two minutes, and his allotted space seemed almost as empty as before. He'd have to work on his wardrobe when he got his first paycheck. "That's one good thing about all this," he grumbled. "At least I'll *get* paid."

With nothing else to do, he idled over to the window and looked out. The trickle of returning teens below had grown into a rush, and the Square was filled as they mingled to chat before scattering across the wet sidewalks to their dorms.

It was a larger crowd than Reed expected, at least two hundred strong with more coming and going all the time. It was like watching a human whirlpool: always shifting and never the same. Everyone below was so different, but here they were, dragged together from across the nation. Forced here, like Reed.

A burning anger shot through him. Why was he here? He should be back in California going to high school and hanging out at the beach with his friends, not living in a prison camp and working all day in a run-down factory. He pressed his fist into the cinderblock wall, ignoring the pain. A smoldering bitterness sparked inside him, building like a thunderhead flickering with stifled lightning. He wasn't even sure who to be angry at, but he was angry. He was very angry.

At the same time, another sensation crept over him: a strange eagerness. What a world! Rows of dorms, an entire city spread across the valley below—there was so much here, waiting for him. His heart beat a little faster. This was a chance to build a life for himself, to find a place in a new world order. He could do whatever he wanted to do, be whoever he wanted to be. He was swept with the sudden longing for more—more from this place, more from life. But, as quickly as it came, the spurt of eagerness sank back into the shadows. None of it mattered. He'd been dragged into this place against his will, and he hated everything about it.

The sound of doors opening and closing at either end of the hall had been incessant for the last few minutes. Voices and footsteps passed by the room. As Reed turned from the window, one of the doors opened again and a cheerful voice rang the entire length of the hall. "That's just girls, bro! Trust me, you just gotta know 'em."

The door shut. There was a quiet response Reed couldn't understand, but the cheerful voice laughed. The footsteps came nearer and, as they stopped in front of Reed's door, the first voice said blithely, "Well, to each his own. Just don't say I didn't try."

With the jingling of a key, the door was thrown open, and two boys entered. They stopped, obviously surprised to find a stranger in their room. The first was close to Reed's height, though perhaps slightly taller, with light hair. The second, coming in behind him, was shorter and thicker with dark hair and eyes.

For a second, they stared at Reed, and Reed stared back. None of them moved until the first boy recovered himself and smiled. "Well, well! Our new roommate finally showed up! I wish Michael had given us a heads up. Anyway, hi! My name's Reagan."

He stepped in and extended his hand. Reed shook it. "I'm Reed."

"Nice to meet you. This," he said, waving behind him, "is Riley. Sweet, so we're all Rs! He's from Jersey, and I'm a Florida man."

The shorter teen stepped forward and shook Reed's hand as Reagan went on. "We're just getting in from work. I see you've unpacked; been here long enough to get supper?"

Reed shook his head. "Michael said you guys would take me."

"You betcha. We were just headed that way." He tossed a small briefcase onto the loft bunk. "Come on! We can get to know each other on the way."

As they left the room and turned down the hall, Reagan began asking Reed about himself. He kept up a steady stream of questions as they exited the hall and clattered down the stairway. By the time they reached the first floor and pushed out the door into the darkening drizzle, his curiosity seemed satisfied, and Reed began to find out more about his roommates. Reagan was nineteen and had lived in Miami, Florida all his life. He and Riley had been roommates since they arrived in the first wave of deportees six months before.

"Six months?" Reed was shocked. He had no idea this had been going on so long.

Reagan shrugged. "Yup. You're one of the latest. I'm sure there's more coming, too."

Reed turned his attention to Riley. As Michael had said, the other boy was quiet, and the little Reed got out of him had to be pried out. Riley was eighteen; he had lived in Newark since he was twelve. Before that, his family had moved from Cleveland to Detroit and then from Detroit to New Jersey. That was all Reed could get out of him.

They had left the dorm by the back entrance and threaded their way through the rows of other dorms. Teens began to fill the sidewalks, pushing out of the buildings and turning in the same direction as Reed and his roommates, toward the dining hall. The Mushroom, a large, brick building with a matching covered porch, sat down a long slope behind the Dorms. Its matronly form presided over a huge parking lot dotted with wrought-iron light posts that already shone in the gathering gloom. Teenagers were everywhere, crowding the wet pavement and pushing in and out of the cafeteria's brightly lit glass doors.

As they worked their way down the crowded stairs, Reagan informed Reed over his shoulder, "Just so you know, we call these 'the North Stairs.' There's another set on the back side of the hill called 'the East Stairs'—somebody was real creative with the names—that comes out behind the Mushroom; nobody ever uses it, though."

Reed tucked the information away for future reference.

The crowd was thick on the sidewalk, with people going both directions, chatting and laughing despite the cold and wet. Reed shivered and hunched his shoulders as he pushed after his roommates. The drizzle trickled down his collar, and his jeans were damp. He was glad when they finally reached the protection of the porch and shoved through two sets of double doors into the warm interior. He shook the water out of his hair and looked around.

The place was enormous, filled with long tables and chairs like a college dining hall. It was already packed, and talk and laughter rose to the high ceiling of arched wooden beams. Three steps led down into the main part of the hall, sectioned off from the entrance by a wooden barrier filled with artificial plants. A counter manned by several women guarded the stairs, and a long line led up to it. Reed wondered how much supper was going to cost.

When it was their turn, Reagan and Riley held out some sort of ID cards for one of the women to scan with a hand-held device. Reed, a little hesitant, did the same with the red tag pinned to his shirt. The woman scanned it without a second glance and waved him through. He joined his roommates on the other side.

"That was easy. So it's free?"

"Absolutely." Reagan stuck his card back in his pocket. "They don't charge us for anything around here. Man, something smells amazing! Come on, I'm starved."

For his first meal in a place called "the Mushroom," Reed's supper was more pleasant than he expected. Reagan and Riley introduced him to their large group of friends and squeezed him in at a long table already jammed with teens talking and eating.

Reed quickly found that, even in such a large group of both boys and girls, Reagan was definitely the favorite. When he first sat down, cries of "Reagan!" went up and, for the rest of the meal, he was the center of attention. His popularity was no surprise. Reagan had a cool, nonchalant way about him. He was witty and fun with a lively laugh and quick smile. He was good-looking, too, with a fit figure; honey-blond hair; pearly, straight teeth; and a handsome face kissed by the Florida sun. Reed thought he looked like a model for a Caribbean travel brochure.

Riley, on the other hand, didn't attract the same kind of attention, socially or physically. He was exactly Reagan's opposite—short, dark hair; a thick, beefy build; and a plain, ordinary face. He preferred to sit back and watch the interaction at the table, saying little, but he, too, could be witty when he chose. Between the two of them, Reed was soon at ease and scarfed down his greasy burger and fries with relative enjoyment.

After dinner, when they had taken leave of the main group, the three roommates strolled out of the cafeteria into the cold night. Reagan stretched and yawned. "Boy, I think I'm turning in early tonight. That was the best supper I've had in about a week. What did you think of it, Reed?"

Reed shrugged, sliding his hands into the pockets of his windbreaker. "It was okay for cafeteria food."

"Well, it's not gourmet," agreed Reagan, "but you'll get used to it. You'll get used to all of it: staying here, working, and all that."

Reed didn't want to get used to it, but he said nothing. They walked in silence down the almost empty sidewalk, its wet surface glinting in the light of the street lamps.

Later that night, when the three were settled back in their room, Michael popped his head through their room door. "I see the 'Rocking Rs' have settled in nicely." He grinned. "Make sure you don't get too crazy in here now that there's three of you."

Reagan glanced up from his computer. "Yeah, dude. It's always a party in here."

Michael chuckled and beckoned to Reed. "Hey, the man's here who's supposed to get you an ID and assign your job. Come on; he's on the first floor." He accompanied Reed down the hall, explaining as they went. "This guy's supposed to take your picture for your ID card and give you a sheet with all the rules. Hopefully, you'll get your ID day after tomorrow. He'll also give you a print-out with your job info. Everybody's hired automatically when they get into the system."

When they reached the first floor, they found half a dozen other boys, all from the bus earlier, waiting in line. A short man with a black moustache stood each in turn against the wall for a picture before waving them on to another man, who took their information and handed them two sheets of paper. After Reed had his picture taken (more like a mug shot, he thought), the other man handed him a job description and a rule sheet. "I assume you know the basic rules already?" he demanded.

Reed felt his jaw tighten, but he nodded. "Yeah, Mi..." He caught himself. "My RD explained them to me."

The man turned away, and Michael shot Reed a wink behind his back.

After the pictures had been taken and each boy grilled to satisfaction, the short man made an announcement. "You will receive your cards tomorrow night here at the same time. They will be used for admittance into the dining hall, your place of work, and eventually into your dorms. If you have any questions, talk to your RDs." With that, he wheeled and marched down the hall, the other man close behind.

"What does he mean by 'eventually the dorms'?" Reed asked Michael as they turned in the opposite direction.

"Aw, they've been talking for a long time about installing card readers on all the doors," the RD explained. "That way nobody could get in without a card. You know, safer and all that." He paused, eyeing Reed curiously. "Well, what job did you get?"

Reed glanced down at the paper in his hand. "I've been afraid to look," he admitted. He flipped the page over and read the company name aloud. And then, "'P Belt 2B. Standard Shift. Red Line.' What does that mean?"

"Sounds like you got a good factory job. That company makes computer hardware and ships it all over the world. You'll be packing parts in Room Two at Conveyer Belt B. You got a regular day shift—eight to five on weekdays, half a day Saturday. The Red Line is the shuttle system that takes all the workers from the Dorms to the factories in that area."

Reed scanned further down the page. "Well, I'm making more than I thought I would. Not bad."

"It's better than some," agreed Michael, "but not as good as an office job. You won't need much, though."

Reed flipped to the rule sheet and ran his eyes down the page. "No smoking, no alcoholic beverages, no possession of firearms, no use of illegal substances." He stopped. "'No attendance of unauthorized religious ceremonies.' What does *that* mean?"

"Just that." The RD held the hall door open for him. "If the government doesn't approve of a 'religious ceremony,' don't go to it. There's a list of acceptable places on the back, mostly government-controlled churches and mosques."

Reed shrugged. "I don't care. I don't do the church thing anyway."

"That's probably a good thing," Michael muttered, more to himself than to Reed. Reed chose not to respond.

When Reed reentered his room, Reagan glanced up from his computer. "So'd they take your mug shot and all that?"

"Yeah," replied Reed, tossing the job description toward him. "Got this, too."

Reagan glanced at the page. "Hey, that's a good place! You're lucky. It's right next door to where Riley and I work. We can ride together."

"Yeah, plus you won't have to put up with *him* all day," added Riley from behind his phone.

Reagan good-naturedly threw a pair of socks at him.

Reed flung himself up onto his bed and watched through half-closed eyes as Reagan's fingers typed furiously on his laptop. "How'd you get to keep that thing?" he asked. "They wouldn't even let *me* bring my phone."

Reagan's fingers didn't stop. "You fought 'em, didn't you? Like, about coming here? That'll do it. They take away your privileges if you're 'dissident.' I didn't, and they let me keep this. They went through it and put on a bunch of bugs and trackers, but it's not too bad. I'll let you use it sometime."

"Thanks," yawned Reed. "That would be nice."

Later, after a shower, Reed lay in bed, still listening to the click of Reagan's typing. *So much for going to bed early*, he thought, smiling. As he drifted off to sleep, he decided that, between Michael and his roommates, maybe things wouldn't be so bad here after all. But, some-where far in the distance, low thunder rumbled over the hills.

CHAPTER 3

B*eep! Beep! Beep!*
Reed jerked into consciousness. It was morning. He could hear Riley slapping around below him, trying to silence the persistent alarm. Reed moaned and rolled over. The room was still dark, barely lit by the gray light that seeped through the closed blinds.

Reagan's groggy voice came from the other side of the room. "I thought you put that thing on radio mode last night."

"Me, too," mumbled Riley, at last smacking the right button to silence the annoying buzz. "Guess not."

Reed groaned and pulled the pillow over his head. "I hate that noise. Wake me up in an hour."

"Sorry," Reagan yawned. "It's seven; time to get up for work and breakfast. If we get there early enough, there might be donuts left."

Reed sat up. "Donuts for breakfast?"

"Only if you hurry. There aren't many, and they go fast. Otherwise, it's cereal and bagels." Reagan threw off his covers. "Plus the shuttle leaves at seven forty-five. If you don't wanna walk, you have to be ready."

A few minutes later, all three were dressed and heading down the hall toward the Mushroom. Other boys were coming out of their rooms, some still buttoning shirts or running hands over their hair. Many, like Riley and Reed, wore jeans and t-shirts. Others, like Reagan, had on dress shirts and slacks.

They left the hall at the back end of the dorm. The stairwell was already filled with dozens more boys from other floors, slamming doors and pounding down the staircase in a crushing pack. They poured onto the first floor and out into the cold, gray morning.

Reed, rubbing the last of the sleep out of his eyes, nearly stopped in his tracks when he stepped out the door. It was rush hour at the Dorms. Hundreds of teenagers covered the Square and filled the sidewalks in a crowd that dwarfed even last night's. More spilled out of the dorms in a never-ending flow, streaming away toward the left side of the hill and the Mushroom. Though no one stopped to talk, most of the teens called to each other or chattered as they went. The noise was terrific. Reagan and Riley, used to the crowd, expertly threaded their way in and out, keeping Reed with them, even down the packed North Stairs.

The Mushroom was like the night before—the woman with the scanner, the smell of coffee and new carpet. But there was one striking difference: the quiet. Forks scraped on plates; the juice machine hiccupped occasionally; no one talked. Compared to the din outside, the silence seemed deafening. Reed wasn't sure he liked it.

The boys were not too late for donuts; a dozen still remained when they arrived, placidly eyeing the world from inside their glass cabinet. But Reed could hardly enjoy his. The room seemed goaded by a driving rush, and even Reagan and Riley stuffed in their breakfast as fast as they could, washing it down with gulps of orange juice. Reed burned his tongue on his coffee trying to keep up with them.

When they finished, Reagan and Riley shoved back their chairs and made for the door. Reed stuffed in the last half of a donut and scrambled to follow, chewing and choking his way across the room. He stumbled into a table in his hurry, banging his shin on a chair, and nearly lost his mouthful.

The other two paused at a counter near the steps, spread with rows of identical brown paper bags. "Lunch," Reagan whispered over his shoulder as he and Riley each swooped up a bag. "Don't miss it." And he was gone.

Reed snatched up a bag and followed. He tried to catch a glimpse of its contents as he lurched up the stairs but nearly face-planted and gave it up.

"Sorry to rush you," Reagan apologized when Reed caught up to him outside. "We're supposed to hurry through breakfast so everybody gets to eat before the shuttles leave. The Council made that *really* clear from the start."

"The Council?" Reed favored his smarting shin. "What's that?"

Reagan shot him an odd look. "You don't know who the Council is?"

"No, how could I?"

Reagan glanced around at the crowd. "Let's go back to the dorm," he said quietly. "We can brush our teeth, and I'll tell you on the way."

They turned up the North Stairs, fighting their way against the crowd that was still pouring down.

"Okay," Reagan began, "So obviously we're here. You have to know a little of what's going on, right?"

"Unfortunately," Reed growled under his breath.

Reagan continued, apparently missing Reed's remark. "Well, after GRO—you know that's what they call this—the government put us in these different compounds in cities around the country. But, since they couldn't keep up with everything themselves, they came up with the idea of putting a six-member 'council' over every compound. They make rules, punish anybody who breaks them, create the jobs—you know, what you'd expect. But it's not like a city council or board of directors; they're government people. It's... different. Very different."

Reagan's voice dropped. "Reed, they're powerful, incredibly powerful. They rule whole cities, not just the compounds. They're part of GRO so they're technically a government agency, but they're almost... autonomous. They have their own offices, boards, police forces, whole bureaucracies. Nobody checks up on them; nobody knows what all they do; nobody even knows how big they really are. The one here keeps the mayor and city council under their thumb. Nobody stands up to them. Even Director Connors can't attend their meetings."

By now, they'd reached the dorm and began climbing the stairs. Though there was practically no one else around, Reagan still kept his voice low, almost whispering. "They run everything, and they've hired everyone—Director Connors, the RDs, the Mushroom workers, the bus drivers, the police. They don't even come to the Dorms them-selves anymore. They let the RDs and Connors take care of most of the discipline issues. But, when they do step in, it's bad. If somebody gets called before the Council, they're in serious trouble. And I mean *serious.*"

"What happens to them?" Reed swallowed back the growing uneasiness in his stomach before it could creep up into his voice.

"Supposedly, they get deported to another city, but I don't believe it. It's too quiet and hush-hush. Besides, after they get arrested, we never hear from them again. Like, ever."

"Sometimes, they don't even get arrested," Riley put in. "There was that one kid who tried to break into one of their offices once. He just disappeared."

"Yeah, he never even made it out of the building."

By now, they were back in their room, brushing their teeth at the sink. Reagan had to stop talking since his mouth was full but, as soon as he could, he continued. "Be careful what you say around other people, too. The Council has ears everywhere. Don't complain too much or say anything bad about them or even mention what you think of them. It could make things… unpleasant." He paused. "Sometimes they put spies right in the Dorms with us. We call 'em 'ringers.' We're not supposed to know they exist, but we usually figure it out. I don't know of any right now, but that doesn't mean there isn't at least one. You have to be careful." He snapped the cap back on his toothpaste.

"This is crazy! Councils? Spies? People disappearing? It sounds like a creepy Netflix show." Reed stood in the middle of the room, trying to process it all.

"It's not a joke." Reagan dried his hands on a towel and turned to face Reed. "It's the new reality. But we're just telling you the worst so you'll know how things work. For the most part, if you do what you're supposed to, they leave you alone. You can actually have a pretty good life here. Just watch what you do and say."

"Oh." Reed rubbed the back of his neck. "Would it be considered 'serious' to… well… give a little attitude to the Director?"

"Not usually serious," Reagan shrugged, tossing his toothbrush into a nightstand drawer. "I guess it depends on what you say. He might watch you closer for a while but, if you shape up, he'll let you alone." He shoved the drawer shut with his knee. "Why? Did you?"

"Well, I didn't say anything *wrong*, but he didn't seem to like my tone very much." Reed paused. "Okay, so he didn't like it at all."

"I wouldn't worry about it," counseled Riley. "Like Reagan said, he'll watch you for a while but, as long as you don't do it again, you're okay. You'd know by now if you weren't."

When they finished in the room, the three left the dorm and turned back down the North Stairs. In the parking lot of the Mushroom, they found a large crowd of teenagers standing in the cold, stamping their feet and rubbing their hands for warmth.

"This is where the shuttles come," explained Reagan as they joined the waiting group. "They can't fit them all anywhere else, so we have to wait out here... and cuss if it's raining."

Reed pulled his jacket closer. "So there's more than one bus?"

"Yeah, just the Red Route by itself—our ride—has six buses. Then there's Blue Route and Green Route. Blue has six, but Green has eight. They're only for workers in the industrial parks since they can't hold all the workers for the whole city."

"Wait, so how many of these parks are there?"

While they waited for their ride, Reed got a crash course in city geography. There were three industrial parks in town. Red, his district, was a short distance from the Dorms and was home to two factories and their offices. The Blue district was nearby and also held two factories. Green, on the other side of town, had only one factory.

Reed shook his head. "I don't get it. How did one town get so many factories? I mean, isn't five a little over the top?"

"Not really." Reagan set his briefcase down and breathed on his fingers. "When you think about all the people that have to work here, it's a wonder there aren't more. This is one of the biggest compounds in the country; last I heard, there were over five thousand kids in the Dorms alone."

Reed stared at him. "Five *thousand*? That's bigger than some towns I know!"

"Yep. And that's just in the Dorms. A bunch more have moved out of the dorms into apartments—sorta on their own but still on the Hill."

"The Hill?"

"Yeah. That's what they call the whole complex—dorms, apartments, the Mushroom, even the factories. It's all collectively 'the Hill.'"

Reed made a note of that. "So they picked this city to dump us 'cause it had so many jobs?"

"Nope. The Council brought them all in. That's what they do."

Just then, a long line of blue buses roared into view from the city below. One after another, they rumbled into the parking lot, stopping with a familiar hiss, until nine of them sat idling in front of the crowd. More waited behind them on the street, stretching around the corner and down the hill.

There were so many. Reed would have been completely lost without his roommates. Reagan and Riley didn't hesitate, pulling him into the crowd past the first three rumbling giants. A screen above the windshield on each declared its route, proclaiming "Green" or "Blue" high above Reed's head in yellow letters.

The crowd split up and surged toward the different shuttles. The first "Red" was filled by the time the boys reached it. Reagan and Riley turned and made a rush for the second with a flood of other teens.

"Make sure you stick with us," Reagan called to Reed. "We'll make sure you get to the right place!"

Reed stuck to them as best he could. He squeezed through packed bodies following Riley's back. He saw Reagan ahead of him elbow his way to the door and up the stairs. Good, he was getting close. Riley was next. He slipped between two shoulders and went up after Reagan, almost stepping on someone's hand. Reed pushed someone else's elbow out of his ribs and put his foot on the step. But, just then, a stout girl shoved her way in, deliberately bumped Reed back with her weight, and heaved up the stairs after Riley. Before Reed could recover his balance, the doors, with a warning beep, slid shut.

He turned desperately to the window. Reagan jabbed his finger toward the next bus over. Reed nodded and made a dash. The crowd was already funneling through the narrow door, but Reed was determined. He wriggled his way in like a mole. There was no way he was going to miss this one.

CHAPTER 4

He didn't miss it. With a little elbow work, he maneuvered his way neatly onboard and found a window seat near the front. He wished he hadn't had to squeeze next to a sleepy boy who smelled of hairspray and oatmeal, but at least he made it.

Once the bus was full, it jerked into motion and swung around, following a string of others out of the parking lot and down the hill. Reed blew out his breath and leaned back in his seat, staring out the window. *What a morning.*

The weather had not improved much since the day before. Though the drizzle had stopped, the sky still hung leaden gray over the city. Reed wondered if the sun ever came out in this part of the world.

The sleepy boy didn't seem communicative, which suited Reed fine. Nursing his sore shin and burned tongue, he looked out the window. In less than ten minutes, the bus rolled to a stop in front of a gated entryway. A small, brick guardhouse stood between black iron gates that swung open when the bus approached. Bold, black letters proclaiming "Red Industrial Park" marched across the brick wall. Beyond, the entry drive split, one road curving left and the other right.

Reed got off the shuttle and found his roommates in the crowd.

"You shoulda tripped her," were Reagan's first words. "If she wanted to play dirty, it could've gone both ways."

"I thought about it," Reed muttered, "but she would've broken my leg if she fell on it."

Reagan laughed.

As the buses roared away, the workers streamed through the open gates. Reed followed his roommates until Reagan stopped at the Y in the road.

"Well, here we are. Riley and I go to the right; you go to the left. We'll meet here after we get off and ride back together, okay? Good luck!" He and Riley disappeared into the crowd moving up the road to the right.

Reed turned the other way. A large cement sign bearing the company name pointed up the road. With a sigh, Reed trudged in that direction, wishing he was going anywhere else.

The road curved through a cluster of small, manmade hills, and the factory was invisible from this point of view. Reed followed the winding roadway through the gentle slopes of dead, manicured sod and bare landscaping until he rounded the last corner. The factory loomed before him. It wasn't the run-down, dirty place out of a Dickens novel he'd been subconsciously expecting. It actually looked very new, very large, and very expensive. He gazed in awe at its forest of shiny black smokestacks, rows of silver generators, and soaring chrome entry as he followed the stream of workers down a final slope and through the main entrance.

In the lobby, a girl stood behind the front desk, taking off her coat. The rest of the crowd poured through a set of doors in the far wall and left them alone. Reed hesitated. With a gulp, he approached. She tossed her smooth, blonde hair behind her shoulders as she settled behind the desk and smiled up at him.

"Umm…" he ventured, leaning his hands against the counter and swallowing again, "I think I'm supposed to work here. What do I need to do?"

The girl's smile broadened. "We've been expecting you for a few days. I can get you checked in right now. Do you have your ID?"

Reed shook his head. "No, just my red tag thingy."

"Perfect! That's all I need." She scanned it into the computer. After a moment of rapid typing, she turned back to him, all business. "All your information is in the company's files now. Most of your paperwork came in last night but, if you'll sign this one form, you'll be all set."

He signed the page she handed across the desk and shoved it back. She glanced down at it and smiled. "Your station is in Room Two, Packing Conveyer B. Take the first hall on the right after you leave the lobby. Room Two will be the second door on your left." Her professional smile became kinder, and she added, "I really hope the rest of your day goes all right. The first day is always a tough one, but you'll make it."

Reed paused as he took his red tag from the desk and looked into her face. She had bright blue eyes that seemed warm and friendly in the echoing chill of the empty lobby. He smiled back. "Thanks. I think I'll make it just fine."

But as he left the lobby and took the first hallway on his right, he began to doubt his own words. Worry crept into the pit of his stomach. This was almost like his first day of high school, and that had not gone so well.

"Relax," he told himself, "there's nothing to be nervous about."

He found Room Two easily. Taking a deep breath, he turned the door handle and pushed; it was locked. He stepped back, glancing around, and spied a card reader next to the handle.

"Idiot," he mumbled, "you could have guessed that."

He held his red tag under the reader's beam. It beeped and the lock clicked. He slipped his tag back into his pocket and opened the door.

He found himself in a huge room with steps dropping down to a concrete floor. Massive steel beams shot across the high ceiling, and half a dozen giant conveyer belts, dotted with machines, covered most of the floor. The day's work had not yet begun, and workers stood in little knots in the aisles.

Reed descended into the room and walked past the first belt. A large letter "A" swung over it, suspended from the ceiling. "B" hung over the next one down. He approached.

The workers gathered around the belt didn't seem to notice him until he came nearer. Then one looked up, and they all stopped talking and turned.

Reed felt his face get hot. *Why do they have to stare?* He cleared his throat. "Is this Conveyer B?"

"Yes," said one of the girls.

That was all. Reed hated this. "Oh. Well, I think I'm supposed to work here."

The effect was amazing. One of the girls squealed, "Yyyeeessss!" loudly and then slapped a hand over her mouth. Everyone else began high-fiving each other and chattering all at the same time.

"Finally!"

"Took 'em long enough!"

Reed stood where he was, unsure if this was a good development. Thankfully, one of the boys noticed his predicament and waved him over. "Hi! Come get settled in."

Reed came. The young man motioned him to an empty space next to him. "Here you go; this station's empty. Sorry about the interesting welcome. We've been short one person for several weeks, and we had to work extra to make up for it. They're excited 'cause now we can catch up on our quota."

"I see," said Reed, setting his lunch by his feet. The other workers had returned to their former conversations and seemed to have forgotten him. Turning to the friendly young man, Reed introduced himself. "Well, I'm Reed."

"Nice to meet you, Reed. I'm Nathan. I guess we'll be neighbors from now on."

"Great. So what exactly are we doing?"

"We're packing computer parts for shipment to different assembly plants," Nathan explained as he unzipped and pulled off his apple-green hoodie. "It's not hard; I'll show you how when they turn on the belt. You just—"

Before he could finish, a whistle shrieked somewhere in the building. There was a click, and the belts began to hum and creep forward. A rhythmic whine began, punctuated by steady beeps and picking up tempo as the belts gained speed. The workers scattered and situated themselves in their stations. When the first of the plastic gray parts rolled down the belt, the first girl picked it up and went to work deftly. Likewise, the second and the third. Nathan took the one that should have been Reed's and showed him how to wrap the part and put it in a small cardboard box for shipping. All these were stacked in larger boxes and set on short belts that ran out through the opposite wall.

Reed was quick and, though his first attempt at wrapping didn't look as good as Nathan's, it was successful. His second was better.

After the first half hour, Reed had the hang of it enough to pay attention to what was going on around him. While they worked, the teens talked. With the droning of the belts, it was impossible to be heard at normal voice level except by those right next to the speaker but, if one shouted, those on the opposite side of the circle could hear fairly well.

Once Reed had his routine down, his coworkers began to ply him with questions.

"So what's your name?" someone called from across the circle.

"Reed!" he shouted back.

"Where're you from?" someone else asked.

"California."

"Ah!" exclaimed everyone, and they began peppering him with more questions.

"Did you live in Hollywood?"

"Did you know any movie stars?"

"Did you go surfing, like, every day?"

The door to the room closed heavily. Instantly, the questions stopped, and everyone bent over their jobs with unexpected attention. Reed paused and looked up in surprise. He caught sight of a man, hands clasped behind him, coming slowly down the stairs, running his eyes over everything in the giant room. Reed picked up the next part and started back to work, watching out of the corner of his eye.

The man reached ground level and passed the first few conveyer belts, looking down the rows of working teens. He paused by one of the machines and checked the parts coming out from under it. Then he examined a stack of boxes ready for shipment. He turned and paced back toward the front of the room, watching. He came straight toward Conveyer B. All the workers kept their eyes down.

The man reached the belt and circled the group. The sound of his measured footsteps on the concrete was almost lost in the drone of machinery. Reed watched the glossy black shoes make their way past each worker. They came closer; they were behind him. They stopped. Reed felt eyes on the back of his neck, boring into him. A cold prickle tingled between his shoulder blades, and he almost dropped his part.

The man didn't move for a moment. He said nothing. Then Reed saw the shoes turning away, moving toward the door. Without a word, the man mounted the stairs and left the room.

As soon as the door shut behind him, the room let out a collective breath. Reed swallowed and looked at Nathan. "What was that about?"

"Just the foreman; he comes in every now and then to check on us. There's no schedule, so it keeps us on our toes. He reports you if you're not working well or seem to have 'attitude.' If you do your job right, there's nothing to be afraid of."

Nothing to be afraid of. Reed pressed down a box flap with his thumb. *Then why do I keep getting the idea there is?*

With the foreman gone, the questions resumed, and the rest of the morning was spent talking about Hollywood, celebrities, and movies. The foreman did not return.

At noon, the whistle blew again, and the workers took a break for lunch. Reed ate with a few of the other teens from his belt, but Nathan sat alone on a packing crate on the other side of the room. That seemed a little strange to Reed; Nathan was a nice guy.

During the rest of the afternoon, Reed found himself watching his neighbor. There was nothing extraordinary about him. He was average height with an average build. His light brown hair, cut short and combed straight down except above his forehead, spiked sharply up above his hazel eyes, as if surprised to see his face so close. His face itself was genial in a nice, homey way. In every way, he seemed to be ordinary. But there was something else, something Reed could not put a finger on. Nathan was not like everyone else, and Reed had no idea why.

CHAPTER 5

Finally, the whistle sounded for the last time that day. The belts turned until the last part was taken off and packed, when their humming rumble finally shut off. The room was quiet for the first time since morning. Reed yawned and stretched his stiff fingers. "That was one of the longest days I've ever had," he commented to Nathan as the workers gathered up their belongings.

"You'll get used to it," Nathan said, smiling as he pulled on his hoodie. "It's not bad after a while. See you tomorrow!"

He was one of the first to leave. Reed closed up his station as he had seen the others do before joining the rush out the door. In the hallway, more workers crowded out of other rooms and poured through the hall. Reed shouldered his way through the crowd.

As he passed through the foyer on his way to the front door, he spied Nathan at the front desk. The young man leaned casually on the counter, talking to the receptionist. She was preparing to leave, but she listened anyway, nodding as she dug through her purse. Just after Reed caught sight of the pair, Nathan straightened and disappeared into the crowd.

Reed wondered what business Nathan had with the receptionist after hours. Their conversation hadn't looked very professional. Maybe he was an admirer. Reed grinned at the thought, then shrugged. What did it matter? He didn't even know the other boy. Dismissing the incident, Reed followed the rest of the workers out the front door into the gathering evening.

The sky was still overcast, but a bitter wind had sprung up, making it even colder than the morning had been. Reed shivered and zipped his windbreaker up to his throat. By the time he reached the park's gate, he was chilled to the bone. Reagan and Riley were waiting for him, bundled up in their warm jackets with hands shoved deep in their pockets.

"Well, how was it?" Reagan's voice sounded muffled through his coat collar.

"Long," replied Reed, trying to keep his teeth from chattering, "but not as bad as it could have been. It's freezing; let's get out of here."

On the bus, he settled into his seat and leaned back with a sigh. The warm air was already thawing him out, and he'd been on his feet since lunch. Life looked more cheerful from this perspective.

When they arrived back at the Hill and unloaded in front of the Mushroom, the line at the cafeteria door stretched back far into the parking lot. Reagan sized it up at a glance. "This won't get any shorter for a while. Let's go back to the room."

They reached the welcome warmth of the dorm and hurried up the stairs into the hall. "Whew!" exclaimed Reagan as he closed the door to their room behind him. "It's way colder out there than it was earlier! I guess it blew in this afternoon." He flipped on the light bar above the sink and tossed his briefcase onto his bed. "Home sweet home! Well, not quite, I guess."

Reed turned away. A rising bitterness suddenly choked his throat. "No, it's not," he growled, jamming clenched fists into his pockets. "And it never will be."

Fortunately, neither of his roommates heard him; Riley had just turned on the tap and was scrubbing his blackened hands.

Reed turned to the window and stared out, unseeing. Blast it all! He was cold, he was mad, and he did not want to be here. What was worse, he'd almost forgotten that. He had been content with his first day. But how could he be? He'd been dragged here against his will—*dragged*. He was supposed to be angry; he *was* angry. He had to hold on to that. He had to. *Never forget and never let go.*

Reagan's voice broke into his thoughts. "Wanna wash up, too?"

Reed nodded and turned to the sink, trying to shake off his dark mood. As the water splashed over his face, the angry blaze died to a smolder. It really wasn't so bad here. Today had been tolerable. Perhaps this place would surprise him. He turned off the tap, shaking the water out of his eyes.

Reagan, sitting on the desk, tossed him a towel. "Here. Ready for supper?"

"Sure," he replied from behind the towel and then, forcing a grin, "I'm starved."

Supper was much like the night before. Reed sat with his roommates and their friends at a long table and found he was beginning to pick up some of the other teens' names. Again, Reagan was the focal point of attention, and Riley put in an occasional word. Reed, who was quite hungry, alternated his attention between the pizza on his plate and the group's conversation.

The talk at the table centered mostly on the latest news of the Hill. The main topic was the prank that had been played in Dorm Fourteen the night before.

"Apparently, somebody decided to give everybody on the hall a surprise," explained one of the boys. "So he got some red drink mix and put it in all the shower heads in both bathrooms." Everyone laughed.

"The only problem was he forgot one of the heads wasn't working right and a plumber was supposed to come fix it. The RD took the plumber up and turned on the shower to show him what was wrong with it." The boy could hardly continue as he choked with laughter. "Oh, dude! The head wasn't working right to begin with but, with that stuff in it, it, like, blew up! Red stuff went everywhere—all over the room, the plumber, and the RD!"

The rest of the story was drowned out as the whole table howled. Reed laughed along with the rest. It felt good to unwind after a long day on his feet, and the laughter was refreshing against the stark melancholy of everything else in this place.

Later, when the three roommates were strolling away from the Mushroom, Reed brought the prank up again. "So do I need to start watching my back? I mean, do things like that shower trick happen around here very often?"

Reagan chuckled. "There's a fair amount of pranking, but the

RDs usually don't get involved. They let us play tricks on each other as long as we don't break too many rules."

"Or they don't get shower nozzles blown up in their faces," added Riley, sticking a toothpick in his mouth.

"So what keeps people from breaking the rules all the time? Or, you know, doing the summer camp or college kinda stuff?"

"Who says anything does?" Reagan flipped up his coat collar. "Stuff like that goes on all the time. But I guess if there was something that kept things from getting completely out of hand, it would be… well, fear—fear of getting caught, fear of what might happen, fear of—you know who. Everybody here lives in terror of the Council. Of course, rules get broken, and all kinds of things go on behind their backs, but nobody dares to cross the Council openly."

He shoved his hands into his pockets. "You'll find out eventually, but they have certain rules they're willing to let slide and some they crack down on hard. Fortunately for us, it usually works out in our favor, so we don't worry about it all that much. We've got other things on our minds." He stared at the sidewalk for a moment. "But who are we fooling?" he said quietly. "Every kid on the Hill lives with a constant fear. We can never escape the Council. It haunts us, Reed. We laugh, play around, have some fun, but it's still there. We can't get away from it."

Reed shivered. Suddenly, the lonely street lamps, the empty sidewalks, and the dim shapes of the dorms above seemed to have fallen under the watch of some spreading, sinister presence, something powerful enough to hold five thousand young people in its inescapable grip. Reed shivered again. A chilling sensation crept up his spine. Eyes were fixed on him—invisible, unblinking eyes. He was being watched.

Reagan mistook the shiver for one of cold. "Let's hurry up and get inside. It's freezing tonight. But remember," he added, "there's nothing to worry about if you just do what they say and don't rock the boat. They'll leave you alone that way."

Reed nodded, but the watched feeling would not leave him. He understood exactly what Reagan meant about feeling haunted. Already, a cold fear was stealing over him. He thrust it back quickly. He had to hold this off. Fear would shut and lock the cell door of his imprisonment in this place, and he refused to resign himself so easily. He would fight it. *Remember: never forget and never let go.*

But, even as the thought crossed his mind, he realized how hopeless it was. He couldn't hold off fear forever. It always came creeping back like a wolf that returns as the fire dies down. Perhaps it really was best to follow Reagan's advice and not stir up any trouble. Maybe he could have a decent life that way.

As the three entered the dorm, another force joined the angry thunderhead within Reed, an icy flow that oozed in, pooling, rising, and filling all the little corners of his mind—fear. A brooding stillness fell across the icy surface, and the hush was thick with a terrible power poised to unleash its fury. But Reed had no concept of the danger. As he swung open the door, he asked Reagan, "Do you think I could use your computer tonight?"

"Sure. Just be careful what you do," Reagan cautioned in a low voice. "You know what I mean."

"Yeah," said Reed softly, "I know."

CHAPTER 6

---✦---

O ver the next couple of days, Reed began to settle into the routine
of life on the Hill: up at seven, breakfast, work, lunch, more
work, off at five, and supper. He even ate each night with his roommates and the same group of their friends. But, the more he learned
about his new home, the greater it seemed to grow and the wider its
possibilities seemed to blossom. It was almost like a coconut, Reed
thought: tough and unpleasant to start with but pretty great once you
got past the outside. A whole new world was opening in front of him,
and the pulsating life of it nearly took his breath away. Everything
was new, everything was different, and everything seemed to be
clamoring for his attention.

Even the girl behind the front desk at the factory wasn't the typical receptionist. Reed hadn't talked to her since their first encounter,
but her constant cheerfulness radiated like sunbeams into the gray
foyer every morning. He could feel it even on his short walks through
the lobby each day.

Someone else who struck him as a little unusual was Nathan.
Everything Reed had observed about him on his first day remained
unchanged. He didn't talk much but, when he did, it wasn't with the
awkward fumbles of a poor conversationalist. Despite his affable
disposition, he kept to himself, even at lunch. Sometimes he took his
lunch and slipped out of the room for the noon break.

Reed watched him day after day. All the little details jumbled together and began to form an overall impression; there was something

underneath the squeaky-clean exterior. It was like the set for a TV commercial, built to be believable but too perfect to be real. Reed's curiosity was roused and tinged with a hint of suspicion.

One day, he decided to get to the bottom of the matter. When the noon whistle screeched, he picked up his lunch and walked over to the crate where Nathan sat by himself. "Mind if I sit here?"

Nathan, his mouth full, smiled and shook his head. Reed sat down. They ate their sub sandwiches and made small talk for a while before Reed got down to business. "So can I ask you a question?"

Nathan bit off the end of a carrot. "Sure, go ahead."

Reed opened his mouth and then stopped. He had no idea how to bring up the subject. His mind groped for anything to say instead. "I was wondering where you go when you leave the room with your lunch sometimes." Random, but it was the best he could do at the moment.

Nathan swallowed his mouthful. "Well," he said lightly, "since my company's usually not in high demand in here, I go eat with friends in another room."

Hmm. Reed finished off a package of crackers. *So he does have friends.* He dusted crumbs off his fingers and tried to make the best of a pointless question. "That's cool. In another packing room?"

"No."

Short answer—very short. It sparked Reed's curiosity. "Well then, where? If you don't mind me asking."

"A break room for the office employees. I know a couple of them."

Office people—why did that ring a bell? Then he remembered: that scene between Nathan and the receptionist. Things were getting more interesting. Perhaps it was time to dig a little deeper.

Reed pulled his mind to a halt. What was wrong with him? It would be the most natural thing in the world if Nathan had a crush on the receptionist, and it was none of Reed's business. He hardly knew the other boy. *Shut your mouth and finish your sandwich.*

That resolve didn't last long. They ate in silence for half a minute before Reed's curiosity overpowered him. "Is one of them that girl at the front desk? You know, the blonde one?"

The top to Nathan's water bottle jumped out of his hand and

rolled to the floor. He scooped it up in an instant. "Excuse me?"

"You know, the receptionist at the front desk; is she one of your friends?"

Nathan replaced the bottle cap deliberately and shot him an odd look. "Yes," he said. "Why?"

"Oh, I was just thinking." Reed swung one leg smugly and tried not to sound overly pleased with his sleuthing. "She seems like a nice girl. How do you know her?"

Nathan was really eyeing him now, more than the situation required, Reed thought. "We're in a small group together," he answered guardedly.

"Cool." Reed bit into an Oreo. "What kinda group?" His instincts warned him to stop his questioning, but he ignored his better sense.

"It's kinda hard to explain…"

The whistle broke in, sounding the end of lunch break. Nathan leapt off the crate.

"Back to work!" he said, snatching up the remnants of his lunch and dashing for the nearest trashcan.

Reed pondered the short interview during the remainder of the afternoon. He didn't know if he'd succeeded in his original mission or if he'd struck on something new. There was no doubt that something was going on between Nathan and the receptionist, but why would Nathan be so nervous about it? It was the most natural thing in the world. But there had been something odd in his manner and face. Reed had been right in the first place: there was more going on here than met the eye.

When five o'clock came, Nathan, as usual, was one of the first out of his station and through the door. Reed watched him leave as he shut down his own station. "Watch," he told himself. "Ten bucks says he'll be hitting up his girl."

Sure enough, as Reed was swept through the lobby in the rush for the door, he caught sight of Nathan by the front desk, arranging pens in a cup and listening. The girl was talking, leaning both elbows on the desk. The crowd swallowed them in an instant, but that was all it took to cement the situation in Reed's mind. He grinned. Sparks were flying, but if Nathan wanted his little game to be a secret, Reed could play along.

Outside, his grin faded. The icy air and sharp wind that seeped through his light jacket smacked him back into reality. "Man, I can't wait to get paid," he hissed through chattering teeth, pulling the windbreaker tight around him. "Then I'll buy a..." He spent the rest of the walk to the gate thinking of all the things he wanted or needed. A thick, warm coat was at the top of the list.

By the time he reached the main entrance, thoroughly chilled, Nathan and his affairs were completely out of his mind. He waited for Reagan and Riley before climbing onto the bus.

After getting comfortably settled and exchanging the usual greetings, Reagan loosened his collar and stretched out his legs. "So I don't know about you guys, but I'm ready for a little fun. How 'bout going into town tonight?"

Reed jumped at the chance. "Sure!" He hadn't seen much of the city so far. "What'll we do?"

"Oh, maybe hang out at a coffee shop or catch a movie." Reagan folded his hands behind his head. "Or we could just walk around if you want to see the sights."

"That would be great! Oh," Reed looked down at his jacket and thought of the relatively short walk from the factory, "but..."

"Aw, don't worry about that," Reagan reassured him. "Between Riley and me, I'm sure we've got one you can borrow. Payday's still a ways off, and you don't want to miss out on everything until you can get your own."

CHAPTER 7

Night had already fallen when they set off toward the city below. Reed burrowed into the welcome warmth of Riley's leather jacket and decided that cold weather wasn't so bad inside a coat. "How far a walk is it?" he asked after a moment.

"That depends on where you want to go." Reagan looped a red plaid scarf around his neck and tucked it inside his pea coat. "It's about twenty minutes to the Boulevard, where most of the good stuff is."

"Good stuff, meaning?"

"You know, the best coffee shops, the cool stores and restaurants, the biggest theaters. It's pretty much the only part of the city worth going to."

They crossed to the opposite side of the dark street. The flat-fronted apartments of the Hill lined their way on both sides, reaching into the black sky. Light filtered out of their windows like small rays of comfort into the shivering night outside.

Reed watched his steamy breath rise through one of the orangey-yellow shafts. The rows of windows, glowing through friendly curtains and soft shades, looked homey and comfortable from the cold street. Beyond the blinds, golden lamplight welled up inside cozy dens and kitchens, trickling out like too much honey on a biscuit. Reed felt a shot of loneliness. "How many kids would you say live out here instead of in the Dorms?" he asked.

Reagan shrugged. "I don't know. Maybe fifteen hundred or so.

Not everybody wants to pay their own rent every month."

"Would you?" Reed was still eyeing the glowing panes.

"And miss out on all the fun at the Dorms? Heck, no! I don't understand who'd want to."

"I think I do," said Reed softly, but his roommates didn't seem to hear him.

It was odd how quickly the desire swept over him. It wasn't something most people would ordinarily dream about, having one of those glowing windows of their own. But then, most people hadn't spent their lives stuck on the outside, looking in. Reed bit his lip and turned away.

He was only too glad when they finally left the apartments behind and entered the commercial outskirts of the city. Brightly lit storefronts and restaurants replaced the brick buildings. Neon signs blinked and flashed overhead, cars sped past, and the empty sidewalks started to fill with people.

"Here we are," Reagan announced after awhile. "This is the Boulevard."

They had reached what seemed to be the hub of all the activity growing around them. The sidewalks teemed on both sides of the street, and streams of cars rumbled past. Signs, storefronts, and brightly lit windows lined the walkways, flashing like a Christmas parade. A few of the outdoor cafés had music playing.

Reed hadn't been out in a place like this since he'd left California. He breathed deeply to inhale it all in one breath. He had missed this. There was nothing quite like the hum of cars and the twinkling of lights on a cold, wintry night.

"Come on," Reagan interrupted his thoughts, "it's cold, and I want some coffee."

A few minutes later, Reed was settled on the outdoor patio of Reagan's favorite coffee shop sipping a macchiato, compliments of Reagan. Riley sat next to him, his feet propped on a chair as he munched a streusel-coated muffin. Reagan was across the table, making short work of a cappuccino and alternating his attention between the street scene and the cream-crowned cup in his hand. Through the caramel-scented steam that curled up from his cup, Reed let his eyes wander the busy thoroughfare. It was a boardwalk of sorts, almost like an outdoor mall—single-storied buildings with glass fronts, brick sidewalks, even a small fountain in the middle of a traffic circle with a rainbow of lights under its frothy jets. It all seemed very new. Perhaps it had come with all the new factories and the new dorms—"encouraged" to move in.

His roommates occupied themselves narrating the street action to one another. Reagan nearly choked when a girl tripped over the curb, sending shopping bags sailing in every direction, and Riley spit muffin all over his shirt when a texting boy ran into a lamp post. Reed, too, watched the little drama, but he hadn't mastered his roommates' humor enough to throw any quips of his own. Besides, the other two were too busy going back and forth with each other to notice anything he said.

"Well, well, what do we have here?" Three girls Reed had never seen before appeared at the table next to them. "Reagan's at the Boulevard, and he didn't invite us? I don't like the way this looks, girls."

The girl who spoke was the tallest of the three and by far the most beautiful. Her deep brown hair, tucked inside the fur-lined hood of her jacket, framed her contoured and flawless face. She pulled a chair up next to Reagan and sat down. "Out with the boys tonight, are we? You could have *told* us you were coming."

Reagan set down his coffee cup and grinned. "Oh, yeah, we're bro datin' it tonight. Nothing wrong with that, is there?"

The girl raised a sculpted eyebrow. "That all depends on who you're with."

They all laughed and began talking at once. Reed smiled and waited to be introduced.

It never happened. The others pulled up chairs and settled into a circle at the far end of the table. He cleared his throat and set his cup down firmly in front of him. Still nothing. Their heads drew close together into a little knot as they whispered and chattered to one another. Reed bit the inside of his cheek and looked toward the street. The sidewalks were still crowded, and the patio, too. A barista brushed by him carrying a load of steaming orders to one of the full tables. But, in the middle of the crowd, Reed was suddenly alone.

Chewing the inside of his cheek, he stared across the street to the crowded sidewalk on the other side. Suddenly, he squinted and leaned forward. That face—where had it gone? He could have sworn it looked familiar, like—there! He'd been right the first time. It was Nathan.

He was strolling on the fringes of the crowd with another boy Reed didn't know, his hands buried in the front pockets of his apple green hoodie. They were glancing over the window displays and storefronts, but they seemed bored. Nathan's friend yawned.

The sight of the pair was like a breath of fresh air on Reed's face. In a flash, he knew he had to catch up to them. Excusing himself from the group, who didn't notice anyway, he got up and threaded his way through the tables toward the open street.

On the opposite sidewalk, Nathan and his friend stopped at an intersection directly across from the coffee shop. They seemed to be conferring about something. Nathan's friend turned to look back the way they had come.

Perfect. Reed dodged a final table and stepped out of the café's walled patio. *Now I won't have to look like an idiot running down the sidewalk after them.*

Still, the two seemed about to move on. Nathan was already starting to walk; his friend, still looking over his shoulder, took a step.

Reed cupped his hands to his mouth. "Hey, Nathan!" he yelled, stepping off the curb. But, as he set foot in the crosswalk, a large truck, going much too fast, barreled past, blaring its horn. Reed jumped back and dropped to the ground, barely ducking under the truck's protruding mirror. The driver shouted something out the window and swerved but roared past without slowing.

Reed blew out his breath and dusted off the knees of his jeans.

"Idiot," said a boy, passing on the sidewalk.

Reed glanced up at him. "Excuse me?"

"Not you; the truck." The boy gave Reed his hand and pulled him to his feet. "Somebody needs to call the cops on jerks like that."

Reed smiled his thanks and turned back toward the street. The corner of the sidewalk was empty. He glanced up and down the crowded thoroughfare, searching for a glimpse of the pair. He saw nothing. *That's weird. They were just there.*

As soon as he could, he crossed the street to the bricked corner where Nathan and his friend had stood not two minutes before.

Again, he surveyed the street in both directions with no luck. "He can't have just disappeared," he muttered, turning in a full circle. "They must…"

Then he saw them. He hadn't realized that the sidewalk came to a corner here to let a narrow, dark alley open onto the Boulevard. But, as he turned, he caught sight of two figures at the far end of the little side road, passing under a street light. One of them wore an apple green hoodie.

Instinctively, Reed took a step after them, then stopped. If Nathan was leaving the Boulevard, he probably didn't want to see anybody. Reed shouldn't chase after him… should he? He glanced back across the street. He could still see the group just where he'd left them, their heads drawn close together in a tight, oblivious circle.

Reed snorted and turned into the dark alley. He jogged, hoping to catch up to the other boys quickly, but slowed to a walk as he neared the end of the street. It would be awkward if he dashed around the corner and ran into them. When he reached the corner, he stopped and peered around the rough cement edge of the building.

This new street was wider than the first and ran both directions behind the row of stores, filled with battered blue dumpsters and lit by half a dozen buzzing guard lights. Reed spotted the two figures instantly. They were already a long way down the alley, passing from one pool of light into another. They were full-out running.

For the first time, doubt shot through Reed's head. What was Nathan doing back here? He stood at the corner, torn. All his previous suspicions about this other boy came back to him. If Nathan was into something he shouldn't be, Reed almost didn't want to know. But what if he wasn't? Reed would always be plagued with questions. He looked back over his shoulder. If he didn't go on, he would have to go back to the coffee shop and the clique on its patio. The decision was suddenly much easier. He turned and ran down the alley after the two disappearing figures.

The two were fast and seemed to know their way well. They twisted and turned in and out of dozens of backstreets and roadways until Reed's head was spinning. The alleys began to grow darker, narrower, and less cluttered.

At last, the two in front slowed to a walk. Reed, out of breath, stopped and tried to gasp for air as quietly as possible. Leaning against a wall, he determined to make a final sprint and catch up to them as soon as he could breathe again. But, just as he straightened up to run, the other two stopped. They were listening, their heads cocked, but they weren't looking behind them. Before Reed could decide what to do, they dove to the side of the street and melted into the shadows behind a dumpster.

Without thinking, Reed did the same, slipping behind a large garbage can and crouching there, heart pounding. He squeezed his eyes shut and tried to think. *Are they hiding from me? Do I wait until they come out again?* He could just make out the silhouettes of the other two—black shapes squeezed in a narrow gap between the dumpster and the alley wall. Before he could make a decision, his eye caught a movement in the shadows further down the street. He fixed his gaze on it, trying to stare it down through the dark gloom of the alley. Something was moving toward him. Then it stepped into the light of the single street lamp, and Reed stopped breathing.

It was a man, all in black with an unbuttoned overcoat that fell nearly to his ankles. He was faceless, or at least the mask of black wool made it seem so, and a badge glittered on the chest of his dark uniform. An assault rifle—cruel and cold with a long, curved magazine that jutted from its belly—was slung over his left shoulder. He walked slowly, checking the street around him as he went.

Reed didn't need anyone to tell him who it was. The feeling of being watched crept slowly up his spine.

The Council.

The man was in sight only for a second before he turned down another street and vanished, but it was enough to chill Reed more than the cold night wind that came moaning up the alley after the figure. He was trembling inside Riley's thick leather jacket. When he was certain the man was gone, Reed let out his breath and fell against the wall behind him. That did it. He didn't know what was going on here, but he had to find out. He glanced down the street to where he had last seen Nathan's silhouette in the shadows. It was gone. Still cautious, he crept out of his hiding place and moved a few yards closer to the spot where he'd last seen the other two boys. By the light of the street lamp, he could easily make out the dumpster and the narrow gap behind it, but the space was empty. Blast. He'd lost them.

He turned and looked back the way he'd come. Now what? He didn't even know where he was. He turned in a full circle, looking for some clue to take him back to the Boulevard. There was nothing but blank walls and dark alleys twisting in a black maze all around him. He sighed. He'd have to wander around until he stumbled onto something familiar or found someone to ask for directions. This wasn't quite the evening he'd been expecting.

It didn't take him as long as he'd feared. It was only half an hour later that he shouldered his way back into the patio at the coffee shop. Reagan and Riley were still there, lounging where he'd left them. The girls were gone.

"Catch your friend?" Reagan asked as Reed approached.

"No." Reed dropped into his chair, surprised Reagan remembered where he'd gone. "I, uh, lost him."

Reagan cocked an eyebrow. "Wait, you mean he didn't see you?"

"Well, it's hard to say. I don't *think* he did. He kinda ran off with somebody else."

"Better hope he didn't see you then," Riley chuckled, dusting muffin crumbs off his fingers. "Otherwise, he was running from *you*."

Reed hadn't thought of that. What if Nathan had heard him shout and taken off on purpose? Perhaps all Reed's questioning earlier had gone too far. The thought hadn't even crossed his mind.

"Well, you can ask him about it tomorrow." Reagan tossed his coffee cup into a nearby trashcan. "You said he works with you, right?"

"Yeah, he does. And I guess I will. But I think he…"

Before he could finish his sentence, he was poked sharply in the back. He turned quickly and started in surprise. "Hunter?"

Sure enough, grinning wryly behind him was the young man he'd met his first day on the bus. They hadn't seen each other since, but the Hill was a big place.

"I saw you over here and thought I'd say hi," Hunter explained, pulling up a chair. His manner hadn't changed much since their first meeting—a little abrupt and slightly reserved with a dry, cool way of speaking.

"Sure, yeah." Reed struggled to get his mind back into the

present and find something to say. "So... where've you been keeping yourself?"

"Oh, I got stuck in Dorm One under Connors."

Reed grimaced sympathetically. "Gee, that's bad."

Reagan cleared his throat. Reed glanced at him and, taking both the warning and the cue, made a quick introduction.

"Your roommates, huh?" Hunter seemed mildly impressed. "I've heard of Reagan from Dorm Four and knew he had a new roommate, but I didn't know it was you."

Reagan looked flattered.

Riley shot Reed a quick wink. "Yeah," he said, "most likely you just heard about his first roommate who was awesome enough to count for two."

Reagan's flattered expression faded, and he glared at Riley in good-natured annoyance.

Hunter gave a brief smile and stood up. "Yeah, whatever. I just wanted to check in with you, Reed. See you 'round."

He turned and disappeared into the crowd. Reagan and Riley watched him go.

"He's a lively one," Reagan observed. "You met him your first day, you said?"

Reed nodded, and Reagan made no further comment.

They left the coffee shop and spent what remained of the night sauntering up and down the Boulevard, admiring window displays, meeting friends, and browsing through an occasional store. Reed relished it all despite the earlier incidents. He even forgot about the girls who had almost crashed the whole evening. But, after an hour or two, he began to wonder when they'd have to return to the Dorms. He had no idea what time it was.

Just as the thought crossed his mind, a loud clang rang out over the city. It wasn't a pleasant noise; it sounded like someone had tried to mix the Westminster Chimes with an air-raid siren. But it was definitely audible above the street clamor.

Everyone on the thoroughfare paused and looked up. A swift stillness swept over the street. For the first time all night, everything was quiet. A cold wind whispered through the bare branches of the planted trees; the fountain splashed and spluttered alone. But, as the last tone died away, the bustling hurry resumed. It was a different kind of busyness, though, as if everyone began hastily winding things down, putting away, and closing up.

Reed glanced over at Reagan. "What was that supposed to be?"

Reagan straightened from admiring a particularly attractive window model. "That's the Council's warning bell. It means we have half an hour to get back into the Dorms before curfew, or else."

Reed snorted in annoyance.

"Nine-thirty already," said Riley with a yawn. "I suppose we should start back."

"Yeah, or it'll be one long night," Reagan agreed.

"And an even longer day tomorrow, if Connors has anything to do with it."

CHAPTER 8

R eed studied Nathan across the room and wondered what to say. The day's work had not yet begun at the factory, and the workers stood in little clusters in the aisles, waiting for the belts to turn on. Late into the night, Reed had planned how to begin this conversation. He had finally settled on a satisfactory method but had forgotten it by the time he woke up. Now, as he eyed the other young man, he settled on a back-up plan and moved toward Nathan.

"So do I need to start wearing more deodorant or something?" He sauntered over. "If it's really that bad, you should've said something."

Nathan's friendly smile turned to a look of complete incomprehension. "Excuse me, what?"

"You know, last night—you sure didn't want to stick around after you saw me."

Nathan looked startled. "What do you mean? I didn't see you last night."

Reed gave an inward sigh of relief. So Riley was wrong. "You didn't? It was at the Boulevard. I yelled to you across the street right before that truck almost hit me. Didn't you hear me?"

Nathan held up a hand. "Whoa, whoa, I'm confused. So you almost got killed by a truck on the Boulevard and you think I was there? Sorry, but I have no idea what you're talking about."

Reed thought for a second. "Well, I guess you missed the part with the truck. By the time I got back up, you were already down the alley. I tried to catch up, but you're pretty dang fast."

For half a second, Nathan seemed to tense ever so slightly; then it was gone. He shook his head.

"Okay, let me get this straight. You think you were chasing me around last night in some back alley at the Boulevard? What on earth—I mean, are you sure it was me?" He sounded confused—almost laughing—but it seemed forced somehow.

"Positive," said Reed. "You were with some other guy I'd never seen before, walking along the sidewalk by J. Crew. Oh, and you were wearing your green Aeropostale hoodie with the white lettering."

Nathan's smile faded a little. "And you, like, followed me?"

"Kind of. I was trying to catch up with you to find out what was going on. I got close, but you lost me. You know, when you hid behind that dumpster."

Nathan's smile disappeared altogether. Without a word, he turned and walked to his station, his forehead creased in a heavy frown.

Reed followed him. "It was you, right?"

Nathan let out a deep breath. "Yeah, it was me." He didn't sound angry.

Reed waited, but Nathan said nothing more. His face was drawn and tight, his brows knitting as he stared at the floor.

Reed had not seen him like this before. "Okay, dude, I don't mean to be nosy, but... what's going on?"

Nathan took another deep breath but kept his eyes down. "I... I don't think I can tell you."

"You mean, you don't know?" Reed had to admit he was relieved; at least Nathan wasn't mixed up in anything.

Nathan opened his mouth to speak, then dropped his head. "I can't lie to you, Reed. I wish I could say that, but... I can't."

Neither of them said anything for a moment. The other workers were still talking in little groups around them. Someone was finishing a cup of coffee nearby; Reed could just catch the rich scent in the air.

Nathan cleared his throat and rubbed the back of his neck. "Look, Reed, I... I can't hide this from you; I mean, you *saw* me. But I can't tell you... I mean... you don't understand... Reed, can I trust you?" For the first time, he lifted his eyes to meet Reed's.

Reed opened his mouth to answer, but found he couldn't. He was caught off guard by the intensity of Nathan's eyes, probing, cutting deep into Reed's mind. He had the uncomfortable feeling they were reading him like a book. Nathan was making his own decision. Reed had to look away.

"Reed."

He dared to glance back.

Nathan was still staring fixedly at his face. "I think I can."

Can? Reed was confused but said nothing.

Nathan's gaze shifted over Reed's left shoulder, and he said, more to himself than to Reed, "But it doesn't look like I have a choice." He stood for another moment, staring into space before he shook himself. "I'm going to tell you something, but only if you promise you will *never* tell another living soul. Ever."

The thought of what he would say to Reagan flashed through Reed's mind, but he brushed it aside. Nathan's serious manner was making him curious and apprehensive. He swallowed.

"I promise." He didn't like the squeak in his own voice.

"I believe you," said Nathan quietly. "But we have to wait until the belt is on. It'll keep other ears from listening."

The whistle sounded, and the conveyer belts creaked and began to roll. The teenagers scattered to their stations as parts began to appear beneath the machines. Nathan waited until everyone else was chattering busily before he spoke. "Do you remember what I said yesterday about being in a small group?"

Reed nodded.

Nathan blew out his breath. "That's where I was going when you saw me last night." He hesitated, then wiped his forehead with his arm. "See, every now and then, a group of kids gets together in one of the apartments. Even on a good night, there's only a handful of us, but we stay for a couple hours."

"What's so secretive about that?" Reed shoved a wrapped part into its box.

"I'm coming to that," said Nathan patiently. "I'm sure you got a rule sheet when you first moved into the Dorms. If you looked on the back, you might've noticed the rule against 'unauthorized religious ceremonies.' That's what our group falls under. See, we're Christians."

Reed felt a dropping disappointment. That was it? Nathan was a Bible-thumper?

Nathan continued his explanation. "We're not an approved religious group since the government hates us so much, so having these meetings is technically illegal."

Suddenly, Reed was all ears. He might not care for religion, but his opinion of the government was much lower. "Hates you?"

"Definitely. They haven't liked us for a long time, but since this new group came into power, 'dislike' has turned into flat-out hatred. That religious rule was aimed right at us. They're hoping to snuff out Christianity on the Hill. We weren't going to let them, so we took to meeting 'underground.' They know we're here—the Council has eyes everywhere—but they haven't been able to find us yet. You probably saw the cop in the street last night; he's one of the guards they put on patrol, trying to sniff us out."

Reed was becoming interested in spite of himself. Not because he cared about Nathan's religion but because the whole idea of secret groups and underground meetings smacked of danger, secrecy, and even a hint of rebellion. "So you have a dozen kids going to illegal meetings every week. How do you keep that a secret?"

Nathan smiled as he wrapped a part. "We never meet at the same place twice in a row, and we're not on any kind of schedule. We keep it low key and quiet." He paused to find an empty box. "Anyway, you probably understand now what was going on last night and why I didn't really want to tell you."

"Yeah, sure. But, if everything's changed around every time, how do you know when and where these things are?" Reed was genuinely intrigued.

"We pass the message to each other whenever we can—on the way to work, on the way home, you know. It works out pretty well."

"So that's why you talk to the receptionist sometimes," said Reed, at last putting the pieces together.

"You noticed that, didn't you?"

"Yeah," Reed grinned sheepishly. "If you really want to know, I thought you... umm... had a crush on her."

Nathan laughed, causing some of the other workers to glance in their direction. "Oh, no," he said, regaining his composure. "We're just friends—more like siblings really. We're all like that in this group."

Reed's curiosity in this whatever-it-was of Nathan's was growing. The mystery of the nameless teens and the intrigue of their underground operation sent a shot of adrenaline through his blood, quickening his pulse. It mixed with something else—a deep and empty emotion he couldn't put a name to. It was like looking into a warm, glowing window from the cold outside.

"So have you always met in the apartments?"

"No, we used to hang out at the Dorms when we all lived there. A few of us moved into apartments at the end of last year so we could have a little more privacy. It's a lot safer, too. It's still risky, but God's been good."

A box from Reed's stack conveniently tumbled to the floor, and he was obliged to crawl under the belt to retrieve it. "How did you ever have top-secret meetings in the Dorms?" he asked, reemerging and dusting off his shirt. "I mean, it's not exactly the most private place in the world."

Nathan hesitated, a box half-sealed in his hands. "No offense, but I don't think I should say, because… well, because it's *secret*. It would be dangerous to tell. It's risky to be telling you any of this. I honestly never would have if you hadn't seen me last night."

Reed finally put into words a question that had been growing in the back of his mind. "If all this is so risky, then *why*? Why do you do it? Why do you risk all this just to get together and have a Bible study?"

It came out more derisively than Reed intended, but Nathan didn't seem disturbed. "I don't think you'll understand, but there's one answer for those questions. It's not a religion; it's… it's *more*."

More. The word stirred something deep within Reed, so deep he could hardly understand it. It came with a flicker of eagerness and longing.

But Nathan wasn't finished. "I don't know how else to describe it. It's more than what anything else can offer, more than what anything else is worth or what it costs us. Danger, hardship, rejection—that's nothing compared to it… or Him."

Reed worked silently, pondering. Then he spoke again. "You're right. I don't understand. At all. Totally clueless."

"I thought so," said Nathan.

Reed returned the conversation to the earlier topic. "So are you the leader of this whatever-you-call-it group?"

Nathan shook his head. "Oh no, not me. That would be…" he stopped. "That would be someone else." The sudden, guarded tone that dropped into his voice warned Reed against more questions.

The rest of the day was quiet between the neighbors. Reed pondered what he'd learned, guessing at what he had not, and tried to drop the whole thing from his mind, all of which met with minimal success.

Five o'clock came. As usual, Nathan was one of the first finished and out the door. Reed searched for a glimpse of him or the receptionist as he passed through the lobby, but saw neither.

When at last, cold, hungry, and pensive, he trudged up to the bus, his roommates were already there.

"Well?" Reagan asked promptly.

Reed had forgotten his promise. He searched his mind for something to say. "It was all a mistake. He just missed me in the crowd."

"That's it?" Reagan sounded let down.

"Yep," said Reed, "pretty much."

He wondered what Reagan would think if he knew the whole story.

CHAPTER 9

The next few days at the factory were quiet for Reed. Except for "Good morning" and "Good night," he didn't speak to Nathan at all. It was hard to say why he didn't. Perhaps, he reasoned, it was because he didn't want to be associated with Nathan in case he and his little group were caught. Or perhaps he was avoiding what might come up in conversation and, even more, Nathan's searching looks.

Dorm life, on the other hand, was anything but quiet. Something exciting and usually loud was always happening. As a roommate of the immensely popular Reagan, Reed was daily swept up in the swirl of social life with hardly a chance to catch his breath. This was a tremendous advantage for him. He could drown out any inkling of homesickness this way. There was plenty of material; Reagan alone attracted enough attention from the female population for all three roommates. Though Reagan was definitely the favorite and Reed and Riley were not stars themselves, they still basked in the light of their luminary roommate. On top of all that, word reached the Dorms that change was coming, and it brought a thrill of excitement to the gray winter evenings.

On a cold night not long after Reed's enlightening conversation with Nathan, Reagan came swinging through the door into their room. "Yo, guess what?"

Reed, sprawled on the top bunk, sat up. "You got a pay raise?" he speculated.

"*I* got a pay raise?" guessed Riley.

"Both wrong! We've all been wondering about this for a long time."

"You found out why we're here?"

"Nope." Reagan missed the cynical gist of Reed's words. "You know that thing they've been building behind the Mushroom? I found out that's gonna be a rec center!"

The front legs of Riley's chair came down with a bang. "No way!"

"Yep," Reagan continued, unwinding his scarf, "it's supposed to have racquetball, a gym with volleyball and basketball courts, weight rooms, ping pong, bowling, an indoor track—you name it! They're even putting an Olympic-size pool indoors and sand volleyball outside."

"Awesome!" Reed jumped down off his bed as if there wasn't a moment to lose. "When's it gonna be done?"

"They say in a month or two, but who knows for sure?"

It didn't take long for the news to spread through the Dorms. Rumors flew back and forth on all the halls, claiming the completion date for the project was anywhere from two weeks to six months away.

Director Connors put an end to all the guesses by issuing an announcement that the building would be open in just over two months. Reed hoped the Hill could wait that long. Some of the teens seemed to think they would die if it wasn't open by tomorrow.

Naturally, all the conversation at the factory the next day centered around the news. The workers could think of nothing else. Reed listened to the chatter and put in an occasional word, but Nathan said nothing. That wasn't unusual, but it made Reed realize that he missed talking with Nathan. It had only been a few days since their last conversation, but Reed felt the estrangement keenly. In a rush, before he lost his nerve, he turned to Nathan. "So are you excited about having a rec center?"

Nathan seemed slightly surprised at the abrupt question, but he pursed his lips. "Kinda-sorta. It'll be nice to have, I guess, but I wish they weren't building it."

Reed blinked. "What? Why not?"

"Have you ever wondered where they're getting the money to

build this thing? Or even how they pay to keep the whole Hill running?"

"Not really."

"Most of us haven't, but that's the thing. The government *doesn't* have enough money to do any of this. It's got to be borrowing from somewhere. Borrowing can't go on forever; one of these days, the creditors are going to want something back. It's going to be a rough day when that happens."

Reed was almost speechless at Nathan's reply. Almost. "You don't want a rec center because of where the money's coming from? Who cares?"

"We should," said Nathan, unperturbed, "because *not* caring is what got us into this mess in the first place. We can't ignore the reason for what they're doing; they're trying to take the place of a God they shoved out of the public eye a long time ago."

"I should have known," Reed muttered. "So it's all about religion."

Nathan heard him anyway. "Kinda. But it's not a religion. It's more than that. It affects everything about us; it's something we're supposed to live."

Reed nearly exploded. "You *say* that, but I've met plenty of Christians whose walk don't match their talk. How do I know *you're* any different?" His grammar tended to slip whenever he was agitated.

Nathan sighed. "You're right. There are a lot of hypocrites. We're definitely not perfect either, but…" He sighed again. "I guess you'd just have to see us for who we are, get to know us as people, and see what you think then."

Reed shot a sideways glance at him. Was that a disguised invitation? A strange but strong desire leapt up in him, like the spurt of a lighting match. He wanted to see what Nathan and this little group of his was like, *really* like. It had nothing to do with religion; the promise of adrenaline and danger were a strong enough hook on their own. Then another thought struck him; the Council had outlawed things like this. This could be a chance to strike back and show who was really boss—a chance to decide for himself. But there was something else, too. It stole over him softly, slipping through the cracks of his mind and past all his other thoughts: the feeling of walking past those glowing windows. He wanted to see it from the inside. All this rushed through his mind in a second.

"Well, could I?"

Nathan didn't seem to grasp the meaning of his words. "Could you what?"

"You said I should hang out with you guys and see for myself. Could I?"

There was a long silence. "You're asking to come to one of our meetings?" Nathan spoke very slowly.

"If you let me," said Reed. He rushed on. "I promise I wouldn't tell anybody. It's a win-win. You get to show me you're not phonies, and I get in on some of this top-secret, Mission Impossible action."

Nathan studied Reed for a long moment, a half-wrapped part in his hands. Reed was beginning to squirm when Nathan broke the silence. "I'd have to talk to the others before I could even say maybe," he said. "You understand we might say 'no' just because of the danger for you and for us."

"Of course," said Reed. The fever of the moment was already starting to wear off, and he was beginning to wonder why he'd asked.

"Then I'll talk to the others but, since today's Friday, it'll be after the weekend before I can tell you something. Even then, I can't guarantee you'll get a solid answer. I can't guarantee anything."

Chapter 10

B y the time Reed stepped out of Packing Room Two, he'd almost forgotten the whole incident. Much to his joy, today had been the long-awaited payday. His mind filled with images of everything he wanted to get as he tucked his first check into his back pocket. He reached the bus before his roommates and was waiting when they trudged up through the cold dusk.

Reagan spoke before Reed had a chance. "Hey," he called, "we've all got some dough now! How 'bout another trip into town?"

"Exactly what I was about to say!" Reed replied, rocking on his toes cheerfully. "I can finally get a real coat!"

After supper, the three set out along the dim sidewalks. This time, Reagan steered them toward a different part of the city away from the Boulevard. "More stuff like you'll want," he explained. "Shopping malls and department stores—it's the practical side of things."

The night was cold, but it wasn't as bone-chilling as nights past. They ambled along for a while, keeping up an idle conversation and occasionally pushing each other into telephone poles for the fun of it. Not five minutes into their walk, Reed felt a strange uneasiness creeping up his spine. He glanced over his shoulder. There was nothing but thick pools of shadow broken by the occasional street light. He shivered. *Quit being ridiculous.* But a few moments later, the feeling returned, settling in his stomach. Again he looked back; again he saw nothing. It happened several more times, and Reed was becoming disgusted with himself when suddenly—

CRASH!

A clanging din exploded out of an alleyway just behind them. Reagan yelled and spun around, dropping into a fetal position with his head wrapped in his arms. Riley dove behind Reed and nearly knocked him over as they scrambled to face the racket. With a yowl, a matted, tawny cat shot out of the darkness. It streaked between Reed's legs, hurtled the curb, and disappeared on the other side of the street, tail flicking wildly. The boys stared after it for a moment, their steaming breath coming in short spurts. Silence settled back over the street. Reed gulped and relaxed the doubled fists he held in front of his face.

Reagan unwrapped his arms from around his head and laughed shakily. "Ha! Just a cat! That's all. I guess all this money makes us a little jumpy... right, fellas?"

Riley and Reed quickly agreed, but Reagan still made them swear not to tell a soul about the embarrassing incident.

They reached their destination without further excitement. This part of the city was mostly shopping centers and department stores, but it was fairly empty for a Friday night. It didn't take Reed long to figure out that, in addition to his other abilities, Reagan was an expert on style. It was no surprise, and once this was established, Reagan took over as Reed's personal stylist. He skimmed through the store, gathering an armful of clothes that he piled into a fitting room and insisting, despite protests, that Reed try them on.

"At least just for laughs," he said, shoving Reed into the tiny room and throwing a few more shirts in after him.

He had other motives. As soon as Reed emerged, Reagan pounced and, popping open the top few shirt buttons, rolling the sleeves just so, and flicking Reed's hair behind his ears, he stepped back, saying. "There! What do you think, Riley? Is that the hottest roommate you've ever seen or what? We'll have girls by the dozens."

Reed colored as he eyed his reflection in the fitting room mirror. He had been told before that he was good looking—blue eyes, black hair, strong masculine jawline and firm chin—but it was different this time. The pale blue Henley with its tight fit around his upper body was not something he would have chosen for himself, but he liked it. Other people had called him handsome before, but hearing it from

Reagan gave the word a whole new meaning. He turned a little in front of the mirror, tilting his face at every angle. "You're just saying that. The girls are too busy with you to notice me anyway!"

"There's plenty to go around," Reagan chuckled, folding his arms and leaning against the doorway. "But when you wear that with those Lucky Brand jeans I've got in there, I just might have to fight for a few."

Riley said nothing but looked Reed up and down from under arched brows.

With Reed's wardrobe settled, the three were ready for something a little more frivolous. They returned to the Boulevard.

Several times during the evening, even amid the street bustle, Reed found himself looking over his shoulder. The uneasiness from earlier was back again, not as strong but definitely present. He tried to relax, but he couldn't shake the feeling. He finally gave up and did his best to enjoy the activity around him anyway.

They stayed at a café, meeting friends and taking in an astounding number of calories until the curfew bell sounded. As they strolled back toward the Hill, Reagan, a collection of bags slung over his shoulder, yawned. "Ah, I love paydays!"

"Mmm…" said Reed, fighting off drowsiness and a sugar high at the same time. He looked back over his shoulder.

Reagan caught the movement. "You've been doing that all night. What's up?"

"Mmm…" said Reed again.

"I know," said Reagan, "he can't speak. The *cat's* got his tongue."

"Hey! You jumped just as much as I did. And who squealed like a little girl?"

"That was not a squeal; that was a… masculine exclamation of surprise. Anyway, the cat's gone. You can stop looking for it now."

Reed did not answer.

CHAPTER 11

✳

The next day was Saturday. Weekend or not, Hill residents were required to work a half day before the weekend could really begin. The roommates, having slept off most of the sugar from their late night, followed their normal morning routine.

"It's just *wrong* to do this on a Saturday," moaned Reed after the alarm shattered the room's silence.

Riley mumbled some incoherent sentence that ended in a sleepy exclamation when he sat up and rediscovered the bunk above him.

"Don't blame me," mumbled Reagan. "It wasn't *my* idea. Man, I hate this!"

The silent, rushed feel of breakfast had become part of a normal morning for Reed. But that morning, as soon as he walked in the door, he knew something was not right. The quiet pressed down on the room with a heavy foreboding. Whispers flitted through the silence like birds before a coming storm. Even the rattle of dishes from the dish pit was hushed and subdued. By the end of the meal, Reed was almost suffocating in the heavy atmosphere. As soon as they finished and escaped back out into the cold morning, Reed drew a deep breath of the fresh air in relief. "What's up with *that*?"

"I don't know." Reagan shook his head and drew his brows together. "Something must've happened. See if you pick up anything at work."

As it turned out, Reed heard about nothing else. Talk flew thick and fast around the belt, some fact and some fiction. No one person knew all the details but, in the end, Reed managed to piece together what had happened from many different accounts.

The night before, a boy from the Dorms had been on his way down to the city just after supper, paycheck in hand. Somewhere between the Hill and the Boulevard, he had been waylaid by a single attacker, robbed, and brutally beaten. The encounter might have ended in a murder except that a group of Hill residents, passing by, came to his aid. The attacker fled on foot. Several of the boys had chased him, but he had shaken them off in the maze of alleys. The witnesses could only say it was a teenager, therefore a Hill resident. The Council and the city police department had already begun an investigation.

Reed felt sick. The uneasiness he had tried to ignore all night came back. His gut had been right; they had walked right past a murderer lurking in one of the inky alleyways. He didn't want to think about it. The sick feeling wore off as the morning progressed, and he had recovered himself by the time noon rolled around. But, when he left the factory at lunch and started toward the park's entrance, he noticed men in heavy overcoats and dark uniforms posted along the winding road. The black figures silhouetted on the hilltops were cut out sharp and grim against the gray clouds. Police. Reed dropped his eyes and hurried past.

When Reagan and Riley arrived at the gate, Reed was waiting by the bus. "So I wasn't just being paranoid last night."

Reagan held up his hands. "Okay, so you were on to something. We came that close to getting mugged, but it was the *cat* that let us in on it, not you."

Reed crossed his arms. "And what did the cat do?"

"Don't you see? That punk didn't know Miss Kitty was there and stepped on her tail or something. She let everybody know where she was, and he thought his cover was blown. He just waited for the next guy to come along."

It made sense, even if it meant Reed wasn't the hero he had hoped. As they climbed into the shuttle, he consoled himself that at least he wasn't the one stretched out on a hospital bed. It was a cheering thought.

When they arrived back at the Hill, they discovered that the Council's investigation was moving ahead quickly. More men in uniform were waiting in the parking lot as the workers unloaded. Officers blocked off the North Stairs, the Mushroom, the sidewalks, even the East Stairs behind the cafeteria. No one was allowed to leave.

When the last bus emptied, Director Connors appeared at the top of the North Stairs, tall and stern against the overcast sky. Two men in black flanked him, arms folded. The guards pushed the teens closer to the foot of the hill as the superintendent quieted the crowd with a lifted hand. "You are all to proceed immediately to your rooms and remain there until further notice." His booming voice carried well in the cold air. "The Hill is under lockdown until further notice."

Immediately, the men in black herded the crowd up the stairs and pushed the teens into their dorms. Reed found Michael waiting at the door to his hall as everyone crowded in. When the last boy filed past, Michael shut the door and locked it from the outside with an ominous click.

"What a day," sighed Reagan, flipping on the fluorescent light above the sink in their own room.

"I'll say," Reed grumbled, tossing himself up onto his bed. "This happen often?"

"No, we've never had anything like this before. I don't know what's gonna happen next. I guess we just make ourselves comfortable and wait." Reagan sighed and kicked off his shoes. "So much for lunch. I'm starving."

They waited. Over an hour later, Michael stepped into the room carrying a clipboard. He glanced around, wrote something down, and left without a word. Nothing else happened for a long time. At last, well after three o'clock, a boy from down the hall stuck his head in and said that Director Connors had ordered everyone down to the Square.

"Here we go," Reagan sighed, jumping off his bed.

"How the heck are they gonna get five thousand people to fit on the Square?" Reed wondered aloud as he pulled a Baja hoodie over his head.

It wasn't easy. The crowd packed not only the Square, but crammed into the spacious area between the dorms like sardines in a can. Reed hardly had room to shiver in the cold wind.

When all the halls had been emptied, the Director appeared at an open window on the second floor of Reed's dorm and addressed the waiting young people through a megaphone. He informed them of last night's events and explained the measures taken that day. The speech was filled with enough "for the safety of all's" and "for the public good's" to make Reed sick. He didn't feel very good or safe with the dark figures of the police visible on the fringes of the crowd.

The superintendent then laid down the law: no one under any circumstances was to leave the Hill that day or the next unless instructed otherwise. They were free to move among the dorms, but no more. Police would be positioned around the perimeter, and violators would be severely dealt with. That was all.

This announcement was greeted with silence by the crowd but, as soon as Director Connors disappeared back into the room, an audible groan arose.

"There went the weekend," said Riley, shoving his hands into his pockets as the crowd dispersed.

"Aww... it's not that bad," consoled Reagan. "Besides, this way I can have a captive audience when I dress Reed up as my fashion model."

Reed made an odd noise somewhere between a sneeze and a hiccup.

Reagan patted him on the back. "Gesundheit. Let's go back to the room, and you can watch the master at work."

In no time, he had Reed "fixed up" like the night before. When he was satisfied with Reed's appearance, he focused on his own and transformed from the corporate office man to the swankified Reagan of the Dorms. He stood next to Reed in front of the mirror. "It'll do," he observed critically.

"Do you do this every Saturday?"

"Not usually. Just special ones."

"And what Saturday isn't special with Reagan around?" observed Riley, spiking up his gelled hair with a comb.

Reagan laughed. "I like the way you think... sometimes."

Reed had not anticipated the response his new look would generate once they left the room. He was noticed, even liked, more than ever before. He hadn't realized before how strong was the correlation between style and status on the Hill. They dove straight into a whirlwind tour of the Dorms that Reagan called "hall hopping." To Reed, it felt more like "whizzing." They went straight from one dorm to the next, meeting people and playing games. The dorms were bursting with activity, throbbing with anything from games of "Sardines" to FIFA championships. When he emerged from Dorm Twenty Four, his ears still ringing from the beat of some enthusiastic hip-hop dancers, Reed began calculating which dorms were left unvisited. "That takes care of all of 'em," he announced, "except ours and Dorm Eleven."

"Don't count Eleven," said Reagan, brushing off his jeans from a slide he had taken in a game of hall whiffle ball. "We won't go there."

"What's wrong with it?"

"Let's just say it's the ghetto of the Hill, and not in the cool way. It's on the east side where nobody ever goes. The Director puts all the troublemakers, misfits, and shady characters there so he can have all his rotten eggs in one basket."

The three returned to their own hall where they found a crowd of boys waiting, ready for Reagan to "get things going." Always willing to oblige, Reagan set things in motion, sending someone to fetch his iPod and borrowing the largest sound system on the hall. He had no trouble with either request. That was how they spent the rest of the day. Reed wasn't sure he had ever had so much fun in his life. If this was the Hill, he loved it.

Much later, after the party had peaked and been broken up by a few of the RDs, Reed and Reagan ambled down the hall in search of the next thing to keep them busy. As they passed one of the rooms, Reed caught sight of a boy leaning against the wall who seemed to be watching them go by. As soon as their eyes met, the boy looked down and seemed to be busy with his phone. Reed had never seen him on the hall before. In fact, he had never noticed him anywhere on the Hill.

"Who is that?" Reed nudged Reagan and gestured back toward the stranger.

"Him?" Reagan glanced at the boy. "Oh, him! I haven't seen him around in a while. He's—"

Before he could finish, a crowd of boys spilled out a doorway and collided with the pair, engaged in an all-out battle of plastic light-sabers and Silly String. Since it was a completely pointless me-lee, they joined in without hesitation. Forgetting his question, Reed joined Reagan in gleefully pummeling anyone and everyone with a saber borrowed from a fallen hero.

He was beginning to really enjoy himself when a hand seized him by the scruff of the neck and jerked him out of the fray. Surprised, he found it was Reagan. His roommate held him back from the rest firmly, watching the scuffle from the sidelines with a look of complete innocence. Reed's incredulity changed to sudden understanding as he caught sight of Michael trotting down the hall. He quickly dropped the saber.

"Okay, okay, break it up! I said break it UP!" the RD bellowed above the din. The fight subsided.

"Everybody get back to your rooms," Michael ordered. "If you're not from this dorm, then get back wherever you belong; it's five minutes till curfew."

He sounded tired and cranky. The crowd began to disperse im-mediately. As Michael turned away, Reed heard him mutter under his breath, "Man, this lockdown's gonna kill me."

As the rest of the boys scattered to their rooms, the stranger Reed had seen earlier slipped through the thinning crowd and out the door, one of the last to leave.

CHAPTER 12

The next day went much the same. No one had to work, but the lockdown was still in place. The Hill residents were forced to amuse themselves among the Dorms. Reed stuck with Reagan most of the day, enjoying his new popularity and adding to his collection of acquaintances. He ran into a few old faces as well, like Hunter. They had a brief conversation, more relaxed and less awkward than their previous two. Reed decided he and Hunter might actually get along well in the future.

The day progressed and the partying continued. That night, sitting at supper in the Mushroom, Reed had to marvel at how they had managed to keep so busy all day. The usual clamor of suppertime filled the Mushroom: loud talk, laughter, clattering plates, and grating chairs. Reed sat with his roommates, listening to the jovial hubbub and enjoying his macaroni and cheese.

Suddenly, a deathly hush fell over the cafeteria. Reed glanced up from his plate. All eyes were fixed on the main door behind him. He turned around. A man in a dark uniform and long black overcoat blocked the steps. He was tall, feet set apart and hands held behind him, and the whole room went cold beneath his stretching shadow. Director Connors stood behind him, flanked by several men in uniform.

"Who's that?" Reed breathed to Riley.

"Vonhauser, the Council's head of police."

Reed's mouth went dry, and he eyed the man in a kind of fearful awe. The silence thickened for several awful moments as the man ran his eyes over the tables. At last, he spoke, each clipped word cutting through the heavy atmosphere like a blade cleaving an apple. "This building has been completely surrounded. All exits are closed."

Everyone turned to the back of the room where an emergency exit opened to the outside. Several policemen had entered and now barred the way out.

The man continued. "Remain where you are. The Council wishes to apprehend a fugitive." He flipped out a leather binder from under his arm. The silence was agonizing. Slowly, he read out a name.

"Joseph Desrok-Mosler."

There was a gasp from across the room. Half a dozen teenagers leapt out of their chairs and scattered like frightened rabbits. One staring boy was left alone. Pools of terror filled his wide eyes with the look of a trapped animal. His fork shook as he laid it on the table and stood up. Two officers from the back wall swooped down on him and marched him to the front of the room.

The towering man frowned down on him from the top of the steps. "On charges of robbery, assault and battery, and attempted murder, you are under arrest by order of the Council."

He stepped aside. The two officers pushed the prisoner up the stairs toward the front door. The rest followed in a single line. Vonhauser, ignoring the remaining teens, snapped the folder shut and stalked out. The door swung shut. They were gone.

The silence hung in the air for a moment more. Then commotion broke out as everyone began talking at once and shoving back their chairs. In record time, the dining hall emptied. As soon as he was outside, Reed let out a long breath. "So they caught their thug. That's a relief."

"Yeah, they caught him," said Reagan, his lips pressed into a thin line. "But that was really quick. *Too* quick. It can only mean one thing."

"What?"

"It means they had some inside help. Boys, I think we've got ourselves a ringer."

Riley's brows met in a troubled frown. "Who?"

"That's the scary part." Reagan knotted his scarf with a jerk. "I don't have the slightest hunch. Whoever it is, they're good. Really good. We've always been able to pick out ringers before. But this time…" He shook his head. "We'll just have to keep our ears open. If anybody knows, we'll be the first to find out. My social web will tell me."

Reed laughed suddenly. "You sound like a spider!"

"He is," Riley assured him. "Trust me."

"Of course! I catch all the shocking and juicy tidbits that wander into my domain."

Reed grimaced. "Okay, never say that again."

At the dorm, they found a notice taped on the door announcing that the lockdown was lifted.

"Finally!" Reagan whacked the paper. "But it doesn't do much good now. The weekend's over."

Riley yawned. "Oh, well. I'm going to bed early. There's work in the morning."

"Ugh," moaned Reed, "At least there'll be something interesting to talk about."

* * *

When he entered Packing Room Two the next morning, Reed's eyes fell immediately on Nathan. Friday flooded back into his mind. He'd completely forgotten about his request.

He shut his eyes for half a second. *What was I thinking? At least they'll say no with this whole ringer theory now.*

He slipped into his station with a nod to Nathan. The other boy shot him a significant look and arched his eyebrows; he had something to tell him. Reed nodded and tuned in to the buzz of conversation flying around the belt. Everyone was talking about the arrest. No one was surprised that Desrok-Mosler was from the infamous Dorm Eleven, but they marveled at how quickly he had been caught. Reagan's ringer theory was already circulating, and everyone agreed it had to be true. Nobody knew who it could be or even dared to venture a guess.

The group conversation slacked off when the belts turned on and work began. It was only then that Nathan spoke. He kept his eyes fixed on his hands.

"Before I say anything else, I have a confession to make. I didn't actually do it, but I set it up." He paused and blew out his breath. "You've been followed for the last two days."

The piece in Reed's hand nearly slipped out of his fingers. He blinked. Followed?

Nathan hurried on. "See, when you asked to come to our meetings, I knew we had to know more about you. We've been suspecting a ringer. So I got the others' opinions, and we all agreed to set our best man on following you—just to be safe. Our guy followed you over the weekend and reported what you'd been up to. There, now I've told you."

Reed's mind raced back over the past two days. It was strange, looking back on things with the knowledge he'd been watched while he did them. He wasn't sure he liked the feeling at all.

Nathan added a sealed box to his stack and looked Reed full in the face. "Please understand it was *only* for safety's sake. I didn't like the idea, but we had to do it. And our shadow only told us things that might be a concern."

That was a relief. Sort of. Reed found his voice. "Oh." He cleared his throat. "Well. That's okay... I guess." Though he had his voice, he couldn't get all of his thoughts back together. He realized he had just wrapped the same part twice.

"So that's the confession," said Nathan. "Now for the news. We all prayed about it and talked for a while, and we decided you can come to our next meeting."

Reed's few collected thoughts scattered in every direction. He wrapped the same part in a third layer.

"Of course," Nathan went on, "you have to promise absolute secrecy. You can't tell anyone anything—where you're going or names or anything like that—but we've decided to trust you. I mean, we didn't have a whole lot of choice since you were on to us, but still..."

Reed managed to stammer out some sort of thanks and assurance of his silence.

Nathan gave him a final look and seemed satisfied. "Okay. I'll be waiting at the East Stairs around eight o'clock tonight. You'll have to figure out how to get away without being noticed if you decide to come. I'd totally understand if you changed your mind after last night, seeing what the Council can do."

The rest of the day was a blur for Reed. *Why did I ask such a dumb thing?* He jammed a part into its box. *What was I thinking? This isn't a TV show; it's a Bible study. What's happened to me? I don't even want to go... do I?*

He wrestled the question around in his mind, getting no answers and no relief. Perhaps he shouldn't go. Or maybe he could go just this once, for civility's sake. There had to be *some* way to get out of this. What was it Nathan had said? Something about Reed changing his mind. Yeah, he'd said he would understand if Reed changed his mind because of the Council.

Reed's independence flared, and his mind steeled into a firm resolve. He didn't care what the Council said; he wasn't going to back out now. Besides, he might still get an adrenaline rush out of the whole thing. It was settled. He was going.

* * *

Back at the Dorms that night, the roommates idled away the evening in their room. Reed kept an eye on Riley's alarm clock, blinking away the minutes on the nightstand. When eight o'clock neared, Reed jumped off his bed and grabbed his jacket from its hook.

Reagan looked up from his computer, surprised. "Goin' somewhere?"

"Yeah," Reed replied, pulling on his coat. "I'm off to meet a friend from work. I probably won't be back till late. See ya." He slipped out the door and shut it behind him. In the hall, he let out his breath. That had come off well. He hadn't even had to lie. He turned down the hall toward the dorm's back exit.

He left the hall and clattered down the empty, echoing stairwell, his thoughts churning. What was he getting himself into? This deal hadn't come with a security guarantee. The Council could easily catch him, couldn't they? But would they?

He reached the ground floor and pushed out into the cold night. Zipping up his jacket, he glanced briefly upward and paused. The sky had been overcast all day with a low, gray blanket that darkened into boiling black as night fell. But now, a small fissure in the billowing clouds had split open overhead. There was no moon and, through the gap, a few stars shone in the velvety blue-black depths beyond. Reed never paid much attention to stars before. They were beautiful tonight, untouched by the clouds that tried blot them out. Their pure, silvery radiance was enthralling, softly enchanting. It held him spellbound for a moment.

A gust of cold wind tossed the hair off his forehead, bringing his mind back to earth. The clouds rolled over the gap again. He shook himself.

"Quit being stupid," he muttered. "You've got places to be. Besides, I think it's going to rain soon."

He turned up his collar and hurried down the sidewalk toward the East Stairs. Hadn't Reagan said these were scarcely used? Good— less chance of being seen. But then a realization struck him. This was *that* side of the Hill, the side where the two "shady" dorms were situated. Reed's confidence came to a screeching halt. How "shady" were they? Desrok-Mosler had been from Dorm Eleven. Were there more like him?

The night shapes and noises around him were suddenly ominous. Every tree had a human-shaped silhouette lurking around its base. The hedges were walls of blackness that hid dark forms. Sighing wind in the bare branches became evil whispers; groans from tree trunks were slow hinges turning in the darkness.

Reed felt cold sweat begin to roll down his back. His shivering doubled, his teeth clenched to keep from knocking together. "Maybe I should go back," he said aloud. It was supposed to make him feel better, but it didn't. The wind threw the words back in his face for the choked whisper they were.

Yes, he should go back. This was too dangerous, and his senses were giving him a final warning. Every hair on the back of his neck was on end. It wasn't too late…

One thought alone kept him from turning and running back to the safety of his room: he had to stay in control. If he gave in now, the Council won. He had to go on if only for that reason. He *had* to.

The head of the East Stairs appeared before him, the trees that overshadowed it looming black against the clouds. He hurried toward them, anxious to make it to the bottom where Nathan waited.

A dark shape stepped from the trees. Reed's heart leaped into his throat, a stab of terror shooting through his body. He opened his mouth, but no sound came out. No one would hear if he cried for help anyway. He was alone. The black figure stepped toward him.

"You're a little earlier than I expected."

Chapter 13

R eed nearly collapsed in relief. Never had Nathan's voice been so welcome. "Oh," he gasped, heart still pounding, "Sorry." He took a few deep breaths.

"You're fine. Come on."

Nathan led the way down the stairs. They crossed behind the deserted Mushroom and turned onto the sidewalk leading into the city. Neither of them said anything until they were a safe distance from the Dorms.

"Did you get away all right?" Nathan slowed to walk next to Reed.

"Yeah, I told them I was going to meet a friend. I don't think they were suspicious." A drop of water landed on Reed's ear. "Great, here comes the rain."

Nathan quickened their speed to a jog. The rain held back its full force until they had turned off the main street onto a side road amid the apartments, then it struck in a downpour. Sheets of water dropped from the sky, pounding on roofs, windows, and sidewalks as the boys dodged through innumerable streets and alleys. Reed became hopelessly lost. He had no idea there were so many apartments on the Hill.

Nathan never hesitated or slowed his pace despite the darkness and the blinding rain. They dodged puddles and avoided the occasional streetlights until Reed thought he could go no further. Nathan at last turned into a final alley and flattened himself against a wall beneath a sheltering eave. Reed followed his example, gasping for breath.

Nathan took a quick look around the corner and pulled back. "Somebody else just got here. We'll wait a few minutes."

Reed leaned his head back against the wall and slowed his ragged breathing. "So where are we?" He could barely see Nathan through the darkness. Thunder rolled in the distance.

"The apartment of two girls in the group." Nathan's voice was low but close. "Sarah and Courtney are hosting tonight."

Reed shook water out of his eyes. The rain seemed to be slacking off. "Does 'hosting' mean they do all the talking?"

"No, it just means we have it in their apartment. Wilson's usually the leader unless somebody else has something special to say." After a moment of silence, Nathan stuck his head around the corner again. "Okay, we can go now."

They crossed the street like shadows. The rain had slowed to a steady, soaking shower that beat rhythmically in the puddles and tumbling gutters. Nathan headed for a door across the road. A single carriage lamp twinkled in the rain. Three brick stairs and a welcome mat—Nathan didn't bother to knock but cracked the white door open. The two slipped in.

Inside, dim light helped Reed's eyes adjust from the dark night. He was in a small entry hall filled with wet coats hung on pegs or slung across a white washing machine. Nathan removed his jacket; Reed unzipped his. He was relieved to find it had kept him surprisingly dry.

"Hello, Nathan! You look wet." A girl stepped suddenly into the hall. Reed jumped.

"Hey, Sarah," replied Nathan, hooking his coat on an empty peg. "Yeah, it's coming down pretty hard out there. I hope I'm not getting your floor too wet."

"It's seen worse," she said, smiling. Then she turned. "And you must be Reed. I'm Sarah. Nice to meet you." She had straight brown hair pulled back in a ponytail that swung as she moved. He glanced at her lightly freckled face but looked down when her friendly but frank eyes met his.

"Same here," he replied, wriggling out of his wet coat.

"We've heard all about you from Nathan," she said. "You're more than welcome. Come in, both of you. Almost everybody's here." She led the way out of the hall and through a dark kitchen toward an adjoining, peach-colored living room. Dim light filtered through the doorway. Reed saw a handful people moving around inside. He hung back, suddenly shy. Maybe he shouldn't have come after all; he felt like he had stepped into someone else's party. Too late now. *Me and my stupid curiosity.* He swallowed hard and followed Nathan out of the kitchen.

The den was a small room with a pink and white couch, a few upholstered chairs, and a large picture window, heavily curtained. Two lamps diffused a warm glow from cream-colored shades. Eight or ten teenagers were scattered through the room, talking quietly.

Nathan stopped at the edge of the light. "I'm sure you'll meet everyone eventually," he said in a low voice, "but I'll give you a little help with the names. You just met Sarah, and that's Courtney over there." He pointed to a girl across the room whose gingery hair curled to her shoulders. "They live together."

Reed did his best to commit names and faces to memory as Nathan continued pointing around the room. The young man on the couch with brown hair and a hawk nose was Wilson, the group leader. He was talking to Gabriel, or Gabe, the dark-headed one who seemed to keep his lips pressed together. Kara, the light brunette with highlights, stood next to black-haired Krista by the window.

"Well, Nathan! Are we playing hide and seek?" A blonde girl advanced to meet them, a smile teasing at the corners of her lips. "Because if we are," she continued, crossing her arms and arching her brows in an attempt to look severe, "then I'm really sorry I didn't give you more time to hide. Just standing there like that makes you look like an unsocial introvert who doesn't want to be around the rest of us."

"Maybe I am," replied Nathan, also folding his arms. "Or maybe we were just standing here having a good time and you interrupted us."

"Oh, I see!" she laughed. "How are you tonight, Nathan?"

"Wet, but tolerable, thank you." He grinned at her, then turned. "Reed, I'm sure you recognize her, but this is Lucy."

Of course Reed recognized her. It was hard to forget the receptionist from the factory, though he had never heard her name. It seemed to fit her well. Funny, he hadn't noticed before how pretty she was.

"Of course." She turned to him. "We sort of met on your first day. I think you were nervous about starting... was it as bad as you thought?"

Reed was surprised she remembered him. "Uh... nah, I guess not. I mean, it wasn't fun, but I survived."

Another girl and a boy came up just then to greet Nathan. He introduced them in turn to Reed, who was beginning to wonder how many more there were.

"This is Katy." Nathan indicated the petite, brown-haired girl with a heart-shaped face. "She's Lucy's roommate at the Dorms. And this," he gestured to the boy, "is Alec, our undercover man. He was your shadow for the last few days."

Reed looked the young man up and down. He seemed about Reed's age, but he was smaller and shorter. There was something about his boyish face and light brown Harvard cut that seemed familiar. It clicked suddenly; it was the new face Reed had noticed on the hall during the lockdown.

"I think I've seen you before," said Reed.

"You have," replied Alec, his eyes twinkling. They were unusual eyes, an extraordinary blue-green color that reminded Reed of a Sprite can. "I'm afraid I got a little careless that night. I wasn't planning on a light saber battle in the middle of the hall."

"Yeah, those are kinda hard to predict. But how'd you stay out of sight before that? I'd never seen you at all."

"I have my ways." Alec raised his eyebrows mysteriously, but he couldn't quite banish the laughter from his face. "I almost didn't the first night, though, thanks to that creep and that stupid cat."

Reed started. "Cat?"

"Yeah, you remember—the one in the alley? I was shadowing you guys toward the Boulevard when I slipped in there. I stepped on it in the dark." He laughed. "We were both surprised, and he bolted through a pile of trashcans. Some guy took off from behind the pile, and I thought for sure you were going to come see what was going on."

Reed was speechless. Two people following them at the same

time in the same alleyway? Unbelievable. No wonder his uneasiness had been so strong.

"Anyway," said Alec cheerfully, "it scared me to death, and you, too, I bet. Thank goodness the street wasn't more crowded than it was. It wasn't my best moment."

Reed decided he liked Alec.

Sarah interrupted the conversation before it could go further. "Does anyone know if the other two are going to make it?" She joined the little circle by the door. "I haven't talked to them since yesterday."

"I did this morning," Lucy spoke up. "They said they would be here if they could."

"Nobody was at their apartment when I passed it," put in another girl. Reed went down his mental list and decided it was Kara.

"We'll wait a few more minutes then," Sarah decided. "Elijah always comes unless something's wrong. I hope nothing *is* wrong," she added, frowning.

"There're more?" Reed whispered to Nathan.

Nathan chuckled. "Elijah and Cody. They work for a private marketing company downtown, so sometimes they can run a little late. I really want you to meet Elijah, though."

Reed eyed him. "Why?"

Nathan shrugged. "I don't know. He's just... different. I think you'll like him."

The door opened and shut quickly.

"They're here!" exclaimed Sarah. She hurried off toward the front hall and returned in a moment with a figure behind her. He was tall and strongly built with broad, strapping shoulders that seemed to fill the narrow doorway. He pushed back the hood of his forest green jacket to reveal dark, crewcut hair and a well-formed, masculine face.

"That's Cody," Nathan said in Reed's ear. "He and Elijah live and work together."

Cody stepped out of the doorway, still removing his coat, and someone else appeared. He was about Cody's height, but his head was bent as he unzipped his navy Northface jacket. Then he looked up and met Reed's eyes across the room. Reed could only stare.

He was slender, and dark brown hair, touched with the tiniest hint of gold over the left temple, swept above his forehead. His face was clean-cut, open, and strikingly handsome. But it was his eyes that held Reed's gaze. They were blue—pure, blazing blue. Not sky blue, or ocean blue, or peacock blue, but an intense, beautiful blue that made even Alec's seem commonplace. And they had a depth to them—a calming deepness that spoke of understanding, perception, and something else Reed could not put a finger on.

"Sorry," Cody was saying, "the boss was out today, and everybody had to stay pretty late. I didn't think we'd ever get away."

"Thanks." Elijah smiled as Sarah took his coat. "I hope you haven't been waiting too long."

"Of course not! Come in."

As the group moved into the living room, Nathan grabbed Reed by the shoulder and steered him in their direction. Reed had a sudden reluctance to meet the newcomers, most likely because Nathan was so excited about it. Or perhaps it was the way Elijah's eyes seemed to cut right through him; it made Reed feel like a shy second grader with cookie crumbs on the front of his shirt.

They made their way up to the newcomers, and Nathan made a quick introduction. Reed smiled automatically, sticking out his hand. "It's—umm—nice to meet you."

Cody said nothing, but he had a very firm grip that made Reed's eyes water.

"It's great to finally meet you, too, man," said Elijah. His voice was not low, but it had a manly tone and a pleasing fullness. "We're glad you could make it."

"Yeah, same here," Reed replied. Without thinking, he dusted off the front of his shirt. He wasn't sure what to say next, but he felt something was needed. "So you guys don't live on the Hill anymore?"

"Well, not in the Dorms," Elijah said. "Cody and I moved into an apartment a couple months ago, but it's technically still on the Hill. Alec says you're in Dorm Four. You probably know Reagan."

"Of course! He's my roommate. Do you know him?"

Elijah raised his eyebrows and exchanged looks with Cody. "Roommate, eh? Yeah, I knew him, though we usually ran in different circles."

Reed wasn't sure how to reply. Thankfully, he didn't have to because Wilson, Gabe, and some of the girls came up to introduce themselves. Reed was grateful for Nathan's help with names beforehand; he would have been completely lost without it.

"We've heard a lot about you from Nathan," Wilson echoed Sarah once the rush of introductions was over. "It's great to have you here."

Reed was beginning to wonder what they had heard. He didn't have a chance to ask, however, as Gabe interrupted the conversation. "Do you think you were followed, Nathan?" he asked, lowering his voice and stepping closer. Reed noticed that he still kept his lips pressed together even when he talked.

"No, I was extra careful," Nathan assured him.

"Did you see anyone on the way over?"

"Nope. It was pouring rain and totally deserted."

"Nobody noticed either of you slipping away?" Gabe pressed.

Nathan turned to Reed. "You'll have to forgive Gabe," he said, only half-joking. "He's kind of like our watchdog and head of security—very good, too. I don't know what we'd do without him."

The conversation would have gone further, but Sarah interrupted. "Since we're all here, let's go ahead and sit down," she announced. "Wilson's about ready to start."

Everyone found a seat of some sort and settled in, although two of the guys ended up on the floor. Reed wedged in between Nathan and the arm of the couch, bracing himself for a long and boring evening.

This isn't half as cool as TV.

CHAPTER 14

Wilson began his talk with some Bible verse about witnesses and living in "the last days," but his words made no sense to Reed. As the evening progressed, some of the others occasionally chimed in with more verses and insights of their own, but Reed lost interest and most of it went in one ear and out the other. After a while, however, a few of Wilson's words caught his attention and jerked his wandering mind back to the present.

"...one of our greatest enemies is complacency," Wilson was saying. "Without that, the Council never could have done what they have. GRO wouldn't exist."

"What do you mean?" Reed interrupted. Immediately, he felt the blood rush to his cheeks. Everyone was looking at him, but the interruption didn't seem to annoy Wilson.

"Well," he explained, leaning back on the sofa, "obviously our government isn't what it used to be, so how did it get all this new power—suddenly, by force? No. It was a slow and gradual turn-over. New groups and new people came to power doing things that should have concerned us, but 'we the people' did nothing about it because of one thing: apathy. We just didn't care. The change came in small steps that seemed insignificant, even good at the time. They got more confident as we got more indifferent, and that's the only way they've been able to get us where we are today. And this is just the beginning. They're not going to stop anytime soon."

"Surely not," Reed objected. "They can't do anything else... can they? I mean, most people in the Dorms aren't happy about what they've done already."

"They aren't?" Wilson raised an eyebrow. "Have you ever heard anyone complain about it? Not about the rules, I mean, but about what's happened?"

Reed frowned. "Well... no, I haven't. How weird! Why aren't they mad?"

"It's what I said." Wilson shook his head. "Apathy. They've been lulled into not caring. Their parents, too. This wasn't a sudden leap to take over the families and split them up. They've been working up to it for years, building trust and drawing kids away. GRO just took things to a whole new level."

"But why would they do that?" Reed fixed his eyes almost fiercely on the other boy.

Wilson leaned forward. "Because it's all about the mind. Never underestimate the power of ideas and the things people will do for them. Ideas are the way into the mind and, if you can control an idea, you can control the world. It starts with us—the young, impressionable future. They saw that and took it. And they were only able to take it because, first, they got us to a point where *we didn't care*."

Wilson returned to his original subject, but Reed sank into his own thoughts. Wilson was right. When Reed stepped back and looked at it, what was going on around him was unbelievable. Who, twenty years ago—or even ten—would have dreamed things would be like this? It was astounding to think about. And nobody cared. *Nobody cared.*

Reed had almost forgotten the hatred and bitterness he'd felt so strongly when he first arrived. Now, it burst back on him like an underworld geyser. He, the one who loved his independence so much, was trapped in an oppressive system built by others' carelessness. He loathed it—he *despised* it—and he was absolutely powerless. He clenched his teeth.

Wilson's talk ended, and the group began their prayer time. Reed shut his eyes mechanically with the rest, but his mind kept working. So he couldn't break out of the system, but that didn't mean he had to be a slave to it. *No, absolutely not.*

At the same time, it wasn't all bad here. Surely he could find a way to keep his independence without giving up everything about this new life. He could use what the system offered to his advantage—go along, play the game, and get what he wanted without letting it control him. It wouldn't be easy, though. He had almost forgotten his anger before; that couldn't happen again. *Never forget and never let go.*

He realized the prayer time had ended. Calming his inward fuming, Reed opened his eyes and looked up. Elijah's gaze was fixed intently on his face. Reed couldn't interpret the expression of the blue eyes, but they seemed to be reading him, getting past his careful guard. He looked away, discomfited, until he sensed the other boy ceased to study him. He was not in a mood to be studied.

Everyone was getting up and talking. Reed stretched and winced as he tried to stand. His side was sore where the arm of the couch had dug under his rib cage. He must have been sitting for over an hour.

Nathan rotated his left shoulder and checked his phone. "We'll have to leave soon to make curfew at the Dorms."

Reed grimaced. "Do we just walk out?"

"No, we slip off alone or in pairs; it can take a while. We'll start off in a minute. I'll let you know when it's time."

Nathan was called over to join a conversation across the room. Reed, left by himself, tried to look intelligent instead of standing awkwardly with his hands in his pockets. He wandered over to examine a collection of china figurines on a whatnot in the corner. He hadn't been there long before Gabe approached him. Reed hadn't paid much attention to Gabe before. He sized him up swiftly. His hair was dark, nearly black, and cut into a classic undercut that swept up off his forehead to the side. He had a finely chiseled face sprinkled with the beginnings of a dark beard with a straight nose and well-defined cheekbones. He seemed to have Arab blood in him, and there was a serious intensity about his whole bearing that culminated in his dark eyes. He still kept his lips pressed together.

The conversation began with some stilted small talk, but Gabe was quick to get to his point. "Look," he began, "I know Nathan wouldn't have brought you here if he didn't think you could be trusted, but we have to be careful. I can't stress enough that you say nothing about this to anybody. You're the only one we've ever done something like this for, and it's very dangerous to have you here. You can't say *anything* to *anyone* at all."

"I know," answered Reed, slightly annoyed. He toyed with one of the figurines in his hand. "I can keep my mouth shut."

Gabe studied him. "I hope that's true," he said quietly. "Frankly, I don't know anything about you except what Alec and Nathan have told me. But remember this: I have my reasons for protecting my friends, and I will do that to the best of my ability." He took a step closer and lowered his voice. "You and I both live in the Dorms and, if anything about this ever gets out, I will know. I'll be watching."

Their eyes locked.

"Thanks, I'll remember that."

Nathan approached. "Ready, Reed? We probably need to head out."

Reed set the figurine back on the shelf and turned away. Gabe never moved.

They put on their coats in the dim hallway as others in the group told them goodbye. Gabe was absent, but Reed was surprised how cordial and warm the rest of them were. When they were ready, Sarah opened the door with a soft "good night," and the two boys slipped outside. The rain had ceased, but a thin mist swirled between the apartments and over the puddle-filled streets. They glided through the damp, white shreds to a side road and began navigating their way back toward the Dorms. After several minutes, Nathan spoke softly. "What'd you think?"

Reed stared up the street in front of them. "Still thinking," he answered. "Everybody was nice, though. Well, almost everybody."

He heard the smile in Nathan's voice. "'Almost' meaning Gabe. Sorry about that. Since he's, like, our security guy, he's always careful about everybody. This new ringer theory has him especially edgy. He's really a great guy once you get to know him. He actually—"

Suddenly, Nathan threw his arm across Reed's chest.

"Stop!" he hissed, staring into the darkness.

Reed froze and peered over his shoulder. Something was moving.

Nathan searched the blackness for a second longer, then he gave Reed a push forward. "Walk!" he whispered. "And look casual!"

Reed did his best under the circumstances, and they sauntered across the open street. Out of the dark on their left, a man appeared, cloaked in the black overcoat and face mask Reed had seen once before. His pulse quickened.

Nathan gave the man no more than a nonchalant glance. Even when their paths almost intersected in the middle of the street, he merely nodded to the black figure and passed by. The man didn't seem to pay them any attention. Nonetheless, Reed could have sworn he felt eyes on the back of his head.

Nathan quickened their pace as soon as they were safely out of the street, but neither of them spoke until they had turned a few corners and left the man far behind.

"Well, that could have been worse." Nathan glanced over his shoulder and stuck his hands in his pockets.

"But he saw us! That can't be good."

"I don't think it will be a big deal. He'll see a lot of kids out right before curfew trying to get back before ten. We weren't doing anything suspicious."

Reed still couldn't shake the chill the man had given him. They walked the rest of the way in silence.

By the time they mounted the East Stairs, he was feeling a little better about the incident. All was quiet, and they were still in time for curfew. Before they separated at the top of the stairs, Nathan broke the silence. "I'm glad you could go."

"Yeah, me, too. See you tomorrow."

Nathan disappeared into the shadows. Reed turned in the opposite direction and walked slowly toward his dorm. Now that he was alone, he let his mind run through the events of the evening. It hadn't been the experience he had been expecting, but one person dominated his thoughts. Elijah.

What is it about that guy? He pulled his coat closer around him as he walked. *Nathan wanted me to meet him for some reason. He seems nice enough, but there's gotta be something else.*

There was something more; Reed felt it somehow. Beyond the outward perfection, insanely blue eyes, and nice personality, something marked Elijah. It was mystifying.

A cold, gentle breeze blew between the Dorms. Reed glanced up. The dark clouds were breaking overhead, and the night sky showed through, clear and deep. Stars were coming out, twinkling to one another in the moonless depths. They seemed so close and beautiful at that moment, yet astronomically far away and unreachable. It all came together in that moment—the stars, the teens he had just met, Elijah. They were all the same, but Reed didn't understand how. It was odd, he knew, but some things only make sense for a brief but clear moment alone under the night sky.

He pushed through the door into the warm stairwell and climbed the steps to his hall, ready for bed and a good night's sleep but, as he reached for the handle to his door, he was slammed in a flying tackle and knocked flat on his back.

"Oh! Whoops! Hi, Reed."

Reed shook his head groggily, trying to comprehend the situation. Someone was sitting on top of him with an elbow on his chest. When his eyes refocused, he recognized his assailant as a younger boy from down the hall. "Sam, what the heck? Did I do something?"

The boy grinned. "Blame Will. He dared me and then sent me out to jump the wrong person. I thought you were somebody else."

"He told you to go knock somebody down when they tried to get into my room?"

"Not exactly. There's more to it, but you don't wanna know."

"Okay, whatever... Do you think you could get off me now?"

"Oh, sure!"

Reed got up and rubbed the back of his head. "Dude, you need to be more careful about who you listen to."

"Hey!" Sam held up his hands. "It was Will, the second coolest guy on the hall! What could I do?"

"Maybe at least *look* first?"

"Okay, sorry. But you're not bleeding and you can still walk, so we're cool, right?"

"Whatever. See you 'round." Reed entered his room and shut the door behind him, rubbing the back of his head.

Riley glanced up from Reagan's computer. "How was it?"

"Swell, especially just now."

"Yeah, that was an awesome thud. What happened?"

Reed dropped onto his bed. "Sam was on some sort of stupid dare and tackled me instead of the person he was supposed to."

"Sam." Riley pursed his lips knowingly. "That explains it."

"You know him? What about him?"

"You'll find out."

Reed sat up and glanced around the room. "Where's Reagan?"

"Living it up in the washateria with some girls. He'll be back before curfew—maybe."

Reed dropped back onto his bed and studied the ceiling through half-closed eyes, a faint smile on his lips. "I wonder how Reagan will ever be able to pick just one," he murmured.

"He won't," said Riley casually.

CHAPTER 15

O ver the next week or two, Reed attended several more meetings in the apartments. He grew more comfortable around the other teens as he got to know them, and he even ran into some of them around the Dorms occasionally.

At the same time, he did what he could to keep up his status in Dorm society. Reagan's predictions had come true; Reed was getting quite popular on the Hill. His memory of names and faces served him well, and he came to know an incredible number of the Dorm residents on sight.

But the deeper Reed got into the culture, the more he became aware that a memory lingered at the heart of the Hill, a name dropped in conversation or woven into a story that seemed to bring his two parallel lives together.

Elijah.

Reed was surprised. Elijah was only one of thousands of teens here, and he had left the Dorms months ago. Why did so many people seem to know him?

This was on his mind one evening as he walked with Lucy, Nathan, and Katy back from supper at the Mushroom. Dusk had fallen over the city below, and shadows crept up the Hill as the sun sank behind a bank of clouds, turning the wispy shrouds to a spread of crystalline orange and pink, like the frozen sherbet bar Nathan was finishing. As they turned up the North Stairs, Reed glanced out over the western glory, burying his hands in the warmth of his coat pockets.

"You know," he said suddenly, "it's really weird how many people around here act like they know Elijah. I mean, he moved off a while ago, and there are so many people here. I don't understand why anybody still knows who he is." Reed wiggled his fingers in the flannel lining of his pockets. "Funny thing, most of what I hear about him has Reagan mixed in somewhere, too. I thought they ran with different crowds."

"Hmm…" said Lucy. She was gathering her golden hair with both hands to keep the wind from tossing it about her face. "They usually did, but some factors can't be helped." She glanced at him. "Has Reagan told you about the way things were before you got here?"

Reed shook his head. "Not really."

"Interesting." She gave up, shaking her hair loose in the cold breeze. "I thought you would have figured it out by now since it kinda involves you."

"Yeah, kinda," Nathan agreed, licking a melted stream of orange off his thumb. "Might as well go ahead and tell him."

Reed eyed them in the fading light. "Tell me what?"

Lucy hesitated before explaining. "Well, before he moved out with Cody, Elijah was kind of a celebrity in the Dorms. You know, he's good-looking and super nice and all that. He was actually more popular than Reagan." She reached the top of the steps and turned to face him. "In fact, Elijah was Reagan's other roommate—the one you replaced."

Reed stopped dead at the top of the staircase and stared at her. "What? I'm not their first one?"

"'Fraid not," Nathan affirmed, sucking his Popsicle stick clean. "It was Reagan, Riley, and Elijah in a room till the end of last year."

Reed was thunderstruck. He looked away, opening his mouth and then shutting it again. "Elijah and Reagan as *roommates*? I don't even know how to process that. I bet all the girls…"

"They did," said Katy, stepping aside to let a group pass down the stairs. "That's one of the reasons Elijah moved off. It was intense. He was getting hit on non-stop."

"But he left? Why in the world?"

"He didn't want it," said Nathan simply. He tossed his empty stick into a nearby trashcan and turned to meet Reed's bewildered eyes. "He's like that. He loves people, and people love him; but he doesn't like being turned into an idol. Everybody knew him back then and kinda worshiped him. You know how the Dorms are about looks and appearance."

"Oh," said Reed. He moved into a walk again, still not sure what to think. "I imagine Reagan enjoyed it, though."

Lucy coughed. "You better believe it. He and Elijah got so much attention. You just hear about them together a lot because they lived in the same room. They were actually total opposites."

Reed was still musing over this new information a few minutes later as he mounted the stairs to his hall. It was a surprise to say the least: someone he'd thought to be a random nobody was actually the biggest icon the Hill had ever known.

And roommates with Reagan? It was like putting two characters from different fictional universes together. Why had no one ever told him? Elijah had said nothing about it; Reagan never mentioned it. Reed frowned. There was something else in all this, something nobody wanted to tell him.

He opened the hall door to find a large crowd of boys blocking his way. They didn't notice Reed as they talked and laughed at something he couldn't see. Something in the center of the group held their attention; curious, Reed pushed his way in.

In the middle of the hall, a boy crouched on the floor with a can of spray paint in his hand, demonstrating his artistic skills on the tiles. Reed studied the artwork for a moment before he recognized an unfinished attempt at a portrait of Director Connors, the face blown ridiculously out of proportion and done in a sickly green and black. Reed couldn't tell who the artist was, however, until he looked up. It was Sam. Reed instinctively rubbed the back of his neck.

The crowd was enjoying the show. Even Reagan stood nearby, throwing in occasional critiques and grinning. Reed had to admit the picture was an obvious but ludicrous likeness. Still, he couldn't believe Sam's stupidity. He shouldered his way into the crowd and called out over the noise, "Sam, what are you *doing*?"

Sam glanced up and brushed his hand across his forehead, leaving a streak of green through his blond hair. "What does it look like?" he grinned.

Reed pushed past the last few boys and crouched down next to the picture.

"But why?"

"'Cause Dylan said it would be really funny." Sam bent back to his work. "And he's the second coolest guy on the hall."

Reed pondered that for a moment. "I thought you said Will was the second coolest guy."

"Not after that stunt Dylan pulled two nights ago," Sam retorted. "He's *awesome*."

Reed stood up slowly. Sam's last shenanigan and Riley's response suddenly made more sense. He stepped back into the crowd; he was in no mood for this tonight. He turned to leave. As he did, he almost bumped into someone behind him. It was Hunter. Reed had kept up with the other boy after their chance encounters, and Hunter now spent a lot of time on Reed's hall. Reed couldn't blame him; most people avoided Dorm One when they could. Hunter caught Reed's eye and smirked.

"A dumb thing to do, but not bad, eh?"

Reed snorted. "He's not known for his intelligence."

"I'll say. Idiot, he's made the glasses too round!"

Reed didn't answer. He turned and shoved through the crowd toward his room.

He was never sure how word of the incident found its way up the chain of command but, by that night, everyone on the Hill had heard it. The next day when Reed entered the hall, he found Sam again on the floor, this time scrubbing up the dried paint. Michael supervised from the doorway. According to rumor, Director Connors imposed several other consequences as well.

The episode was forever attached to Sam's name. Apparently, he was notorious for a number of idiotic exploits in the past, but this latest one topped them all. The mere mention of his name was enough to bring a sneer or a laugh.

At first, Reed shied away from all the talk. The blatant ridicule and mocking laughter made him uncomfortable. But then, he reasoned, it was the truth—most of it, anyway. And some of it was really funny. Besides, nobody else was hanging back; they all thought it was great. It was like having an inside joke with everyone on the Hill.

Besides, it wasn't like he particularly cared for Sam anyway.

He "tested the waters," so to speak—hesitantly at first, but then more boldly as he warmed to the idea. Everyone else was doing it, so why shouldn't he? It didn't bother him as much as he'd thought it might, and he found he could enjoy it.

But his pleasure was short-lived.

CHAPTER 16

***

It was a Saturday, barely a week after the paint incident, that Reed ran into Elijah in the Dorms. Winter was beginning to loosen its grip on Nature's throat, and the earliest forerunners of spring were appearing on the Hill. Tiny flowers of timid purple and yellow peered out of the dead turf, and early buds sprinkled a few of the trees. Though the cold still held the upper hand, the early afternoon had warmed to a milder temperature than normal. Reed was outside catching a little sun when he spied the other boy.

Elijah was alone, taking the sidewalk that cut through the center of the Dorms, dressed in jeans and a navy hoodie. Reed had never seen him outside the straight-from-work setting at the apartments. It was a rare opportunity, perhaps the chance to get some answers to the many questions Reed had about him.

"Hey!" he called, quickening his pace. "Mind if I walk with you?"

Elijah turned and smiled. "No, not at all."

Reed caught up and fell in step beside him. "What're you up to?"

"I was going to visit friends outside the city. You're welcome to come if you want."

Reed had been hoping he would ask. He had nothing else to do, and he'd been looking for an opportunity to find out more about Elijah. They had never spent time together apart from the rest of the group.

He looked out over the valley and pursed his lips as if weighing his choices.

"Sure," he said at last. "Why not? If you don't mind, I mean."

"Not a bit." Elijah slid his hands into the stitched front pockets of his hoodie. "I hope you don't mind walking. It's a pretty good ways."

Reed didn't mind.

They turned onto an adjoining sidewalk that ran north and east off the Hill and out of the city. But, before they were even out from between the Dorms, someone called out behind them.

"Yo, 'Lijah!"

Reed recognized the voice immediately, and a soft groan escaped his lips. He didn't want to turn around, but he did, only because Elijah did first. Sam was coming toward them, trying to look nonchalant and failing miserably.

"Hi, Sam." Elijah smiled. "How's it going?"

Reed was a little surprised these two knew each other. He wondered how Elijah could sound so genuinely pleased to see the other boy.

"Oh, ya know, I'm hanging." Sam shrugged. He was trying to sound cool. Reed didn't think it went so well. "I haven't seen you in a while. I guess we've both been busy." He reached them and pretended to notice Reed for the first time. "Oh, and it's Reed, too! This is quite a crowd."

"Two's company," said Reed dryly.

"Whatchya guys up to?" Sam hung a pair of bug-eyed sunglasses on the front of his striped shirt, apparently missing Reed's remark. Reed felt slightly disappointed.

"We were just headed off the Hill to visit some friends," Elijah explained, half unzipping his hoodie and pushing up his sleeves. "How about you? You got something planned?"

"Oh," Sam waved a hand, "nothing much. I'll probably work on a special assignment my boss gave me. He said nobody could do it like I could. After that, I'll probably just hang with the rest of the cool peeps. I got asked to go to the Boulevard later with some of them. Did you, Reed?"

Reed blinked, stung. "No, actually," he said. "I thought I'd stay here and graffiti the floor with the other losers."

The jab was unmistakable. Reed felt Elijah's eyes on him, but he chose to avoid them. Sam, however, grinned.

"Really? I might be able to give you a painting lesson sometime. Ya know, Michael said mine would have been pretty good if it hadn't been painted on the floor. Maybe I'll do it on the wall next time. Anywho, I've got places to be. See ya."

"Sure, Sam," Elijah answered. "Take care."

Sam swaggered off, and Reed and Elijah turned back onto their original course. They walked in silence. Reed was beginning to wish he hadn't made that comment in front of Elijah. Reagan and his friends would have thought it was hilarious, but it seemed out of place now. He watched his feet and tried not to step on the cracks in the concrete.

Elijah finally spoke. "That wasn't very nice, Reed."

Reed kicked at the sidewalk. "I know. But he kinda started it. And besides, he's just *Sam*."

"You think he was insulting you? I think he genuinely hoped you were going to be there. He admires you, Reed. It's really obvious."

"Sam? Me?" Reed was taken back at the suggestion and stepped on a crack by mistake. "You mustn't know him! Did you hear what he was saying? Everything was all about hisself and how cool *he* is."

His grammar always slipped when he got worked up or very uncomfortable.

"Exactly," said Elijah calmly. "He wants to make you think he's cooler than he is. He talks big about himself because he feels inferior and scared. He wants to impress you."

Reed wasn't sure how to respond to this idea and even less sure that he liked it. He pulled at his ear in agitation. "But it's not just me. He's so annoying to everybody! He's always doing the stupidest stuff, and he sucks up to somebody different every day."

"That's because he's looking for affirmation." There was something sympathetic and sad in Elijah's voice. He was looking away at the ring of misty blue hills surrounding the valley. "It's all a front. He wants to fit in so badly that he tries all these different ways to get attention. He gets it, all right, but it's not the kind he wants." The blue eyes turned to Reed's face. "Reed, he's so unhappy. People like him always are. Whenever somebody's rattling and making that much noise, it means there's something broken on the inside."

Now Reed really wasn't sure how to respond. He tugged at his ear again. "But why me? Why doesn't he go after Reagan or somebody like that?"

"Maybe he just wants to be your friend. Maybe he thought you were different. Everybody else ridicules and scorns him, and perhaps he thought you wouldn't."

Reed kept his eyes down.

Elijah added softly, "Just because everybody else is doing something doesn't mean you have to do it, too."

Reed stuffed his hands into his pockets. "But he didn't seem to care about what I said," he tried.

"He's been cut down so many times that he's learned to hide his feelings. He didn't look like it, maybe, but he cared. Words always go deep, especially cruel ones from people we don't expect."

Reed bit the inside of his cheek and looked away. He was starting to see the point. Suppose Elijah was right. What if Sam actually had hoped Reed would be in that group tonight? To get a thrust like that from a supposed friend... He looked at the ground. "I'm sorry."

"That's good, but it's not me you need to say that to."

"I know." That was all he said, but Elijah seemed to understand.

By now, the Hill and the city had fallen behind them, and they were walking a gravel country road instead of a concrete street. Bare woods lined the way, broken by stretches of brown field and white board fence. An occasional house dotted the landscape, but they were few and far off the road. The two were alone with the early spring.

Elijah inhaled deeply and broke off a twig from a nearby tree. "It's wonderful to be out of the city, isn't it?"

Reed dared to glance at him for the first time. "Sure," he replied.

After a few more minutes of silent walking, they turned up a white rock driveway thickly overhung with trees.

"So exactly who are we visiting?" Reed had neglected to ask this before.

"It's a family we met in our first few weeks here," Elijah answered, flicking the twig from between his fingers. "They have a small farm and, well, not much else. All of us in the group come out here whenever we can 'cause they need help around the place and we need to get out of the smog."

They emerged from the tree-lined driveway into a spacious yard, brown but sprinkled with tiny white flowers. A wall of woods blocked out the rest of the world on three sides. In the center sat a little gabled house—low, brick, and simple. Behind it lay a farm, mostly sloping fields and tree-lined fencerows. Not far from the house, a weather-stained barn and white board fence presided over a large pond. It was a pleasant place.

"Yijah!" cried an excited voice.

A small figure shot around the corner of the house and bounded across the yard toward them. Without a word, Elijah dropped to his knees and threw open his arms. A boy, perhaps three or four years old, flung himself upon the teen, throwing his arms around Elijah's neck. "I knew you woulds come," he said in a lisp. "Mommy said you mightn't."

"Of course I would!" Elijah loosened the boy's arms so he could breathe. "How are you? Have you been a good boy?"

The child pulled back and looked him gravely in the face. "I twy-ing," he said somberly. "But... but I not always. Mommy says I been a good boy *today,* though."

Elijah's expression matched the boy's in solemnity. "Well, that's good. You just keep working at it till you grow up."

The little boy pondered this, and a look of shy sweetness stole over his face. "When I grows up," he lisped, "I wants to be just yike *you.*" He tightened his grip and buried his face in Elijah's shoulder.

Elijah grinned and wrapped both his arms around the boy. "Aww... that's so nice! But, when you grow up, I want you to be just like Jesus."

The little boy nodded. "Him, too."

Reed stood off to the side and watched this little scene, feeling awkward. He didn't like kids, and he wished Elijah wouldn't make a big deal about this one, even if he was fairly cute. Dark hair set off a pair of wide brown eyes, and his features were adorably serious. He and Elijah made quite a pair. Watching them, Reed felt the familiar sensation stealing over him that he was locked outside a bright window, looking in.

The little boy at last lifted his face away from Elijah's shoulder and caught sight of Reed for the first time. He blinked, mouth slightly ajar, at the unfamiliar figure.

Elijah suddenly remembered his guest and turned back to him. "Reed, I want you to meet my friend, Ethan. Ethan, Reed came to help us today."

"Hello," Reed said obligingly.

The little boy put two fingers in his mouth and looked down.

"Aren't you going to say something?" prompted Elijah. Ethan shook his head and hid his face again.

"Well, fine then," Elijah laughed, and he hoisted the boy up in his arms.

As he did, a slender silver chain dropped out of the collar of his white t-shirt. It had been invisible, hidden under the material, but the movement swung it out in plain sight. A pendant of some sort dangled down in the V of Elijah's unzipped hoodie. It caught Reed's eye immediately; Elijah didn't seem like the necklace-wearing type. The pendant was an odd shape, too, unrecognizable at first glance.

Before Reed could look closer, Elijah slipped it back inside his shirt with one swift movement. Reed's gaze shifted up to meet his. The other boy looked back at him steadily with no anxiety or shame, but offered no excuse.

Before they could say anything, two girls rounded the corner of the house, carrying a large basket between them. They stopped at the sight of the three on the driveway.

"Why, Reed!" exclaimed one. "What are you doing here?"

It took Reed a moment to recognize Lucy. She wasn't the professional office girl he was used to seeing. Her golden hair was pulled back into a ponytail, and the sleeves of her faded blouse had been rolled up past her elbows. Judging by the flush of her cheeks and the water splashed on her apron, she'd just finished washing something. Funny. Professional or not, she still looked very pretty.

"Oh, hi!" said Elijah, shifting the squirming Ethan over to his back. "I just ran into him on the way out here. He came along to help out."

"How nice!" Lucy came forward with a radiant smile. The second girl followed, obliged to go where the basket went, but she eyed Reed with obvious doubt. Lucy turned to her. "Marielle, this is Reed, the one you've heard us talk about. Reed, this is Marielle, Ethan's sister."

The girl smiled politely and murmured some greeting, but she shifted her weight and shot both Lucy and Elijah uncertain glances. She was younger than they were, perhaps fourteen or fifteen, with a slender, pointed face. Her straight hair, dark like her brother's, fell past her narrow shoulders.

"I wish you had been here a little earlier to help us hang out the laundry," Lucy continued gaily, tucking a strand of hair behind her ear. "It appears somebody ran off with all our clothespins."

Ethan peered over Elijah's shoulder. "Oops. Sorry. But Yijah got here!"

"And you just *couldn't* wait." Lucy patted him on the cheek. "But maybe now you can make up for it and help 'Lijah while he works."

The little boy nodded, bouncing up and down on Elijah's back.

"Then we'll finish fixing the barn roof from last week," Elijah said over his shoulder. "You can hand me my tools. Anything else?"

"Mother wondered if somebody could work on the back door," Marielle informed him, taking the empty basket from Lucy. "The knob won't turn again."

Elijah nodded. "All right, we'll start with that, won't we?"

"Yeth!" Ethan swung his feet gleefully.

"Reed can help on the roof when you're done with that," Lucy added. "We'll find something to do until then."

Marielle led Elijah and his eager charge toward the back of the house. Lucy and Reed came behind at a slower pace.

"How did you get hooked up with these people?" he asked her when the other three were out of earshot. "I mean, why did they pick you guys out of all the kids on the Hill?"

"They didn't pick us. We asked to help them," she replied, rolling down her left sleeve. "We met their family through the church not long after we got here and offered to do what we could."

"You went to a church here? I thought they were all government-controlled."

"Most are, but not ours. It's…" she stopped and stared at him, eyes wide. "It's… underground. But don't mention that to anybody, not even that it exists. I shouldn't have said anything."

"I can keep secrets. I'm getting kinda used to it."

"It's not that I *doubt* you." She began to work on her other sleeve. "But you have to understand that, when our group agreed to let you visit, we chose to take the risk on ourselves. We can't ask the whole church to do that. It's made up of old people and young couples and families with little kids." She stopped for a second, staring at nothing, before she went back to fixing her cuff. "Our Hill kids' group is just an off-shoot. We're young enough to risk it. The rest of the church couldn't without risking whole families."

"You make it sound pretty big."

"It's a fair size." She finished with her sleeve and laughed. "You didn't think we were the only Christians in the whole city, did you?"

Reed chuckled uncertainly and changed the subject. "So you met this family, and they needed your help. Why doesn't their dad do all this stuff?"

Lucy dropped her eyes. "They don't have a father anymore," she said quietly.

"Oh." For a moment, the only sounds were their slow steps on the rock driveway. "Well, at least the kid seems to have hit it off with Elijah."

Lucy laughed. "Yeah, he has. Ethan's *so* adorable it's hard not to like him, and 'Lijah loves kids."

They walked in silence for a moment. At last, Reed could contain his curiosity no longer. "Lucy, do you know anything about that chain Elijah wears?"

Her smile vanished. "Why do you ask?"

"I caught a glimpse of it and couldn't tell what it was. Do you know?"

She looked down and smoothed the front of her apron. "If he hasn't told you, I'm sure he has his reasons."

"I didn't ask him about it, and he doesn't volunteer a lot about himself, if you know what I mean. Surely you can just tell me what it is."

She didn't reply at first. When she did speak, her voice had fallen from its normal, happy pitch. "It's not my place to tell you. He has reasons for everything he does, and he'll tell you if he wants to."

"All right then," said Reed, a little nettled at her stubbornness. "I'll ask him."

She whirled on him in an instant. "Don't you *dare!*"

He stepped back, stunned. Her bright face was transformed by a look of sudden fierceness that matched the fury in her voice. She was trembling, and a warning glitter flickered in her eyes... or was it the glistening of tears? Either way, it shocked Reed and left him speechless.

His astonishment must have shown on his face for she spun away, inhaling to bring herself under control. "I'm sorry, Reed."

He remained silent and let her regain her composure. She turned back after a moment, all ferocity gone, but her face still worked with strong emotion. "I should not have said that like I did. Forgive me." She sighed. "You have to understand that it's not for *my* reasons that I won't tell you. It's for his sake. Talking about people behind their backs is never good, but especially not in this situation. That pendant comes from his past, and the story behind it is very personal. Don't ask him, Reed. Just don't. He'll tell you if he wants you to know." Her eyes sought his.

Reed said nothing for a moment but, at last, he conceded. "All right."

They resumed their walk. A bird twittered in the woods. Everything else was quiet.

Reed broke the silence. "So do we actually have to do any of these chores or can we just chill for a while and call it a day?"

Lucy laughed suddenly. "Reed! It won't be all that bad! Have you ever planted a garden before?"

And that was how Reed spent the rest of his Saturday afternoon—slicing potatoes, digging holes, filling them back in, and hammering on top of the barn roof. Lucy and Elijah found plenty to keep them all busy. Reed could think of no excuse to stop while they continued. *What did I get myself into?*

During his stay, he learned there were four more children in the family, all of whom still lived on the farm and expected him to remember their names. There was a Meagan and a set of twins with "L" names he couldn't remember for sure. Another boy everybody called Matt seemed to be the oldest, but Reed didn't care to ask. It was a relief to meet the one and only animal on the farm, a silver gelding by the name of Patton, who didn't expect anything from him and seemed more laid back than the rest of the rambunctious brood.

At the end of the day, he was introduced to Mrs. Shelly, the matriarch—a kindly, care-worn woman with a slender, patient face and straight dark hair just beginning to gray. She thanked them sincerely for their help and hugged Lucy and Elijah. She refrained in Reed's case, however, and shook his hand instead.

When the three teens left the farm at last, Reed realized he had completely missed the biggest social day of the Hill's week. On top of that, he had dirt on the knees of his favorite jeans, a splinter in his right thumb, and a terrible ache in his back. *What's the point?* The other two might be satisfied with a hug for all their pains, but what did he get out of it? It wasn't the afternoon he'd expected. What was Reagan going to say?

CHAPTER 17

"**B**OR-ring," yawned Reagan, lounging in his chair with his computer on his lap.

It was warm indoors tonight. It was quiet, too, except for the lulling hum of the fluorescent lights overhead and the far-off rumble of the central heating unit.

Reagan's remark was prompted by a dull evening following a mediocre day. Reed, lying in his usual position on the bed, grunted.

"You'd think they'd give us a little more to do around here at night," Reagan continued, circling his finger listlessly across his touchpad.

Reed grunted again and stirred. "I guess that's what the new rec center's supposed to do when it's finished."

"Humph! *If* it ever gets finished. It's taking them forever."

"The government at its best. Are they ever fast?" Reed rolled onto his back and rubbed his eyes. "But they've got until April or May. After that, I guess we start filing complaints with Connors in written form."

Reagan chuckled. Reed rolled off his bunk and stood up, stretching. "Well, no use just lying around." He yawned. "I'll go see if anything's happening on the hall."

"And if it isn't?"

"Then I'll start something wild and get everybody else in trouble when Michael finds out."

Reagan laughed outright. "Now you're talking! I've trained you well."

"What can I say?" Reed made a humble bow. "I'll be on the hall. The room's all yours; don't have too much fun without me."

He stepped out the open door and looked both ways. To his left, two shirtless boys were having a wrestling match on the tile floor amid a small circle of onlookers. To his right, the hall was empty—almost. A few pairs of feet stuck out of rooms too crowded to hold all the boys who tried to squeeze into them. Reed decided to try this direction first. He wasn't in the mood to get pulled into a WWE match, despite his boasting to Reagan.

He sauntered down the hall, looking into different rooms and weighing his options. After passing his third open door and declining another set of enthusiastic invitations, Reed heard someone calling behind him.

"Hey! Reed!"

He turned.

Hunter had pushed his way out of the first room Reed had passed and was coming toward him. That was no surprise; Hunter usually sought him out when he was visiting on the hall.

"Hey!" Hunter caught up and fell in step beside him. "Where were you on Saturday? I looked for you all over the place, but you weren't anywhere."

Reed shrugged. "I went off the Hill with a friend. Why?" he added teasingly. "Did you miss me?"

"Yeah, everybody did. You're, like, half the fun around here now."

The serious reply caught Reed off guard. He rubbed the back of his neck. "Psh! Whatever."

"I'm serious! A lot of people think so, especially Allie."

Reed made an odd noise in his throat. Allie was a pretty girl from Dorm Eight, one of the social butterflies of the Hill. Everyone knew her, and she was considered a fine connoisseur of boys.

"Ridiculous!" Reed declared. He felt his face getting hot nonetheless. "Allie thinks any decent-looking male that has a face and breathes is fun."

"Really?" Hunter shot him an odd look and arched his eyebrows. "I doubt she notices when each one is missing and asks about him."

"Did she?"

"Duh, yeah! Her and half the other girls. But nobody knew where you'd gone. Who did you say you went with?"

"Oh." Reed floundered for an instant. He stopped to take off his socks, balancing himself against the wall. "You wouldn't know him. He's not in the Dorms." He had a strange reluctance to reveal Elijah's identity. Perhaps it was the same reason he sometimes avoided Nathan at the factory. Or maybe he was still smarting from Elijah's gentle but effective rebuke.

"Oh, one of the *apartment* people." The disdain dripped from Hunter's voice.

"Something wrong with them?" Reed straightened and stuffed the socks in his back pocket, resuming his slow walk barefoot.

"Oh, I just think they're ridiculous. I don't see who would want to move out and leave all the Dorms' fun unless they're flat-out boring… or have something to hide."

Reed darted a glance at him. Hunter knew something. His mind raced for a way to convince the other boy to reveal his secret. He leaned closer. "What do you mean?"

Hunter stopped in the middle of the hall, looked both ways, and lowered his voice. "I've been thinking about it. I wouldn't be surprised if the ringer actually lives *outside* the Dorms. It would make perfect sense. That way, he—or she—could hang out with us whenever they wanted but not have to worry about being watched the rest of the time. They wouldn't have to deal with curious roommates, curfew, RDs, anything."

Reed breathed a little easier; Hunter was on a different track. Still, his idea made sense. Good sense. Reed hadn't thought about that before. The idea sank in.

"I'd be careful around those people if I were you, Reed," Hunter warned. "You never know what they could be up to."

Reed had to agree. He moved into a walk. "I take it you're not keen on the Council's spies."

Hunter snorted. "I'll go further than that. I hate the Council!"

The statement carried every bit of feeling that could be fit into the four words. Reed glanced at him, shocked. No one ever dared to say something like that out loud. But Hunter kept going, his passion rising with each word.

"All they do is boss us around and keep us tied up with all these stupid rules and lockdowns! I can't *stand* being under somebody's foot like this. I don't need them, and I could do way better on my own!"

Reed wasn't sure what to say. He couldn't deny that he sympathized deeply with Hunter's feelings, but he could hardly believe his friend's brashness. His hatred made him far too reckless. Caught up in their conversation, the two had ceased paying attention to the hails coming out of the many open doorways they passed. But, as they neared the end of the hall and their discussion, Hunter stopped abruptly. "What's that smell?"

Reed, who hadn't been paying much attention, inhaled deeply and then wrinkled his nose. The scent was ever so slight—hardly noticeable, in fact—but it was very odd. "I don't know. I've smelled it down at this end before. Somebody said it was something in the attic."

The explanation didn't satisfy Hunter. He continued sniffing, turning his head in all directions. "It smells almost like something burning." He walked back and forth, intently following his nose, and then stopped before a closed door. "And it's strongest right here."

Reed joined him and breathed in again. It was stronger now, and it did smell like something burning but with a hint of something sour and musty. It was beginning to seem vaguely familiar. His brain groped to identify it, but he couldn't quite put his finger on what it was.

Hunter was eyeing the door, one of the few closed on the hall. "Hmm… I say we go in and see what's happening."

Reed offered no objections, and Hunter turned the handle (knocking was obsolete on the hall) and pushed. The door didn't budge. He put his shoulder to it and leaned with all his weight. Reed joined him. Slowly, it began to swing back with an odd sliding noise. As it opened, the smell rolled out to meet them in an overpowering wave. Its strength registered instantly with Reed. It was an odor he had often smelled in the less-frequented places of his high school back home. The door opened just wide enough for both of them to see into the dim room.

A fog filled it from floor to ceiling, turning objects within to hazy shapes that floated in the mist—ghosts of chairs, desks, beds. There were people, too. Half a dozen boys drifted in the swirling sea like figures in a bizarre dream. They lounged on the beds, chairs, and nightstands, thin wisps of smoke curling from their lips and the rolls in their fingers. They seemed completely unaware of their visitors until the reeking billows set Reed coughing. One look at the dull faces and reddened eyes that turned toward the door showed what kind of vapors filled the room. Another glance revealed why the door had been so reluctant to open: towels stuffed in the crack and piled on the floor to keep smoke from escaping into the hall. Through watering eyes, Reed recognized several faces from his hall and the neighboring dorms. A few, though, were strange. All stared at them wordlessly. Hunter was the first to break the silence.

"So... whatchya guys doing?"

There were low, murmured replies. One of the group spoke up. "Catchin' butterflies, o' course."

Slow laughter slithered out of the haze. Reed decided to try a more effective approach. "Don't you know you could get caught? You'll set off the fire alarm in a minute."

The boy nearest the door stood up, fishing in his pocket, and produced a small battery. "We've taken care of that." His voice was low and gravelly, almost more of a growl. He was one of the few Reed didn't recognize. "Everything's fine. Why don't you guys join us? There's plenty to go 'round."

A murmur of assent rose from the rest of the room, but Hunter shook his head. "No, thanks, I'll pass this time. But where'd you guys get the stuff?"

"Why does it matter?" the boy said. "If you want some, take it. That's all you need to know."

Hunter shrugged. "All right. Just don't let Michael catch you. Old Connors would roast you alive if he found out."

"I bet he would." The boy eased himself back onto his seat on the nightstand. "But he won't find out. He's been trying, and he can't."

"Well, he won't hear about it from us," Hunter assured him.

"Good. Are you sure you don't want to stick around?"

Both boys nodded. "We probably should be going," added Hunter, reaching for the door handle. "If we keep the door open much longer, the whole hall will find out."

The group inside agreed, and Hunter swung the door shut on the darkened room. Reed breathed in the hall's clear air like a man coming up from the underworld. "Wow."

"Yeah, pretty much." Hunter stepped back and shook his head. "They're a little over the rainbow. I wonder where they got that stuff."

They turned back up the hall in the direction they'd come. Reed sighed. "Well, that was interesting, but we still don't have anything to do."

A commotion erupted from one of the rooms at the opposite end of the hall. Both boys stopped, listened for a moment, and then broke into grins.

"On second thought, that sounds fun," Reed amended.

"Yeah, I've been waiting for this all night," Hunter agreed, dashing up the hall.

Chapter 18

Reed chose not to mention what they had discovered that night to anyone. He had heard rumors of a drug trade on the Hill and suspected many people knew about it already. Why turn them in anyway? Life was good for him right now, but he knew it could be boring sometimes. This was just their way of dealing with it. It was fortunate he and Hunter had been alone when they made the discovery; no one else had seen anything. Or so he thought.

It was the next morning before work that Reed ran into Gabe on the crowded Square. The two of them often saw each other around, but they never spoke by mutual agreement. Gabe claimed it was for safety's sake. Reed had a feeling there was more to it than that. It caught him off guard, then, when Gabe accosted him in the crowd.

"Hey." Gabe appeared out of nowhere and blocked his way. "I saw smoke coming out of a cracked window on your hall last night. Did something happen?"

It was phrased as a question, but it struck Reed like a demand. He stiffened but stopped grudgingly.

"Maybe," he shrugged, avoiding Gabe's eyes. "Do you think I would know?"

"Yes, I do." Gabe crossed his muscled arms. "I can tell by your face. What was it?"

"Just some guys who lit up and had a good time." Reed felt a spark of dull anger. He looked Gabe full in the face. "What's wrong with that?"

"What's wrong with it? You know just as well as I do! The Council's been trying to find that group for months. Did you report them?"

"No," Reed retorted. "Why should I? It's their choice, and it ain't hurting me."

An odd look Reed couldn't interpret swept Gabe's face, but it passed quickly.

"It's illegal, Reed. You know that. I thought you'd have better sense than to get on the wrong side of this. The Council *will* find out, and then what'll happen to you?"

"The same thing that'll happen to everybody else on the Hill," Reed shot back. "I didn't take any, and it's not like I'm the bad guy for not being a snitch. They can do whatever they want. Who are *you* to judge them? And who says it'll be found out?"

Gabe did not reply, but turned and disappeared into the crowd. Reed rolled his eyes. "I don't know why he's ticked off," he muttered. "I certainly didn't start this conversation."

"Hey, Reed!" The chipper voice came from behind him, welcome and familiar. Reed turned, trying to shake off his sullen thoughts. Nathan threaded his way through the crowd toward him with a backpack slung over his shoulder.

"Yo!" said Reed. "What's up?"

The boys saw each other daily. Besides working together at the factory, Nathan always guided Reed when he chose to attend one of the meetings in the apartments. Maybe he could get the sour taste out of Reed's mouth.

Nathan dodged a final knot in the crowd and joined him. "Look, it's not like I'm stalking you or anything," he began, shoving his ID card into his pocket, "but I saw you talking to Gabe just now, and I think I have an idea of what it was about."

Reed made a wry face but said nothing.

"Yeah, I know; he can be a little blunt sometimes. But you have to understand something about Gabe: it's not always easy to understand him."

"Well, if you do," Reed said, a sudden thought coming to him, "then tell me what he was doing outside last night looking up at third-story windows."

"I don't know." Nathan shrugged. "He does a lot of things I don't

see the point of. I don't understand what he does all the time, but..."
His eyes met Reed's. "I trust him."

Reed looked away. Nathan was a nice guy, and Reed usually listened to what he said with respect, even if he didn't agree. But it was different this time. Something in Gabe's manner and that fleeting expression didn't sit well with him. It soured his already second-rate mood and left him eager to end the conversation. Taking leave of Nathan, he pushed his way into the crowd, ready for an exciting day to clear his mind.

* * *

"BOR-ring," yawned Reagan. It was another warm, lazy evening on the hall and, as usual, Reagan was seated in his desk chair. The night outside was rainy, and drops spattered against the window in a pulsating rhythm. Reed, lying on his bed, only grunted.

"This is sad," Reagan continued. "Really sad. Two nights like this in a row. We've gotta get things going around here." He slid his bare feet off the desk.

Reed grunted again. Reagan glanced up at him. "You're not being very helpful."

Reed rolled over with a yawn. "What can I say? I tried to get something started last night, which means it's your turn tonight. Besides, you're a master at this kinda thing; you'd do way better than the rest of us could anyway."

Reagan grinned. "A very flattering way of saying you don't want to get up. True, I may be the master, but I've shared a little of my craft with a chosen few. You did pretty well last time, and Riley's not too bad. He's always finding something to do."

"Maybe he attends classes on how to be as cool as your roommate," Reed suggested.

Reagan chuckled. "You think so? I'd say you were a total suck up if it wasn't that everything you say about me is true." He closed his computer and stood up to stretch. "Well, no use just lying around here. I'm off to find something to do. You can borrow the computer while I'm gone." He swung his arms to get the blood moving. "You know, I feel like killing some zombies. Maybe I'll go play Kevin's

X-box." He sauntered toward the door, buttoning up his shirt. "I'll be on the hall."

Reed didn't move until after the door had shut behind Reagan. Then, with a yawn, he rolled off the bed, stumbled over to the desk, and settled himself in the chair, his back to the door. He slid Reagan's computer over in front of him. This was one of the highlights of his night. With the click of a mouse, the entire world was at his fingertips and he never had to leave his chair. The problems of the day, the boredom, even the room itself all faded away. Time even ceased to count its minutes.

Tap! Tap! The sharp noise roused Reed from his trance some time later. Annoyed, he wondered who it could be. Knocking was supposed to be obsolete on the hall, and he did not want to be bothered. He sighed. "Come in," he said without looking up.

Tap! Tap! The noise was repeated, quicker and more urgently.

Good grief! Can't they open the door themselves? He called out a little louder. "Come *in*!"

Tap! Tap! It came again, louder and sharper than before. Reed slapped his palm on the desk and tore his attention away from the computer. "Why don't you just…" But as he lifted his eyes from the screen, he froze in mid-sentence. His chair tipped over backward, and he fell to the floor with a crash. The thud, as jarring as it was, hardly shocked him compared to what he saw. Plastered against the dark, streaming window were two hands with a wet, urgent face between them.

Reed pulled himself to his feet and approached the window at a slow limp, staring. Any face against his third-story window in the middle of the night was wild enough, but this was one he recognized.

One of the hands waved him to hurry, and the face puckered in its urgency. Perplexed, Reed undid the latches, swung open the double panes, and Alec tumbled inside, dripping and panting.

"What the…" began Reed, but Alec cut him off, his brows drawn together under his dripping bangs.

"I don't have much time. There's going to be a shakedown tonight sometime after curfew. All the RDs are in on it, and Director Connors has called in the police."

"Shakedown?"

"Yeah, like a search of all the rooms. They're doing it in every dorm. I came to warn you." Alec gulped and bent over double to catch his breath.

"Uh… well, thanks, but what are they looking for? How do you know about it?"

"Gabe found out and let me know. I have no idea what they're after, but it must be something big. Maybe us." He met Reed's eyes.

Reed's stomach tightened. "Are you going to run for it?"

"No, we can't. Besides, we don't know if they're really onto us or not."

"Do you want me to tell everybody else and spread it around?"

"No, don't." Alec straightened up. "Lucy insisted I give you and *only* you some sort of warning." He hesitated. "And I had to bring you this, too. For safe keeping." He swung a red drawstring pack off his back and dropped it on the floor. "Just in case. Since this is yours and Reagan's room, they won't expect to find something like this in here. But hide it somewhere good anyway. It's already ten; I gotta go." He turned and swung one leg back over the windowsill.

"Wait!" Reed stopped him. "How did you get up here?"

Alec paused, straddling the sill. "It's pretty easy, really. From here, I'll pull up onto the flat part of the roof and go to the back end of the building. There's a partial ladder for maintenance. I take that half-way down and then get over into the spruce tree by the door. I could jump straight into this tree, but it's a little wet tonight." He slid out of the window and stood on the raised brick edging that surrounded it.

"But how did you know which room was mine?" Everything was happening so fast that Reed was still trying to grasp the situation.

Alec paused again, the hurry in his face fading a little. "This used to be Elijah's room," he said. "I came and went a lot back when he was here."

The slamming of a door echoed through the pattering rain. They froze. Low voices drifted up from the Square, followed by the click of boots on brick.

"They're here!" exclaimed Alec. "That was fast! I'll see ya later." He vanished into the darkness without a sound.

Reed shut the window quietly after him and turned back to the room. His head whirled. It was all so sudden, he hardly knew what to think. The red pack lay on the floor at his feet. He bent and picked it up, doubts and suspicions leaping through his mind. It was heavy. He pulled open the top and peered inside.

Books. He drew one out and turned it over. *Holy Bible*, the dusty blue cover proclaimed in a silver script. Katy's name was engraved on the bottom right corner. He pulled out another, burgundy, bearing Nathan's name in gold lettering. Three more remained in the satchel, probably belonging to Alec, Lucy, and Gabe.

He stuffed them back into the pack and cinched it shut. Now he understood. They had sent these to him "for safe keeping" in case they didn't make it through the night. The severity of the situation was beginning to sink in. If Bibles were found with the full names of these five etched on the front, the game would be up. It all depended on this bag.

Reed gazed at it dangling from his outstretched palm. He held in his hands the key to their safety or their downfall—in a way, their lives. They trusted him. He lifted his chin. He had to hide this well. But where?

There was a noise at the window, which Reed had forgotten to latch, and Alec slipped in again.

"They brought more men than I thought!" he panted. Water streamed down his drawn face and into his dripping t-shirt. "We're completely surrounded. I can't get out!"

Reed pushed past him and stuck his head out the window. Sure enough, in the light of the lamp posts, he could make out figures scattered across the wet Square below. Already, a group of men was moving toward the front door of Number Four. He pulled in his head. "They're on their way now. You can stay here, but we'll have to act fast."

Alec nodded. "Got a towel?"

"Yeah." Reed's mind worked quickly. "But that won't do it. They'll still see your clothes are wet. We're close in size; you can borrow some of my stuff." He delved into his wardrobe as Alec whipped off his wet clothes. Reed found the smallest sizes he had and tossed them onto the bed. He turned back, glancing around the room.

"Uh-oh, you're leaving spruce needles all over the floor! They're all in your hair, too! Umm... here's my towel. Go rinse off in the showers. Quick!"

Alec swooped up the dry clothes and the towel and darted out of the room.

Reed's next move was to borrow Riley's towel and soak up the puddles of water around the window and where Alec had been standing.

The wet clothes! Reed snatched them up from the floor, rolled them into a tight bundle, and tied them with Alec's belt. Now what? There was just enough slack at the end of the belt that maybe... He dashed to the window again. Cracking it open, he hung the buckle over the catch used to prop it open and dropped the clothes down below the sill outside. There. The window closed just enough to appear shut, or at least cracked to let in some fresh air.

Reed turned back and swept the room with a final glance. That seemed to take care of everything.

The sound of slamming doors and muffled voices came up through the floor. The officers had already worked their way up to the second floor.

Alec returned, still drying his hair, but looking fairly decent in the black Henley and silver gym shorts.

"It's normal for us to have company up here," Reed said, taking the towel from him. "Just find somewhere to look natural." He slung the towel over the end of his bed.

"What about the backpack?" Alec pointed to the desk where Reed had left the bag.

Reed slapped his forehead. "Shoot, I forgot! Where can I put it? Think, think!" He pressed his fists against the sides of his head.

The noises below were subsiding, but the stairwell echoed with enough racket to alert the whole dorm. Reed ran his mind over the room in desperation. Not under the bed... not in the drawers... not on the top of the shelves...

A sudden idea seized him. He grabbed the pack and leapt up onto his top bunk. The suspended ceiling was constructed of individual foam tiles set in a metal grid. He pushed up one of the tiles and slid it to the side, shoving the satchel through the hole into the attic. The tile slid back easily and left no trace it had ever been moved.

Reed collapsed onto the bed. He hadn't been a moment too soon. The sound of heavy feet filled the hall and drew nearer. The door to the room was thrown open, and a man in uniform barged in. "Everybody out by order of the Council!" he barked. "Move!"

A hot rush shot through Reed's body. He tightened his jaw and glanced at Alec. The other boy met his fiery look with a calm, warning gaze. Reed hesitated a moment longer and then yielded. He slid off the bed, grabbed a hoodie for each of them, and followed Alec out of the room. It grated him horribly.

The man's words were being echoed up and down the hall. Boys spilled out into the hallway, wide awake, half-asleep, and everywhere in between. They were herded toward the stairs as fast as they appeared. No one seemed to have any idea what was happening and obeyed in confusion. They poured down to the first floor and into the night.

Despite the freezing cold and the light rain, the Square was already crowded with the rest of the Dorm residents. They milled in a confused mass, calling out to each other like lost sheep. Reed and Alec pushed their way through the crowd toward a tree at the edge of the Square. The bare branches would offer some shelter from the rain.

As they shouldered through, Reed felt someone smack his right arm. He turned and glimpsed Hunter, his face set and tight. He hissed in Reed's ear as he passed. "See what I mean? The Council!" He cursed.

Reed had no time to respond before he was swept out of earshot.

They reached the shelter of the tree and found a relatively dry spot beneath it. Pulling the navy hoodie over his head, Reed settled on the edge of the bricking next to Alec and surveyed the scene. Lights shone out of every window, and figures could be seen inside ransacking the rooms. Officers kept the crowd under control, corralling everyone on the Square with shouted commands and human chains. The RDs mixed with the teens, assuring them it was just a passing search and they would be allowed back inside shortly. Reed caught sight of Michael in a soaked t-shirt and shorts, trying to reason with a knot of unhappy young people while one girl cried on his shoulder.

"I wonder what set this off," Alec mused aloud. His bright eyes narrowed as he took in the confusion around them, and he pushed the hood of Reed's white-and-blue hoodie up onto his head.

Reed shrugged. "Dunno. I guess they must have…"

A realization exploded in his mind. He knew what this was about. Just last night he had stumbled upon the drug ring that had been on the Council's wanted list for months. *Months*. It couldn't be a coincidence. But how did they find out?

Alec glanced at him curiously. "They must have what?"

"They must have picked up something from their ringer," Reed finished, hastily gathering his wits.

Alec nodded. "Yeah, I guess so. I'd give just about anything to know who that is."

Reed would have as well. His mind ran backward over everything that had happened since the night before. Maybe one of the other boys had discovered the foggy room after Reed and Hunter's visit. Or could somebody have smelled the smoke after they left the door open? Had someone seen it through the window?

Wait. The window. A horrible truth dawned on Reed. Somebody *had* seen that window last night. And someone had met Reed on the Square that morning and forced the information from him. It was the only other person who would know. But that would mean... *Gabe— the ringer?* It seemed bizarre, impossible. But why else would he be so pushy to find out what had been happening? Why else would he make it his business to look in third-story windows at night? And why else would he be so suspicious of everybody else?

Reed was stunned. He realized his mouth had sagged open, and he shut it quickly. *But I can't tell anybody yet. It's just a suspicion.* Still, he could keep his eyes and ears open. Things might begin to make a lot more sense now.

The night wore on. The sudden fury of the shakedown subsided as midnight approached, and the officers returned to the Square. Only later did Reed find out they carried with them several pounds of illegal drugs, confiscated from the room near the end of his hall. They also arrested several teens connected with it, both boys and girls.

Once the officers departed, the RDs announced that everyone could return to their rooms. The crowd dispersed, grumbling and still not sure what had started all the hubbub. As everyone broke up, Alec turned to Reed. "I haven't said this yet, but thanks, Reed. Thanks a lot. You saved me and all of us from goodness knows what. That was quick thinking. I'll get your clothes back to you tomorrow."

"Sure, whatever." Reed shrugged. "I'll find a way to give yours back, too. They're hanging out my window right now. But, really, it was nothing. I was glad to help."

"Well, I'm grateful to you, and I'll always remember this." Alec's blue-green eyes had never been more sincere. "If you ever need anything, you can come to me anytime."

"Thanks. Oh, and I'll figure out some way to get the backpack to you. We'll have to be really careful, though. They're going to be watching everything for a while."

"Yeah, they will, but you're a smart dude. You'll be just fine."

"Good night."

"G'night, bro."

CHAPTER 19

S pring had finally come. Buds burst open in a spray of color that settled across the countryside. Flowering trees tinged the greening woods with white and pink, and warm breezes played among their bright, fresh leaves. A shade of green crept over last year's dead sod, sweeping around the Dorms' sidewalks and trees. Wildflowers burst out of the hillsides and laughed up at the returning songbirds. The whole world was coming back to life, and it lifted Reed's heart toward the blue sky and dazzling sunshine overhead.

This place wasn't so bad, he decided as he strolled the country road. Things had drastically improved since he formed his first impression months before. He sucked in a deep breath. As he walked, every fiber in his body soaked up the beauty, the warmth, and the bright sunshine. An early afternoon on a perfect Saturday... *Why on earth did I let myself get talked into spending it at the Shellys'?*

Everybody else on the Hill would probably be out tanning and sharing the latest gossip. Things had slowed down after the shakedown, almost two weeks earlier. It was remarkable how quickly the event had faded into the past. Most of the teens seemed to have forgotten about it as soon as their clothes dried.

Reed shrugged off his thoughts and glanced over at his companions. Sarah, making some sort of daisy chain out of wildflowers she'd gathered along the road, was chatting with Cody. The two of them had offered to guide Reed out to the Shellys' farm for the afternoon. Though he probably could have found the place on his own, he was grateful for their company and continued offers of friendship. That was the only reason he agreed to come out here and work—a friendship.

An amiable silence lapsed between the other two. Sarah had been doing most of the talking and stopped to gather a few extra flowers from the roadside. Reed took advantage of the moment to ask a question that hung at the back of his mind. "So are we going to be the only ones there today?" He picked up a pebble and tossed it from hand to hand. "I mean, I know Lucy and Alec are coming, but is that all?"

"Oh, no," Sarah replied, adding an aster to her growing chain as she resumed her walk. "I think everybody's supposed to come help with the annual spring chores. I think even Gabe is going to be there."

Reed caught the rock in his right hand. Silence.

She cocked her head at him. "Oh, come on, Reed! Gabe is fine. Surely you've noticed how he's softened up toward you over the past week or two!"

Reed had to admit there had been a change in Gabe's attitude. Still, he had his suspicions.

Sarah wound a Black-Eyed Susan into her garland. "He was a little touchy at first, but he's suspicious of everybody. He just has to warm up. After what you did during the shakedown, I think he's starting to accept you. Alec told him about it. He really was grateful and, I think, kind of impressed."

Reed tossed the rock away and changed the subject. "Is Elijah supposed to be there?"

Sarah laughed, and Cody grinned. "Are you kidding?" he said. "I don't think Ethan could survive a Saturday without him."

They found the farm already bustling with activity. Every door and window of the little house was thrown open to catch the spring breezes that ruffled the spreads of sweet-smelling clover. Half a dozen girls flitted in and out of doors, shaking rugs, hanging out curtains, and emptying mop buckets in the grass. Two boys were working on the roof while others moved furniture and mattresses out into the yard. Little Shellys were everywhere.

"Sarah, honey!" Lucy flourished a dust-cloth from a window as the three approached the house. "It's spring cleaning! Mrs. Shelly isn't feeling well, so we put her to bed and told her we'd do it!"

"Of course," Sarah called back, quickening her pace. "Anybody got an apron?" She vanished inside, draping her daisy chain over the doorknob.

"Hey, guys!" Alec popped a sweaty face over the edge of the roof. "You look fresh."

Cody squinted up at him. "Thank you. I'm afraid you don't."

Elijah appeared next to Alec, silhouetted against the bright spring sky. "He isn't, poor Alec. It's been quite a day so far, and he's always gotten the worst end of the deal."

Alec nodded agreeably.

Elijah rested a hammer on his thigh and wiped the sleeve of his white t-shirt across his forehead. "Maybe now that Reed's here, they can swap out. If he doesn't mind, he could help me on the roof for a while. We're almost done." As no one objected to this plan, they made the switch with the help of a ladder. When Alec was safely on the ground and Reed perched on the roof, Elijah leaned over the edge once more.

"Oh, and Cody, there was a heavy box or something in the bedroom that Gabe and Wilson left. Could you take care of it?"

Cody waved. "You got it, bro."

"Thanks, dude! You're the best."

As the other two disappeared into the house, Reed chuckled. "So is Cody, like, freaky strong or something?"

"Something like that." Elijah smiled as he moved back up the roof. "Or maybe we just live together, so we boss each other around all the time."

After a brief seminar on the art of roofing, they settled into the work of replacing worn-out shingles. It wasn't a hard job, but it was hot and dirty. Reed began to sympathize with Alec.

After a few minutes, Cody reappeared below. Reed glanced down and paused, hammer mid-air. Cody carried on his shoulder an old fireproof safe the size of a large microwave. It looked heavy. What caught Reed's attention was Cody himself. His muscles were enormous under the weight, swelling to a size Reed wouldn't have believed if he weren't seeing it. Katy fluttered behind him, kneading her hands and asking continually if he was sure he didn't want any help.

Elijah glanced down and smiled. "Ah, Katy! She's always worried he'll hurt himself. She shouldn't, though; he'll be fine."

Reed said nothing, but gaped in silence until Cody had safely set his burden on the grass. Even then, he had to assure Katy several times he was fine. The sight of the two together amused Reed. Katy, all of four-foot eight-inches high, seemed to have shrunk next to Cody, who had never looked so massive. Reed looked up at Elijah and grinned. "They make quite a pair."

Elijah straightened and smiled again. "Yeah, they do."

Reed ventured another glance down as the two disappeared back into the house. He chuckled. "I'm not sure which one sets the other off more. They'd make a cute couple."

"Cody wouldn't mind if Katy's agreeable."

Reed's grin faded, and he glanced at Elijah. "Wait, really? Cody has a crush on Katy? I never would have guessed!"

"You weren't supposed to." Elijah returned to his work. "Cody's going about it the right way. Don't say anything to anybody yet; it's not public knowledge. Me and Lucy know, but nobody else is supposed to yet."

Reed sat back on his heels, pondering the news. "But she's so small, and he's so... so..."

"Freaky strong?" Elijah looked up with twinkling eyes. "Toss me that nail, would you?"

Reed handed it to him. "Well, yeah. Why the heck did he pick little-bitty Katy of all people? With a bod like that, he could have bagged any girl he wanted, maybe a model or something."

Elijah paused his work and rested on his hammer. "There's more to this than looks, Reed. If you just go for size or appearance, you're bound to be disappointed. There's always somebody bigger or prettier, and you've gotta go deeper and look for things that matter. Looks are just on the surface; they're not the most important thing." He picked up his hammer again and slid a new shingle off the pile.

Reed stared at him for a minute and then mechanically did the same, blinking down at his hands. Looks weren't important? His view on the subject couldn't be any more different, but he held his peace. He hadn't done well last time he tried to argue with Elijah.

They worked in silence. Reed pounded a nail into the roof and reached for another. Where did Elijah get these ideas of his? *Nobody thinks that way anymore. How can he say stuff like that?* He shot a glance in Elijah's direction. *Duh, look who's talking.* Here was the young man who had literally been too hot to live in the Dorms. Of course he could say looks weren't a big deal; he already had all the looks he needed and didn't have to worry.

Then again, Reed pondered as he added a second nail next to the first, he *was* the best-looking kid on the Hill. Why would he want to say something like that? Shouldn't he be saying looks are everything? He could get anywhere or anything he wanted.

Reed put down his hammer and scratched the back of his neck. He didn't understand this guy. He glanced in Elijah's direction again. Stranger still, the heartthrob of the Hill was spending his leisure after-noon working on a random widow's roof, sweat dripping off his perfect face and nails sticking out of his mouth. *Why?*

Ever since he had met these people, Reed had been asking that question, hunting for what made them so different. Here it was again, and yet, it still eluded him. They had told him time and again their ex-planation—God, Jesus, salvation—but he still couldn't—wouldn't—believe it.

Fortunately, most of the roof work had been taken care of before Reed arrived. The little that remained went quickly. When it was done, he straightened and surveyed their handiwork with pride, for-getting he hadn't done most of it.

Elijah brushed off the hopelessly blackened knees of his jeans and gathered up the tools. "We're finished here. Let's go down and see what we can help everybody else with."

Reed squinted up at the sun and sighed. He should have known they weren't done. Picking up a load of tools, he backed down the ladder. Elijah took the quicker route and dropped straight from the roof to the yard below, landing easily on his feet in the new grass. At the impact, however, his silver chain jolted out of his collar. The arcane pendant slipped out of his t-shirt and dangled down onto his chest.

It caught Reed's eye with a flash of afternoon sun. He'd almost forgotten about the strange object in the weeks since he'd first seen it. Now, the flash brought everything back in an instant—the memory, the mystery, the curiosity. But, in half a second, the flash was gone again. Elijah's fist closed over the bright glitter and dropped it back inside his shirt.

Reed turned his head away and kept climbing down the ladder. He suddenly felt an astronomical distance from Elijah, now gathering tools on the grass. Before, there had been a growing friendship, a mutual liking and friendly camaraderie. But this secret—this thing—was between them, pushing them worlds apart. Reed prided himself on having keen perception, but this situation baffled his senses. Elijah seemed so pure and clear, but this object—whatever it was—seemed to represent a different side Reed had not seen, something completely foreign.

What is that thing? he wondered, dusting off his jeans at the bottom of the ladder. *He guards it like the Hope Diamond. I'm not supposed to ask, he won't tell, and I can't even get a good look at it. How the heck will I ever find out?*

CHAPTER 20

Reed didn't have much time to wonder about the pendant the rest of the afternoon. Most of his will and energy was focused on surviving each task that loomed up before him. Though the roof had been taken care of, Patton's corral required repair, several door hinges wanted replacing, the windows needed work, and the yard cried for attention. After all that, there was still the garden. This was a large, tilled plot behind the barn that Reed had visited on his last trip to the farm. Planting new seeds, thinning young shoots, weeding around the growing plants—the garden promised to be a black hole of work, sweat, and back pain.

After several hours of chores, the teens took a break under the spreading branches of a great oak behind the house, overlooking the pond. Reed stretched out on the thick carpet of shady grass and closed his eyes, wondering again how he'd gotten talked into this. Every disgruntled muscle in his back and knees complained from the hours of bending.

The other teens, scattered around the dappled shade, seemed unaffected by the fatigue. They acted more pleased than exhausted.

"Well, we knocked out all the inside cleaning, the outside repair work, the yard, and a good bit of the garden," Sarah listed, counting on her earth-stained fingers with each accomplishment. "That's awesome, guys!"

"Don't forget the barn work," added Gabe, lying on his stomach in the grass with his head pillowed on his arms. Alec had been giving him a backrub until the twins, Luke and Lizzy, began dropping leaves down the back of Alec's collar from the branches above. He had been forced to mount the tree to bring an end to it, and he had not returned. Hushed whispers and muffled giggles from above suggested an armistice had been reached on the terms of a story. Gabe would have to do without his backrub.

"Yes, and the barn," amended Sarah, adding to the tally on her fingers. "Did I forget anything else?"

"Marielle and I took care of the laundry," Lucy put in. She, Katy, and Krista had formed a massage train near the edge of the shade. Gabe looked slightly jealous.

"Cody fixed the light switch in the hall, too," added Wilson, staring into the sky with his hands clasped behind his head.

"And Wilson got the lawnmower up and running," Kara finished from across the circle where she was braiding Courtney's hair. Nathan was asleep and didn't say anything.

Sarah gave up counting. "Well, I'd say that was an incredible day's work."

"And I learned how to caulk awound windows!" exclaimed Ethan, bouncing up and down in the excitement of the moment. This was not a kind or wise thing to do, since he was using Elijah, propped up against the tree trunk next to Cody, as a recliner. But Elijah took it well and never even opened his eyes. His eyebrows did go up and down with each bounce, however.

"Did you?" said Lucy, smiling at the little boy's enthusiasm. "Then I'm sure you're practically a professional." Elijah's eyebrows skyrocketed. "That is definitely worth adding to the list."

Sarah smiled and clasped her hands around her knees. "Can you count, Ethan, and tell us how many things that was?"

Ethan studied his fingers deliberately, his tongue sticking out in concentration as he lifted them one by one.

"Nine!" he announced suddenly.

"Very good!" Lucy exchanged surprised looks with Sarah. "You can count fast!"

The little boy grinned and then added shyly, "Thanks, Cody."

"What? Cody!" Lucy gasped. "That's cheating! You can't tell him the—*ouch*!"

She broke off in surprise as a large piece of bark thumped on top of her head. There were giggles in the tree.

"Hey, you up there!" she called into the branches, rising to her knees. "What are you doing?"

"Who says it's us?" replied Alec's merry voice. "It might be the squirrels."

A young acorn bounced off her upturned face. More giggles erupted, accompanied by a muffled snicker that definitely did not come from any squirrel.

"Squirrels, my eye!" she retorted. "Alec, am I going to have to come up there and *get* you?"

"You might," the voice replied. "But I'd like to see *you* try to climb a tree."

Lucy considered that. "Then I'll send Cody up! Or Gabe! Or I'll…"

Her voice trailed off, and a twinkle stole into her eyes. Slyly, she reached back and took out the rubber band holding her ponytail, shaking her golden hair loose. Squinting one eye, she aimed her metal-banded weapon along her fingers deliberately. "Or I could try… THIS!" She let fly her pink-and-silver missile with a snap. There was an echoing pop in the tree, and a satisfying "ouch" rewarded her aim.

That started a war. The opposing sides recruited allies and began an all-out campaign. Reed remained neutral on his back in the grass. He was tired, and this wasn't his kind of fun. It would take a lot more than acorns to bring back his sapped energy. Sure, it wasn't too bad now, sprawled in the shade playing games, but that was nothing compared to the hours of work they'd all put in. A twig hurtled dangerously close to his nose. He couldn't comprehend what these people were thinking. The Dorms offered so much more. Why come all the way out here just to work their fingers to the bone? To build muscle? *Heck,* thought Reed, *I'll take the Hill any day and go to the gym later.*

The war might have gone on until the tree had been divested of all its new acorns, but Marielle and Meagan emerged from the house with a pitcher of lemonade and tray of cups. That ended the conflict and brought those in the tree down to earth, though Alec had to make two trips. After he reached the ground the first time, Lizzy insisted she could not come down by herself and must be carried down on Alec's back.

Once everyone settled, Marielle took on the role of hostess. She poured the lemonade with all the dignified sobriety of a fourteen-year-old and began a "proper" conversation. "Mother says to thank all of you very much for your hard work," she said as she filled the last of the mismatched cups. "She wishes she could come out and thank you in person, but she isn't feeling very well. She says to ask how things have been going 'out there' for all of you."

The reference to the Hill as "out there" amused Reed, but he hid his smile behind his faded blue glass. The lemonade was making him feel better already.

"Well," Sarah took a sip from her plastic yellow cup, "I guess you could say they're fine. I'm not in the Dorms anymore, but it seems to have calmed down after that search thing a few weeks ago. I don't know of anything else. Oh, except that concert coming up."

Marielle's prim hostess demeanor vanished, and she nearly dropped her glass in her lap. "Oh, I know! I've heard so much about that!"

"Yeah," Reed agreed, finishing off his lemonade. "Everybody's talking about it. They're, like, the greatest group ever."

"Group?" Marielle turned to him, puzzled. Then realization dawned on her. "Oh, you mean *that* concert—the Hordes of Hell."

"Marielle!"

"No, really! That's the name of the band!"

"Heck, yeah, it is!" said Reed. He enthusiastically spit an ice cube back into his glass. "The whole Hill's gone crazy over their latest single! Everybody's going to hear them live."

"Well," Sarah hesitated, "I was actually talking about the lead from the Broadway *Les Mis* that's coming through on tour. I really don't want to go to the other one. Marielle, how did you know about it?"

"Like he said," the other girl shrugged. "Everybody's gone crazy over them. There're posters and billboards plastered all over town, and the newspaper's hardly talked about anything else. I hate it. They give me the creeps."

Reed hardly noticed this last comment. He sat up and stared at

Sarah.

"You don't want to go to their concert? They're the biggest thing right now!"

"I don't really care how big they are," said Sarah frankly, sliding her cup back onto the tray. "I just don't like them. I mean, they're not even mainstream! They are *way* out there." She dried her hands on her lap. "Besides, their pictures give me nightmares. I probably couldn't sleep for weeks if I saw them in person."

"Oh, come on! It can't be that bad."

"Well, most of their stuff *is* censored on YouTube," Lucy countered. She was brushing bark out of Lizzy's hair across the circle. "But I think you're missing Sarah's point, Reed. What she meant is that whatever's 'in' right now shouldn't determine your standards of right and wrong. You'd be changing them every day if it did. There has to be something steadier to base your principles on."

Reed opened his mouth to reply.

"But," Sarah said suddenly, plucking the cup out of Meagan's hand and plunking it inside her own, "all that's to say, Marielle, that it's been pretty slow around the Hill lately. Not much going on!"

"Yeah," added Alec. "Except supper, and I'm starved."

Everyone laughed, and the strained stillness broke and melted under the sound like a sandcastle dissolving under a wave. Everyone seemed to be talking at once. The girls split off into chatter among themselves, and all the boys began teasing Alec—almost all. Reed leaned back onto the grass moodily, feeling outnumbered.

Why'd Sarah have to cut in like that? He brooded up at the leaves. *I was just about to let 'em have it.* Of course, he realized, that was exactly why she had broken in, and Alec, too. One more second and Reed would have blown his top. Then they all would have been sorry, him more than anyone else. He wanted to pull the grass over his head. They'd all been watching, too.

The only one who hadn't seemed to pay any attention was Elijah. Ethan, still in his lap, had soaked up the conversation, mouth slightly ajar, but the older boy had never even opened his eyes. Reed hoped he was asleep. He wasn't.

Ethan was quick to lose interest in the "big people" talk and, as the banter moved away from the central conversation, he laid his head against Elijah's shoulder. The shift in his weight pulled the collar of Elijah's t-shirt down his chest, showing skin and a large portion of silver chain. It caught the light that filtered through the leaves with a tiny sparkle. The glitter captured Ethan's attention. He reached up wonderingly and ran one finger up and down the shiny links. Elijah offered no objection. The jewelry obviously fascinated Ethan. Wrapping it around his finger, he began to lift the chain out of Elijah's shirt. Reed held his breath.

"Tan I see it?" the little boy whispered.

Nothing moved except Elijah's hand. It shot up and gently untwined the chain from around Ethan's little fingers. "No," he whispered back without opening his eyes. "Not right now."

"Otay." Ethan blinked at the forbidden object. "Someday when I grows up," he whispered, "I wants to wear one, too."

Elijah said nothing for a moment. He seemed still, but Reed could see his throat move as he swallowed. Then, in the same soft whisper, Elijah replied, "I hope you never have to, Ethan. Never."

The other teens, still busy ribbing Alec, hadn't seen the incident. Only Reed heard the little exchange. He turned his head away and stared out over the rippling face of the pond. Here it was again, this thing, and this time not even Ethan could touch it.

"I hope you never have to, Ethan. Never."

Reed's curiosity roared up like a fire doused with oil, fed by returning doubts and suspicions. *What in the world is that thing?*

CHAPTER 21

That question still plagued him hours later. Moodily, he lay on his bed, watching Reagan iron. Dusk was falling outside. It was quiet except for the hiss and sputter of the iron as it slid over the smooth material. Reed lay with his chin on his folded arms and stared at the small puffs of steam that rose from Reagan's work.

Reagan endured the silent observation patiently. He said nothing for a long while and kept on with his chore before he finally glanced up from the shirt he was working on. "You're awfully quiet tonight," he remarked. "Something wrong? Jilted maybe?"

Reed stirred slightly. "Nah, just thinking."

"'Bout what?"

Reed was about to brush aside the question with a casual "nothing" when a thought struck him. The answer to his endless wondering lay right under his nose. Reagan.

He had lived with Elijah for months. If Lucy wouldn't tell Elijah's secret, perhaps Reagan would. Reed pushed up to his elbows. "Reagan, do you know anything about that chain-pendant thing Elijah wears?"

Reagan kept ironing, but his eyebrows nearly escalated off his forehead. He shot Reed a curious look. "You know 'Lijah? You never mentioned it before."

"Well, you never told me he was your old roommate, either. Somebody else did."

"He didn't, eh?" Reagan held up the finished shirt and eyed it.

"To answer your question, I don't know anything about it. He never took it off; he even slept with it on. He always kept it inside his shirt, and I never saw it. That's all I know." He took a coat hanger in his mouth and buttoned the shirt onto it.

"You don't have any idea what it's for or why he wears it?"

"Not at all." Reagan hung the shirt in his shelf space with a click and turned back. "He never volunteered, and I never asked. But I know it's not just for looks."

Reed had surmised that much. A guy generally didn't keep a pendant hidden inside his shirt if he wanted everybody to see it.

Reagan slung a pair of slacks over the ironing board and looked up. "But why do you want to know all of a sudden? And how did you meet my old roomie anyway?"

A convenient cough saved Reed from answering right away. He rolled to his back, mind groping for a reply. "Oh, you know, through a mutual friend." He breezed on. "Have you seen him lately?"

"Nah. Not since he left. Still as hot as ever?"

"Yeah, I guess. He's been working out a lot lately."

Reagan shook his head and began pressing the slacks. "Sad. He was really something! It's too bad he had…"

The door burst open, and a boy rushed in. "Guys!" he panted, "The Hordes are coming!"

Reagan almost dropped his iron. "What?"

The boy was out of breath and could hardly speak. "They're coming! There's a carnival… and a concert… and… and…" he handed Reagan a flyer and bent double, heaving for air. Reagan scanned it and looked suddenly relieved. "Oh, *those* Hordes."

Reed sat up. "What is it?"

"Apparently," Reagan said, still reading for himself, "somebody's bringing in a street fair… carnival… thingy for the Hill the day after the Hordes of Hell concert. Oh, sweet! The band's gonna be there all day for us to meet, and they're giving *another* concert on the grounds that night! Dude!" He whirled to the dark-haired messenger. "Where'd you get this, Will?"

"Michael gave it to me," the boy puffed, dropping into a chair. He was a rather thick person that could take a while to catch his breath once he lost it. "Said it's kind of a promo before the rec center opens."

RANSOM GREY

"Freakin' *awesome!*" Reagan was moonwalking circles around the desks. "So the rec center's opening, I get to meet the Hordes of Hell, *and* I get out of my tight spot!"

"Tight spot?" Reed paused in his own jubilation, much to the bed springs' relief.

Reagan didn't hesitate. "I couldn't decide on just one girl to take to the concert, but now I get one for each night!" He stopped. "But that means double tickets. Ouch."

"No tickets," Will piped up. "Hill people get into the first one on their ID cards, and the one after the carnival's free."

"This just keeps getting better!" laughed Reagan. "I knew I liked this place! But there's still the rec center to get ready for. Man, I gotta get my tan going again and start doing supersets at the gym."

"What does that have to do with...?" Will looked puzzled.

"Pool," said Reed, winking at him.

"Ohhh." Sudden understanding swept the other boy's face.

"You got it!" Reagan said, calming down enough to slip on a shirt from the pile on his bed, taking time to make sure it looked all right with his shorts. "Now I've gotta go see if this has gotten around yet. Oh, dude, this is... this is... sweet!"

136

CHAPTER 22

I t didn't take long for the news to travel through the Dorms. It spread like wildfire, leaving in its wake a trail of ecstatic teenagers. It also left behind a jumble of drama, crushed dreams, and scandals as the teens immediately began pairing up for the big event. It was enough to keep Dorm society busy until "The Day" arrived.

The night of the first concert began with a crowd that completely packed the Square, grass, and sidewalks of the Hill. It was an early Friday evening after a clear and perfect day. The late afternoon sun shot through the fluttering leaves above the teeming sidewalks and cast dancing shadows on the grass. The air was vibrant with anticipation. The throng of teens laughed and jostled each other, filling the spring evening with their happy babble. Expectation—it flavored the atmosphere like a spice.

Reed sucked in a deep breath and gave his hair a final sweep off his forehead. This was the life: not a care in the world or a cloud in the sky. He reveled in the joy of being young as he shouldered his way through the crowd toward the corner where he was supposed to meet Allie.

They usually met at this corner whenever they were going out, "whenever" meaning perhaps half a dozen other dates. It had been almost two weeks since Reed had decided to follow up on Hunter's tip. Allie, never one to turn down masculine interest of any kind, had been more than receptive to Reed's advances. He was now ranked as one of the top figures on the Hill in both social status and looks.

In fact, it was whispered that she'd had her sights set in his direction long before he paid any attention to her.

He arrived at the corner by Dorm Eight. It was empty. Unperturbed, he settled under a nearby fir tree for what could be a long wait.

"She's always late," he told himself. "The makeup never goes on as quick as they think." While he waited, the constant stream of traffic down the sidewalk in front of him carried past a number of familiar faces. Several of the guys looked at him sympathetically and made brushing motions on their cheeks. Riley went by with another boy and flipped him a thumbs up. Reed hadn't seen much of him lately; he hung with several boys from Dorm Fourteen constantly and was never in the room. Reagan passed not far behind, a girl on each arm. Reed chuckled. The free tickets had freed him up more than he'd imagined.

"Umm... Reed?"

He jerked around in surprise. Lucy and Katy had come up next to him quietly and stood on his left, eyeing him.

"Oh," he said, scrambling to his feet. "Hi!"

"Hi."

They continued to eye him in awkward silence. Reed coughed, dropping his eyes, and noticed for the first time that both girls were dressed for a formal event. Katy wore a knee-length dress of deep blue and had curled her hair. Lucy's fell smooth and straight over the shoulders of her lacy white top. He decided he liked her hair that way.

"Gee, you're all dressed up."

The girls looked at each other, and Lucy smiled. "Well, yeah," she admitted. "It might be a little overkill for a concert, but we decided to have some fun with it."

"So you changed your minds? You're coming after all?"

"No," they both said quickly and again looked at each other.

"We're going to see the tenor from *Les Mis* Sarah was talking about." Katy pushed her hair behind her shoulder. "That's tonight."

"We're supposed to pick up Marielle on the way and meet some of the others there," Lucy added. "Have you changed *your* mind?"

"Nope." Reed stuck his hands in his pockets. "But are *you* sure? Everybody else is going."

"I don't care what everybody else does," Lucy laughed. "I'd rather be free to do my own thing than what everybody else tells me to."

Reed had never thought of it that way before. He wished he hadn't.

Lucy grew serious again. "Umm... Reed, not to pry or anything, but are you waiting for somebody?"

"Err... yes, actually."

As if on cue, Allie emerged from the dorm, mincing over to where Reed waited.

"Hey, babe!" she said, tossing her bleached bangs off her forehead. Judging by the way she batted her eyes at him, she was pleased to find him waiting. Her pleasure was short-lived, however, as she caught sight of the other girls. Her coy smile melted like a snow cone dropped on a radiator.

"Oh. Lucy." She eyed them. "I certainly didn't expect to see *you* tonight."

"Uh... same here," replied Lucy, her voice almost matching Allie's pointed tone. But her eyes were fixed on Reed in an astonished stare. He looked away and studied the crowd.

Allie went on. "Oh! And what a... quaint top. It doesn't look like anything I saw where I shop."

"No, it wouldn't." Lucy finally took her gaze from Reed and looked at Allie for the first time. "It... hmm... never mind. Oh, those are quite the jeans! Did they come like that or did you sit in something... unfortunate?"

"Oh, yeah! All the *fashion* people are wearing them. The girls are crazy about them."

"I'm sure they are." Lucy smiled sweetly. "Well, we don't want to keep you. It was nice to talk to you again, Reed. Perhaps we'll see you around sometime."

"Oh, yeah. Sure. See ya."

The two girls disappeared into the crowd. Reed and Allie turned in the opposite direction and fell in with the flow of teens. Reed decided to speak before Allie had a chance to say anything. "I didn't know you knew Lucy."

"Yeah, sorta. We never really clicked. Some people liked her an awful lot, but I never cared for the old-fashioned style. I try to keep more with the times."

Reed could have guessed. Allie, with her halter top, flat-ironed hair, and profuse mascara made quite a contrast to Lucy, despite their similar height and figures. He wondered if Allie would ever consider letting her hair fall over her shoulders the way Lucy's did.

She slipped her hand into his and pressed up against his shoulder. "Oh, come one! We are going to have the *best* time. How am I supposed to have fun if you keep your face like that? Smile, handsome!"

Reed looked down at her and grinned. "Better, gorgeous?"

"SO much better. You are freakin' adorable." She squeezed his arm and then gasped. "You've been hitting the gym again, haven't you?"

"Yeah, Reagan and I have been going a lot lately." He grinned at her again. "You like it? I've gotta keep it up or I might lose you to the competition."

"Oh, shut up." She leaned up and kissed him, right there in the middle of the sidewalk.

The rest of the night went better than Reed could have hoped. The concert was everything the billboards had set it up to be, from the rainbow of searing lights to the second largest smoke machine in the country. The crowd was ecstatic. Crawling into bed much later that night, Reed—hoarse, exhausted, and a little hard of hearing—was prepared to do it all over again.

CHAPTER 23

"Hey, Reed, wait up!"

Reed paused on his trek up the North Stairs from the shuttles the next day. Like any Saturday, he had been obliged to put in a half-day at the factory. Everyone had been let off a few minutes earlier than usual, however, thanks to the carnival and the concert scheduled for later that afternoon. He turned back to see who called him and, with mixed sensations, saw that it was Lucy trotting up the stairs after him. He swallowed and stopped to wait for her. As soon as she caught up with him, he spoke. "Look, Lucy, if it's about last night, I just want to get one thing straightened out."

"Oh." She looked at him. "I wasn't going to bring up last night but, if you want to, go ahead."

"I think I will." He took a deep breath. "So I know you and Allie don't get along, but there's no point in hiding that I'm dating her. I was going to tell all of you eventually, but I just never got around to it. And it's not like we're gonna run off and get married next week, but we're both happy with where things are going. I could tell last night you thought… well, I didn't know what you thought, but I didn't know if you'd ever speak to me again."

"Oh, no, Reed!" Lucy shook her head. "I'm not mad at you. Not at all! Just… concerned. I admit I was a little surprised that you would fall for a girl like Allie, but I'm not sure you know what you're getting into. She's not quite what she looks like." She pursed her lips. "Okay, take that back, maybe she's exactly what she looks like, just not to *you*." She started up the stairs again.

Reed followed her, frowning. "What do you mean? I know her. We've been going out for three weeks now. I think I've got a pretty good idea of what things are like."

Lucy turned and looked him straight in the eye. "Reed, I understand what you're saying. But I know how girls think, especially this type, and trust me: things aren't the way you think they are. Things are a lot more open and laid back for guys, and they assume everybody else is that way, too. But it's a lot more complicated with girls. Trust me, Reed, there is a lot going on under the surface that you have no idea about. She's in this for more than you know, and she *will* try to get it."

"From me? Why?"

"Err... talk to one of the guys about that. I'm just warning you from a girl's perspective."

"Warning? You make it sound like I'm being hunted or something."

"You *are*, Reed." Her serious tone startled him. "Things get around in girls' circles that guys never know about. Believe me, there are more girls than I can count who would love to get their hooks into you. Allie's not the only one, but she's definitely the closest."

"What?" Reed could feel his face getting hot. "Nobody's got any hooks in me! That's... weird! Look, I'm just dating a girl, and maybe that goes somewhere and maybe it doesn't. If it doesn't, too bad. If it does, who's to say that would be so awful? You make her sound like a scheming..."

Lucy sighed heavily. "Reed, you're a smart guy. But women have defied men's understanding for thousands of years. If you don't understand what I mean by 'complicated,' that's okay. Just believe me when I say it is. But you don't think it would be bad if anything comes from this? Oh, Reed!" She shook her head and looked away for a moment. "I don't want to poison your mind, but you have to understand. She's a bad girl. There are things about her you don't need to know and I wish I didn't. You might not even realize what's going on until it's too late, but she will work every skill in her power to get what she wants from you. It will *not* be good. Please believe me, Reed!"

He stared at the concrete, unsure if he should be angry, scornful, or frightened. If she'd meant confuse him, she'd done a good job. Her words poured into and overflowed his brain like too much water in a sink. Her main point, however, sank in.

When he finally spoke, he kept his eyes averted. "Well, if it makes you feel any better, I'm not going to be with her this afternoon. She's going to hang with her girlfriends at the street fair."

"Oh, good." She sounded relieved. "I mean, that'll give you some time. You need to talk to one of the guys—Nathan or Alec or 'Lijah or somebody. They're all going to be around this afternoon, and I'm sure they can talk you through it much better than I can. Elijah's especially good to talk to." She stopped in the middle of the sidewalk and met his eyes. "Will you promise me you'll talk to one of them? For your own sake?"

He looked down. "I'll try."

"Good." She smiled and relaxed. "I'll see you later."

She turned toward her dorm, leaving him to ruminate on her words.

He went up to his room but found it and the entire hall empty. Most of the boys had gone down to where the road in front of the Dorms had been blocked off and the carnival had already started. He changed out of his work clothes and retraced his steps. His mind was on overload trying to process everything Lucy had said. He wasn't sure whether to accept it from someone with inside information or to reject it as coming from a jealous girl with a grudge. After all, the two of them didn't get along. He felt that he should even be angry at Lucy for some of the things she had said about his girl, except they matched something he had felt deep in his gut all along. He needed to sort out his thoughts, find some way to make sense of it all.

Preoccupied, he pushed out the door into the sunlight and ran directly into someone going past on the sidewalk.

"Whoa! Sorry, bro. My fault," he apologized, not even looking up. "I didn't see you there."

The other boy eyed him strangely. "Reed?"

Reed's head jerked up. "Elijah! I didn't expect you to... I mean, you don't... that is... Did Lucy send you over here?"

"Lucy? No. I haven't seen her all day. Should I have?"

"Well, no." Reed rubbed the back of his neck. "It's just that she was insistent about you. I mean, insistent that I talk to you, and you just happened to show up."

"Ah." The word carried complete understanding. "And you don't want to talk about it, but you kinda… have to?"

"Exactly!" exclaimed Reed in relief. "It's personal but, by myself, I can't even… Ugh! This is frustrating."

"Well," Elijah said slowly, "I was just going to walk around, maybe skim the street fair thingy. You're welcome to come along, and we can talk as we go. It might help you straighten things out."

It was exactly what Reed had been wishing for. He accepted the invitation.

They turned up the deserted sidewalk at a slow pace, side by side. Starting out was awkward for Reed. He opened and shut his mouth several times without saying anything. It was harder than he had thought it would be. He hated opening up, especially on something this personal.

"It's okay, Reed. Don't tell me anything you don't want to, but don't hold back what you need to get out either."

That helped. How did Elijah always know just what to say? Reed tried again. Once he got started, it became easier, and before long, he found himself unloading the whole story of the night before, Lucy's reaction that day, and his own confusion.

Elijah listened attentively, hands in his pockets, his eyes wandering over everything they passed. He said nothing but allowed Reed to go on until he ran out of steam.

"…and that's when she said I should talk to you," Reed finished. "I didn't think I would 'cause I couldn't even sort it out myself, but then you just happened to come along and… you know."

"I see," Elijah mused. "Wow, I'd be confused, too. She laid on a lot all at once. But what is it that's bothering you the most?"

Reed watched the shadows play across the sidewalk thoughtfully. "I want to know what she meant when she said Allie wants a lot more from me than I think." He looked up. "I'm already doing all the good boyfriend stuff. What else could she want?"

Elijah was silent for a moment. "Is that what's *really* bothering you?"

Reed dropped his eyes and pulled at his ear. "Well…"

"Get it off your chest, Reed."

"Okay, fine. I admit I was a little bothered when Lucy said flat-out that it would be bad if anything came of this relationship. I mean, how would she know? That's something for me to decide! Why can't people just mind their own business and let me live my own life?"

The only sounds were the rustling of leaves and a few faint echoes from the carnival in the distance.

"Feel better?"

Reed let out a deep breath. "Yeah."

"I see where you're coming from, Reed. It's a valid point." Elijah slid his hands into his back pockets. "There *are* some things a guy has to decide for himself. But let's go back to your first question: what else does she want from you?" Elijah kept his eyes on the sidewalk in front of him. "I really hate to go into this, but you need to know some of Allie's history. Lucy was right; she's a bad girl. You're not the first boy she's gotten in with. She started out as a little-known, pretty flirt, but she's been climbing the social ladder steadily over the last few months. How? She works her charms on guys like you. Each time, she sets her sights on a boy a little higher in the social strata than she is. She's pretty and smart; the guy falls for it. She pulls him down to her level and then uses him as a footstool to take her next step up. Sometimes, she only goes far enough to get what she wants. But it's no secret that others… well, you know, went all the way."

Reed said nothing. Elijah continued. "You are her next and per-haps final step. What does she want from you? Think about it, Reed. You know as well as anybody you're in the top crust here. Everybody knows you; you're Reagan's roommate. That practically makes you a deity to most of the girls."

A half-smile flitted across Reed's face as Elijah continued. "And, on top of that, you're a very attractive guy. Any girl would love to get her hands on you. I think that's what Lucy is so worried about. This girl wants to use you, Reed, for your position, status, looks, the whole deal. It's more than just 'all the good boyfriend stuff', more even than just getting to the top of her ladder. She wants… well, you know. She's planning to have her cake and eat it, too."

Reed tugged at his ear again. He was not fond of being referred to as cake to be eaten, and this wasn't the kind of conversation he'd been expecting. "Okay, so maybe she doesn't have a stellar record, but that doesn't mean other people can tell me what relationships I should and shouldn't have."

"True." Elijah took his hands out of his pockets. "But, Reed, we're both guys. I know what this is like. When a girl shows interest in us, it's flattering. Somebody noticed us! It makes for a great feeling, but it can go to our heads. We have to get past the emotional high or else we can't look at anything straight. Allie likes you. Great. But would pursuing this relationship really be best for you?"

"Hold it!" Reed threw up his hands. "Everybody's acting like I signed a contract in blood or something. It's not that way! If we want, we can call it off and this can all just be for fun. It's the thing to do!"

"You mean so you can have somebody to go to concerts with?"

"Well, yeah, pretty much."

"I understand that. I mean, everybody wants that kind of companionship and intimacy. But you're getting out onto thin ice with this one. You can go along and play the game now, but you'll find out it's not going to give you what you really want. It might be fun for a while, but what it is and what it leads to is so... unsatisfying."

As they talked, they had passed through the Dorms and come to the front of the Hill. They stopped beneath a young maple overlooking the road. Below them, the carnival had been set up on the cement street and was already in full swing. From where they stood, they had a clear view of the spinning rides, rows of brightly colored booths, and enormous crowds that lay in a gleaming panorama beneath the afternoon sun.

Elijah's gaze wandered over it all. Then he sighed.

"Unsatisfying," he murmured more to himself than to Reed, "but what else can you expect in a place as fake as this?"

Reed blinked. "What?"

"Artificial, fake, phony. Just look at it." Elijah swept his arm to encompass both the scene before them and the entire Hill. "The whole GRO set-up is so unrealistic. It's a plastic bubble detached from the rest of the world. It's almost like putting one of those desktop aquariums at the edge of the water at the beach. It doesn't make any sense. We're not made for this. We're supposed to be challenged, learning, and growing to make the world a better place, but we're stuck in this playground instead. It's not *good*."

"Hey," Reed turned up his palms, "we're kids! We don't have to worry about being grown up yet. Besides, what's wrong with aquariums? I mean, the water's warm, you don't have to worry about getting eaten, and hey, there's lots of other cute fish."

Elijah chuckled. "Yeah, whatever. I meant that this place was designed just to keep us locked away from reality. It's intentionally built to keep us small, to stunt us. There's a purpose behind it all, Reed. Like Wilson told you before, it's all about ideas." He stopped and sighed. "And there's something else about aquariums: they break easily."

Neither said anything more for a moment, and they watched the carnival scene in silence. Reed broke into a grin. "What the heck are we talking about? I mean seriously, how did we get onto aquariums?"

Elijah laughed softly. "I guess we kinda got off track. But it all ties together somehow; life's just a big, tangled knot sometimes."

"You can say that again. Well, anyway, I've said all I wanted to. I really just needed to talk it out. Thanks for listening."

"Anytime," replied Elijah. "And don't worry; I'll keep it with me."

Reed felt a rush of gratitude. "Thanks," he said.

They had hung back from the crowd as they talked but, as the conversation ended, they moved down the slope to join the teeming mass of young people on the road. The laughing, chattering flood engulfed them. The teens were enjoying themselves to the fullest. It was one giant party, with music blaring somewhere in the background and spinning lights on both sides of the thoroughfare. The smell of kettle corn and corn dogs flavored the air. Someone brushed past with a massive cone of blue and purple cotton candy. Reed noticed that many of the kids carried posters, cards, and CDs of the Hordes of Hell with them. *Autographs,* he thought. *Sweet, so they really are here!*

The crowd was thick, jostling and pushing, but he managed to stick close to Elijah. He liked the feeling of being one of so many people, of fitting in and matching up. He grinned; living in a bubble wasn't bad all the time.

Pop! Pop! Pop! Pop!

The sound was faint but clear, even above the din of the crowd. Reed paused. *What's that?* he wondered. It sounded like fireworks.

Pop! Pop! There it was again. It stopped. *It must be fireworks,* he decided, *but in the middle of the day?*

No one else around him seemed to notice the noise. The crowd went on with its carefree, noisy business uninterrupted. Reed turned to Elijah. "What the heck was that?"

Before Elijah could answer, a scream sliced through the air. It was piercing, bloodcurdling. It stabbed through the party atmosphere like a knife through fabric and shot chills down Reed's spine. Though he'd never heard anything like it before, the sound was unmistakable. It was the cry of a girl in terror—absolute, unmitigated terror.

The laughter and talk in the crowd died instantly, and everyone grew very still. An uneasy hush fell across the whole carnival; even the music stopped.

The scream came again, shrill and paralyzing. Others joined it, not only girls' shrieks but boys' hoarse cries. They grew louder, wilder, and sharper.

The crowd began to shift uneasily, droning like wary bees. Reed struggled to hear over the rumble, trying to understand what the cries meant. He could not make it out. The popping sound began once more; it seemed to be coming closer. The screams doubled, tripled, spread in every direction.

Suddenly, a few teens burst through the mass of people at the carnival's center, fighting their way toward the Dorms as fast as they could. One of them was a boy Reed knew. Reed grabbed his elbow as he rushed past. "Jordan! What's going on?"

The boy's eyes were frantic as he turned on Reed, struggling wildly to free his arm. "It's—it's a gunner!" he shouted hoarsely, breaking away. "He's shooting!"

CHAPTER 24

The effect was instantaneous. His words leaped from mouth to mouth and swept through the mass of teens in half a second. Like a bomb, panic exploded in the crowd. Shrieks and screams split the air. Everyone began frantically pushing, trampling, trying to run, but no one knew which way to go. Hysteria broke loose like a wild animal as teens crashed through dividers, beat down booths and counters, even knocked each other down in a frenzy to escape. There was an ear-splitting groan, and one of the towering rides swayed and crashed to the street, overturned by the stampede. The chaos choked the very air, but the unrelenting gunshots cut through it all, drawing steadily nearer.

Panicked, Reed whirled around. Elijah was not by his side anymore. Reed caught sight of his friend off to the right near the edge of the crowd. Alec was there, too. But, before Reed could move in their direction, the two boys turned and plunged into the heart of the frantic mass. At the same instant, Gabe flashed past him in the same direction.

The shots, pounding in a ceaseless, deadly rhythm, were closing in on him. Not twenty yards away, teens began dropping. Those nearby fought wildly to scatter, but the surrounding crowd was a wall, too thick for them to go far. It was a slaughter.

Without warning, a girl not five feet from Reed spun and dropped to the road, her long brown hair falling around her into a growing, red pool on the cement. Reed stared, horrified. There was no more time;

he had to get out now or he… he would be next. It was surreal to even think it. *I have to get out of here.* Without a second's hesitation, he turned and dove into the crowd.

The terror-stricken mass fought him for every step. His progress was agonizingly slow. With each ragged breath, his heart raced faster, beating against his ribs in a throbbing, clutching, growing fear. Someone's elbow struck him in the jaw. He knocked it aside and kept going. But the shots weren't getting further behind him; they were gaining on him. He couldn't move fast enough in this crowd!

Suddenly, Reed was slammed from the side and hurled to the ground by a boy running for his life. He felt the concrete smash into his body and the boy's foot dig into his back. He heard the boy curse as he stumbled over Reed's body and then a strange, sickening thud. A choking gasp, and the boy fell full length on the concrete, unmoving.

Reed lay where he had fallen, stunned by the impact. One more second—half a second—and that bullet would have buried itself between his shoulder blades. He made no move to rise. Something in the back of his dazed, terrified mind told him to stay low. He wasn't sure he had enough strength to sit up anyway. The shots continued, and he heard the bullets ripping through the air above him.

The panicked cries and screams began to lessen. Waves of teenagers were fleeing either up to the Dorms or down to the city.

They're leaving me. The thought sliced through Reed's dulled mind like a hot iron. He was about to be left alone with an armed murderer. Without the crowd, there would be nothing between the two of them, nothing between himself and the unthinkable. He would be dead in seconds.

You can't stay here! You have to move! Gathering his quivering strength, he rolled to his stomach and began to crawl painfully across the pavement toward the Dorms. Horror cudgeled his mind and goaded him on, screaming to his terrified brain. *Move! Move! Move!*

He grimaced, clenching his teeth as he dragged himself across the rough concrete, but his frantic mind felt nothing, understood nothing. One thought occupied his entire being and clutched at his heart. *If I don't make it… if I don't make it…*

The cement ripped several buttons off his shirt. It scraped the skin of his forearms tender; he was missing a piece below his left elbow. He could taste dust in his dry mouth and feel grit in his eyes. The stretch of concrete was eternal. *There's no way you can make it in time.*

He wasn't sure how far he had crawled before it happened. The firing cut off. He stopped moving and dug his cheek into the rough surface, cringing. It did not start again. He lay for another moment, waiting. Nothing happened. Cautiously, he raised his head. Still, the shots did not resume. Taking a deep breath, he struggled to his feet, rubbing his arms, and looked about him dumbly.

It was horribly still. A handful of other teens remained standing on the road. The collapsed ride lay not far away in a heap of twisted yellow metal like a mutilated Titan. Shredded canvas hung limply from booth frames and overturned counters.

It was over.

But the ones standing were not the only ones left on the street— not nearly. Reed passed his hand over his eyes to clear his mind from the nightmare, but the ghastly vision did not depart. Most of the crowd had vanished, and left where it had once been were bodies, scattered on the ground. They had been kids not half an hour ago, living and laughing; but now they were groaning, bleeding, dying. Bodies—kids—just like him.

Like a curtain, his previous blind terror fell from Reed's mind. A new sensation rushed through him, pushing back everything else. *Just like him.* It was strange, foreign, but suddenly he wanted nothing more than to help them, to do something.

Apparently, he was not the only one who had the sudden awakening. The others who were left broke from their trances and fell to work immediately, going from victim to victim, looking for signs of life.

Reed dropped down next to the nearest boy and rolled him over. He started when he saw the face. It was Will, who had first brought the news of the carnival to Reed and Reagan. He was not breathing. Reed sat back, staring. So this was death. It seemed different now with the horror of its reality lying in his lap. This was what he'd escaped only minutes before. One shot was all it took, and there was nothing he could do about it.

He dropped his eyes from the still face and saw that Will's hand still clutched a CD of the Hordes of Hell. It was shattered by the bullet that had taken his life and dyed a deep scarlet.

Reed stood up slowly. There would be time for sadness. Now, others needed help. Sirens began to wail in the city below. Ambulances were on the way, but they would be too late for some. Reed hurried on to the next form.

Some of those who had fled to the Dorms began to trickle back. Some of them, after staring at the scene for a moment, also set about helping the fallen. But not all. The shock was too much for many; they collapsed against trees or fell to their knees wailing, rocking back and forth. The rest worked on.

The returning trickle turned to a rush. More teens appeared on the road and began helping feverishly. Shirt sleeves, whole shirts, bottoms of jeans and skirts, scarves, and fair prizes became bandages. Belts turned into tourniquets and makeshift stretchers. There was a strange sense of urgency and kinship like nothing the Hill had ever experienced. It was a single heart, a single drive, a single truth in three simple words: *just like me*. Friends or strangers, it didn't make a difference. They were fellow humans, and that was all that mattered.

For the next two hours, they did what they could to clear the roadway for the emergency vehicles, comfort the wounded, and help load them into ambulances. Some of the victims could walk on their own or with help from other teens. Others could only be moved by the medical staff and had to wait for assistance. These were the worst, often crying hysterically and begging someone to stay with them. Several had to be extracted from the wreckage of the fallen ride.

By the end of it all, Reed was exhausted. He paused to survey the scene as the last ambulance roared down the road into the city. Dozens of other Dorm residents, looking just as tired as he felt, remained and watched the sun set red in the west.

They had done it, Reed realized. Catastrophe had struck, but they had rallied together. They may have run at first, but they had all done their part in the aftermath. Reed felt proud to be one of them.

As he turned back up the hill, he caught sight of a familiar group half-way up the slope. Lucy, Katy, Kara, and Sarah were gathered in a little knot near the Dorms. He hurried to catch them. As he neared, he realized they were not alone. Alec, Elijah, and Gabe, looking no better than anyone else, were with them. Reed hadn't thought about the three after they had vanished into the crowd but, seeing them now, he was relieved of a subconscious worry. They were still alive and walking.

"Well," Alec greeted him as he joined them, "you're a sight for sore eyes. You're not hurt, are you?"

"Me?" Reed glanced down at the remnants of his shirt and realized for the first time it was covered in blood. "No, just tired. That's somebody else's."

"Same here," observed Elijah, eyeing his stained arms. "We probably need to wash this off outside. It's really not safe."

They found a faucet on a wall of one of the dorms and took turns rinsing their hands and faces. As Reed leaned against the wall, waiting for his turn at the water, the adrenaline that had carried him through the long, traumatic ordeal gave out. All the emotions he'd forced back rushed over him, not to be stopped, and he was suddenly tired, heartbroken, and sick. The full horror of what had happened and what he had seen struck him in a crushing reality. His former pride faded and, instead, he felt cold and shaken to his very core. All it had taken was one man, one gun…

Reed had a sudden thought. "Hey, what happened to the shooter? He just stopped all of a sudden, and I never heard anything about him."

"Somebody took him out," replied Gabe, drying his hands on his thighs.

"Somebody?" exclaimed Lucy. "You mean *you* did."

"I did not," countered Gabe. "Alec and 'Lijah did most of it."

"You know what I mean."

"Wait," Reed interrupted, "you guys did it? How? He had a gun!"

"Well, we tried to talk him down first," said Alec, shaking the water from his arms, "but that didn't go over very well. In the end, it took three of us, but we got him." He paused and rubbed his jaw. "It wasn't quite as easy as I wish it had been, but we had a few things in our favor. Never mess with 'Lijah in a fight."

Elijah had his face in the stream of water and couldn't reply.

"What happened to him?" Katy asked timidly. "Did you… did you… kill him?"

"Oh, no," Gabe assured her, "Just incapacitated him. The police took him after they got there. Maybe he won't have too many internal injuries or concussions." He paused. "Okay, so maybe it's wrong, but I really don't care if he does."

The momentary distraction passed. Reed leaned his tired back against the wall, absorbing the warmth that radiated from the bricks, and tried to right his shaken psyche. There was so much horror, so much pain. The others must not see him like this. He had to pull himself together.

Elijah, drying his face and arms, looked up and met Reed's eyes. "How are you holding up?"

Reed only shrugged. Elijah straightened and joined him by the wall. "It's okay to not be okay, dude," he said, leaning against the warm bricks. "We're all shaken up. Somebody tried to crack the fishbowl, and we can't just walk that off."

Reed rallied his failing spirits. "He tried," he answered, "but he didn't, did he? Maybe the Hill's tougher than you think."

Elijah cocked his head and searched Reed's face. "Do you really believe that?"

"Of course! Didn't you see the way everybody pulled together? I love this place."

Elijah stared into the distance but said nothing. Sarah approached before Reed could say anything else. "'Lijah, I hate to bother you, but would you mind walking us home? It's not that far, but I don't want to take any chances tonight."

"My pleasure," Elijah replied, awakening from his distant mood. "Cody might be wondering why I'm not back by now. I should get going."

After they had all finished washing, he and the two girls started down the sidewalk toward the apartments. As the others turned toward the Dorms, Reed, on a sudden urge, turned back and called after the figures disappearing into the dusk, "Hey, 'Lijah! Thanks for earlier. I'll keep working on that knot."

Elijah waved. Gabe gave Reed an odd look. "What was that about?"

"Oh, nothing." Reed forced a half-smile and a shrug. "Anyway, I'm tired, and I need to go make sure my roommates are okay."

Lucy looked concerned. "Do you think they might've gotten hurt?"

"No, but it's a good excuse to go up and get into bed."

CHAPTER 25

For several days after the awful event, Dorm society was in complete upheaval. Besides tightened security, another shakedown, and the natural trauma, everyone faced the awful business of finding out who had escaped the massacre and who had not. As he had hoped, his roommates were unharmed, but Reed knew nearly all the victims from his extensive circle of acquaintances. Will was his only close friend to be fatally injured.

As the dust began to settle, bits of the story behind the shooting came to light and were carefully pieced together. The gunner, a resident of the notorious Dorm Eleven, had been armed with two handguns and nearly a dozen magazines of extra bullets. He'd targeted the street fair since the crowd would be one of the largest the Hill had ever seen. The rest was not hard to follow. He had maneuvered to the center of the carnival and opened fire, changing clips as he emptied them. How he came by the firearms or the ammunition was a complete mystery. He was interrogated but refused to reveal anything. Word spread not long afterward that he committed suicide in prison.

The count of his victims came up in reports from the city: sixty-seven dead and more than ninety wounded. The staggering number was attributed mainly to the density of the crowd. With the odds stacked so high in the murderer's favor, it was indefinite at first what had ended his killing spree. The police had found him unconscious on the scene, his guns lying nearby. The puzzled authorities could make nothing of it. An explanation was finally offered when a handful of witnesses reported the murderer had been attacked and overcome by three unarmed young men. No one could identify them. An announcement was issued, publicly praising the unknown heroes and asking that they come forward to be recognized. They did not, however, and their identities remained a mystery—to most.

Reed was one of the few enlightened. He was more than a little proud to know the three boys the whole country was asking about, but he kept his secret at their request. He sat silently through wild speculations at the Mushroom and the factory, trying not to laugh at the fantastic powers attributed to his friends.

But things could not stay on such a high forever. A form of normalcy returned as the turmoil faded back into everyday life on the Hill. Reed, strolling between the Dorms a week or two later, marveled at how quickly the terror seemed to have been forgotten. The parties had already resumed as if nothing had happened, and expectations were on the rise as the delayed opening of the rec center drew nearer.

But he couldn't forget. No matter how hard he tried, he could not erase the image of Will lying in his own blood or the sound of the ripping bullets. They haunted the edges of his memory day and night, slinking in the shadows of every ordinary thought like sleepless specters. The closest he could get to relief was distraction.

Going back to what he had learned during his early days on the Hill, he immersed himself in the rush and swirl of everything the Dorms offered. The bubble was unbroken, but Reed was more shaken than he wanted to admit. Moments like these, walking alone under the trees, were the only times he let himself reflect on the dark horrors of the past.

"Well, it's nice to see you alive, too. Thanks for noticing."

Reed's thoughts scattered. He hadn't realized someone had come up beside him.

"Oh, hi, Sam." Reed made an effort to sound less grudging than he felt. "I was just thinking. I see you made it through all right."

"Yep," Sam responded, swinging his lanyard around one finger. "Never even saw the guy. I suppose you heard about Will?"

"I found him."

"Oh." Sam was obviously not expecting that. After a moment of rare silence, he added, "Yeah, pretty sad. But the worst part is that we missed the concert that night. I mean, that is literally the worst! The Horde packed up and left so quick, I never even got to meet 'em!"

Sam talked on and on. It was all old, pointless gossip, and Reed couldn't care less. Finally, when Sam paused for a breath, he took the chance to get in a sentence.

"I don't suppose you've heard from your friend Dylan, have you?"

"Dylan, from our hall?" Sam crinkled his forehead. "No, I guess I haven't. I should drop into his room and check on him. He might be wondering about me, too."

Personally, Reed found that doubtful, but he granted that it was a possibility and urged Sam to find out. Sam agreed without much persuasion. He had even started to leave before he paused and turned back. "Hey, are you going anywhere tonight?"

Reed nodded quickly. "Yes. I mean, most likely."

"Oh. Then I guess I won't see you later?"

"Probably not."

Looking disappointed, Sam turned and trotted off. Once he was out of earshot, Reed blew out his breath. He'd done his best to cut back on the jabs and criticisms after his conversation with Elijah, but he still found the other boy trying at times.

"What was all that for?" Reed muttered, resuming his walk. "The way he talked, you'd think nothing happened."

Then it struck him. Sam was talking as if everything were normal because he wanted it to be that way. The Hill was Sam's life supply, and any blow to it struck at him deeply, like an ax on a tree trunk. No, Sam had not forgotten. Maybe he wasn't so different from Reed after all—seeking distraction from his pain, burying himself in the system.

Reed picked up a stick from the sidewalk and began to break it into tiny pieces. Maybe it wasn't just Sam. Perhaps the whole Hill still remembered all too well. What if this flippancy, which Reed thought was forgetfulness, was only a cover? Could it be that they were all only pretending to go on? Reed felt something close to sympathy for Sam. Still, the kid could be annoying.

"Goin' somewhere?"

Reed jumped. Again, someone had joined him while he was deep in thought. He needed to start paying more attention.

"Oh, Hunter! I didn't see you." He tossed away the stick.

"Obviously." Hunter's dry manner hadn't changed. "I've hardly seen *you* in over a week. At least you're still alive."

"Everybody keeps saying that like it's weird. Is there a reason I shouldn't be?"

"Maybe," Hunter shrugged. "I wasn't actually there, but maniacs like that usually go for the high-profile targets first. You're lucky he didn't hunt you down."

Reed swallowed and glanced at him. "You weren't there? Why not?"

"I just didn't feel like it. I had other things to do."

Reed could hardly imagine what might keep someone away from a free carnival, but Hunter went on without explanation. "So I just heard you tell Sambo you might be going out tonight. Got anything in mind?"

Reed did, actually. There was going to be another meeting with the group in the apartments. Reed hadn't been to one in several weeks, and he felt it was time to make another visit. But he couldn't tell Hunter *that*; he had to think up some kind of answer. "Oh, yeah, kinda sorta, I guess." He kicked a fir cone off the sidewalk. "Reagan wants the room tonight, so I'm gonna meet a friend and we're going into town." True, he was supposed to meet Nathan after supper before going to the apartments.

Hunter nodded. "That's got potential. Any idea what you'll be doing?"

"Nah," Reed shrugged, "I'm just winging it." Also true. He really didn't know where he was going or what the others had in mind for tonight. Reed congratulated himself on his clever answers but took the opportunity to change the subject. "I haven't seen you on the hall all week. Where've you been keeping yourself?"

It was Hunter's turn to shrug. "I've been really busy. I don't know how much I'll be able to come up to the hall anymore with all the stupid new security junk. They might think I was spying." He spat in disgust.

Reed grimaced. "Surely it won't be that bad. They just put the card swipes on the doors like they'd always threatened... and a few other things."

Hunter snorted. "You'd be surprised. Have you ever thought about what card swipes have to do with gun control? I'll tell you: nothing. They're just trying to squeeze more of our freedom out of us. They're always looking for ways to take a little. Anyway, I've gotta go get some things done. I'll see ya 'round, maybe later tonight."

"Sure, if we're not all under lock and key by then."

Hunter smirked as they parted.

CHAPTER 26

The sun was still well above the horizon when Reed met Nathan at the bottom of the East Stairs. The daylight forced them to be extra cautious. They cut back behind the Mushroom and came out on a sidewalk that ran down toward the city. The street was quiet; a soft breeze carried the far-off echo of honking horns and rumbling traffic up from the bustling town below.

Reed decided it was finally safe enough to speak. "Whose place are we going to?"

"Well," Nathan paused and checked the road over his shoulder, "right now we're going to Cody and Elijah's, but that's not where the meeting's supposed to be. We've actually changed to meeting outside the city in the last week or two. It's warm enough now and safer than staying on the Hill. I'm going to drop you off with the other guys and go back for the girls at the Dorms."

"Oh." Reed stepped around a fire hydrant. "But why couldn't the girls have just come with us? It would save you a trip."

Nathan shot him a sidelong glance. "Don't take this the wrong way but, 'cause of you. You're too well known. Chances are somebody would recognize you in the daylight, leaving the city with me and a bunch of girls. That would be bad for everybody."

Reed hadn't thought of that. He didn't ask any more questions until they arrived at the boys' apartment. It was just like any other apartment on the quiet side street—flat-front, red brick, green shutters framing the windows. Cody, still dressed in slacks and a plaid dress shirt, let them in through the white front door.

"Just getting away from the office?" asked Nathan as they stepped into the cool interior.

"Yeah, we had to work a full day today," Cody replied, closing the door after checking the street both ways. "The boss needed some overtime."

"'Lijah still there?"

"Nope, he's gone already. I'm supposed to wait at the Gorge till you bring the girls."

"Awesome." Nathan put his hand on the doorknob. "Then I'm out of here. See you later." He slipped out but then poked his head back in. "Oh, and Cody, try not to talk his ear off." With a wink in Reed's direction, he was gone.

Cody kicked off his shoes and began unbuttoning his shirt. "Make yourself at home," he told Reed with a casual motion around the room. "I'll be back in a sec." He disappeared down a hallway as he peeled off his shirt. Reed was left to study his surroundings.

The room was a comfortably furnished den, definitely belonging to Texan bachelors, but neater than Reed expected. A five-pointed metal star over two feet in diameter hung on the wall above an over-stuffed, brown leather couch. A matching loveseat and a couple of recliners formed a semicircle around the metal and glass coffee table. Floor lamps, chests, bookshelves, carpet—everything was in the same family of beige, brown, and stained wood. Reed thought it was relaxing and homey. He settled himself on the couch and sank into the cool leather with a sigh, propping his elbow on its ample arm. He was just beginning to get really comfortable when Cody reappeared, looking much more at ease in a black T-shirt and jeans. He dropped the window shades and opened the door as Reed regretfully stood up.

"If you're ready," was all Cody said.

Reed quickly came to understand the irony of Nathan's earlier remark; Cody was a man of few words. On their entire walk, any conversation was started by Reed. The other boy wasn't unfriendly. On the contrary, it was the most genial silence Reed had ever experienced; Cody just didn't talk. Reed tried several different approaches, but finally gave it up. He wondered how different the situation would be if Katy were present.

They left the city by the road that led to the Shellys' farm, and Reed wondered if that was where the meeting would be. But, halfway to the farm, the other boy turned off the road into the trees, and they struck out through the woods.

The trees were thick, but the undergrowth did not impede their pace. Walking was easy and pleasant. The woods were beautiful, wrapped in fresh green and dotted with an occasional snowy dogwood or wild cherry. The late afternoon songs of wild birds resonated under the leafy canopy and echoed off the sun-sprinkled floor of the forest.

The boys tramped for some time, stepping over logs and under branches, until Reed began to hear the sound of running water. Then, unexpectedly, they broke out of the trees into a good-sized clearing, spread with a thick carpet of rich grass. Before them, the ground sloped up, rising toward the center of the open space and then falling gently away to the other side. The sound of the water was barely audible now.

Cody stopped and spoke. "This is what we call 'the Gorge.' It's kind of a landmark for finding your way around here. You can follow the stream down from where it crosses the road by the Shellys' farm and it brings you right here."

Though amazed at this lengthy speech, Reed noted the valuable information.

His announcement made, Cody dropped down without another word, leaned his back against a tree, and closed his eyes. Apparently, there was nothing to do now but wait.

Reed wandered out into the clearing and up the little slope, stooping to pluck a dandelion as he went. But, at the top, he jerked to a halt and stared down, completely unprepared for what lay before him. The ground vanished at his feet and dropped straight down into a narrow gorge perhaps ten or twelve feet wide, but completely hidden by the rise of the land. A stream surged through the perpendicular, gray walls over thirty feet below in a rapid but deceivingly smooth current. The water was dark, thrown into shadow by the cliffs on either side.

Cautiously, Reed dropped the dandelion over the edge. It fell, spinning slowly, to the surface below. Instantly, the current swept it away, the bright yellow crown bobbing for a second on top before it was sucked beneath the black water. Reed stared in fascination. It was strangely beautiful, this deadly and relentless flow. Anything in its grasp would be lost forever in the dark, rushing water. Reed felt almost guilty for dropping the sweet yellow flower, but something about its fall moved him strangely.

He tore his eyes from the mesmerizing stream and turned from the gorge. Voices and footsteps were coming through the trees behind him. Cody rose, stretching, just as Nathan and the girls entered the clearing with Gabe close behind.

"Hello, Reed!" Lucy called cheerfully. "How do you like the view?"

"Breathtaking, especially when you're not expecting it."

Gabe was not so genial. "I didn't know he was coming," he said, eyeing Reed. "Does he know how to get out here?"

"I don't know, but he's here now," replied Nathan, slapping Gabe on the back. "And what's it matter anyway?"

Gabe regarded Reed sourly, but said no more.

Without further delay, they left the clearing together and turned deeper into the woods. Reed slipped into a spot next to Lucy at the back of the line. They tried to carry on a conversation, but it lagged quickly. It was obvious to both of them that he had something on his mind. Everyone else was talking quietly in pairs, but Reed still lowered his voice until only she could hear him. "Lucy, why does Gabe hate me?"

She didn't seem surprised at his question. "I don't think he dislikes you, Reed; he's just suspicious." She plucked a new leaf from a young oak and ran it through her fingers. "Honestly, I wouldn't be surprised if he *did* like you deep down. But you know he's our protector, and he takes that seriously."

"But I've been coming for months. Doesn't he trust me yet?"

"I don't know. He's hard to understand sometimes. Alec's his roommate, and he knows him best. You should ask him."

At the sound of his name, Alec dropped back to join them. "Talking about me?"

"Reed was just asking me why Gabe doesn't trust him," Lucy told him. "I said I didn't know, but that you probably understand him best."

"Oh."

"What's really weird is how it changes!" Reed exclaimed, hardly noticing Alec's half-hearted response. "I thought he was softening, but tonight, it's like I'm a crook or something."

"Sorry about that," Alec apologized, sticking his hands into his pockets. "He picked up some news today that worried him. That's why we're out here now. *They* seem to be moving toward something, and he's afraid they might be on our trail. The tightened security isn't helping, either."

Reed didn't need to ask who "they" were, but he wasn't sure how this involved him. "So?"

Alec took his hands out of his pockets and began popping his fingers one by one. "He's nervous about what they're doing, what they know, and how they know it. He's keeping *any* possibility under suspicion."

"Wait." Reed stopped walking. "Any possibility? You don't mean that he suspects *me*? He thinks *I'm* the ringer?"

Alec dropped his eyes and reluctantly nodded.

Reed exploded in a choked whisper. "What? That's ridiculous! Do you really think I..."

"Reed!" Lucy broke in sharply, looking him in the face, "Alec didn't say the rest of us thought that. We don't! Remember, Gabe is just suspicious of everyone right now. It's nothing against you. He'll probably get over it in the next week or so."

Reed was not reassured. It took the rest of the walk for the other two to calm him down. They finally succeeded in cooling him off, and Lucy promised she would talk to Gabe when they reached their destination.

This turned out to be a clear glade the size of a large room, spread with short grass, but it was unlike any place Reed had ever seen. The floor of the clearing sank down into the earth five or six feet, deep enough for a grown man to stand in and still keep his head below ground level. The forest trees stopped just shy of the edge and spread their branches high above the sloping green walls. The floor was perfectly smooth. It might have been a crater or a pond ages ago.

None of the others had arrived yet. The group climbed down the bank and spread out on the grass in the bottom to wait. Reed noticed that Lucy sought Gabe out and began talking with him earnestly on the other side of the little basin.

Reed settled down alone on the clearing floor and leaned back against the slanted side, staring into the sky. Above him, branches swayed in an evening breeze. Rays from the setting sun struck them, turning each fluttering leaf into a drop of vivid green gold.

Reed studied them, hands clasped behind his head, and began to reason over what Alec had just told him. Why shouldn't Gabe suspect him? After all, he was their only link to the outside world. In fact, the more he thought about it, the more he realized how suspicious he might have looked at times. For one thing, he was always asking questions. He knew this was only because of his bothersome curiosity, but would they understand that? And he always knew everything that was going on in the Dorms. That came from being part of Reagan's social web, but it certainly could appear questionable.

Someone sat down beside him. Reed brought his eyes down and found it was Gabe. The other young man said nothing. Neither did Reed. After a moment, Gabe spoke. "Did your week go all right?"

Reed relaxed and smiled inwardly. Lucy had gotten through. "Sure," he replied. "But everything's still kinda crazy around the Dorms."

Gabe agreed, and silence fell again. A bird sang somewhere in the treetops. "I guess we really haven't talked very much, have we?" Gabe kept his eyes fixed across the clearing. "Sorry. I've been way too edgy lately. Well, not just lately."

"It's fine," Reed answered, his gaze also far away. "I understand. Looking back, I probably seemed pretty suspicious sometimes."

"I still didn't handle it right. There's no excuse, and I'm sorry."

The others were right; Gabe was a nice guy when you got to know him.

The rest of the group arrived, breaking up the conversation. Alec voluntarily set off to keep watch while everyone else got comfortable in a circle on the basin floor. Reed, cross-legged between Nathan and Courtney, was grateful the grass was soft.

Once everyone else was settled, Wilson opened his Bible and spread it on his knee. "Well," he began. But he never got the chance to finish his sentence.

A clear sound cut through the silence of the surrounding woods. They all heard it: a steady, thumping beat from deep in the heart of the forest. They froze, hardly daring to breathe. Gabe stiffened and snapped into watchdog mode.

The sound became recognizable; it was hoof beats pounding over the forest floor. In a moment, a rider came into view, ducking under the low branches at a swift trot. It was Marielle, and she was mounted bareback on Patton, the Shellys' silver gelding. A general sigh of relief went up as she reined in at the edge of the dell.

"Marielle!" exclaimed Sarah, getting up. "What brings you here? Is something wrong? Is your mother okay?"

The girl did not dismount. "You have to get out of here now!" she cried, pointing toward the encircling woods. "Matt just came back from town and passed a bunch of men coming this way. It's the police and the Council, and they have dogs! Mother sent me straight out to find you. There's not much time!"

She was breathing hard, and Patton danced under her.

"How did they…"

"I don't know!" Marielle exclaimed, looking like she might cry. "But they're after you guys!"

Alec dashed out of the woods on the opposite side and came sliding down the bank. "They're coming!" he gasped. "At least twenty of them. They're less than half a mile out, and they brought the K-9 unit!"

Gabe spun around and fixed his eyes on Reed. No words were necessary. Reed knew exactly what he was thinking. Before he could say anything, Wilson turned to the group. "We all know what to do. Now, we just pray like it's our job and do it. Reed, you stick with Nathan." He turned back to Marielle as everyone else hurriedly got ready to leave. "Will you be all right?"

She nodded and wiped her eyes. "I haven't gotten off since I left the farm, so they can't trace me. There's nothing wrong with riding in the woods. I'll pray for you guys."

She wheeled Patton and galloped away into the trees, her dark hair drifting out behind her as she disappeared through the gathering dusk. Everyone else scattered into the woods. In less than ten seconds, the basin was empty with no sign that anyone had ever been there.

CHAPTER 27

R eed stuck to Nathan without asking questions. They darted
through the woods, dodging and twisting between the trees at an
all-out sprint. No one else was in sight.

For Reed, everything had become surreal. He was running for his
life, hunted by the police and a pack of dogs. In the back of his mind,
he saw the black figure from that night in the alley—the clear shape
of the rifle and that cruel, curving magazine. *This isn't supposed to be
happening. If I get caught...* He didn't want to think about it.

He followed Nathan closely, hoping he knew where to go. They
leapt over logs and briars and ducked under branches but never
slowed from their full run.

Why was he doing this? Why had he decided to come tonight
of all nights? Why had he ever started coming in the first place? "I
knew my stupid curiosity would get me into trouble," he moaned to
himself.

On they ran—jumping, ducking, dodging, circling until Reed
thought his lungs would burst. Once, they even took to a brook and
waded through it for a hundred yards.

How cheesy, thought Reed. *That's the oldest trick in the movies.*
It had better work this time.

How long they ran, he had no idea. The sun's glow faded from
the sky into a gray twilight under the trees. He had a terrible stitch
in his side and was beginning to stumble. He didn't know how much
farther he could go.

At last, they burst out of the trees onto a clear downhill slope and ran full speed toward the bottom. It took Reed a moment to realize they were running straight toward a woodland lake, several acres in size but, even when he did, it was too late to stop.

They reached the edge and plunged in without even pausing for breath. The cold water struck him in the face and knocked the precious air from his lungs. He struggled to breathe and then struck out across the lake, swimming. It was agony after running so far, but he pressed on, mostly because he would drown if he didn't. Breathe, stroke, breathe, stroke, breathe—the cycle was endless. Darkening water and gray sky blended together before his blurry eyes.

At last, Reed felt the bottom rising beneath him. Sand and rocks met his clawing fingertips, and he struggled to his feet and staggered out onto the shore, heaving like an asthma patient.

The others were wading out of the water as well, dripping and out of breath, to draw together on the dry land. Reed joined the growing circle and realized they were not on the opposite shore. They were on an island in the middle of the lake. Apparently, he was one of the last to arrive. He bent over double, still struggling to catch his breath.

"That was fun!" exclaimed Lucy as she wrung water out of her hair. Her eyes sparkled, and her cheeks were pink with the exercise. "I hadn't swum in a long time."

Reed looked up and stared at her incredulously. *Fun?*

Elijah caught her eye and grinned back. "Yeah, that was pretty great! We left a nice trail for them to follow all night." His blue eyes were fairly dancing as the water ran over his face from the hair that hung in dripping spikes on his forehead.

"What I want to know," said Gabe quietly, "is how they knew where we were."

The others fell silent. He turned his dark stare upon Reed. "*You* wouldn't happen to have any idea, would you?" The tone in his voice and the flicker in his eyes left no doubt about his meaning. It was an accusation.

"Gabe!" flashed Sarah. "We are *not* going to blame *anyone*! For all we know, one of us could have slipped up!"

But even as she spoke, Reed saw doubt in her face. She would not meet his eyes.

169

"Whatever happened, we can be sure it was unintentional," added Wilson. Reed searched his face, but he looked down uncertainly.

"We need to move into the trees," Alec urged them. "We'll have to leave one at a time toward the south, and we can't let them see us waiting when they get here."

Reed, crushed as he felt, realized their plan. When the trackers arrived at the lake after following a dozen confusing trails for hours, they would reason that their quarry was hiding on the island. To reach them, they would need a boat, which would take even more time and a great deal of trouble. While the police were busy with that, the young people would slip away to the shore and make their way to the city, leaving trails easily confused with their previous tracks.

They all moved into the cover of the trees near the center of the island. One by one, over the next hour, they slipped silently away through the darkness.

* * *

Reed felt awful. Even though he knew he hadn't done what Gabe accused him of, he couldn't shake the feeling that he was somehow responsible. He hadn't defended himself. What could he say? Besides, he just wanted to get away, to hide.

As he trudged up the road toward the city, leaving the woods and the lake behind, he brooded over it all. He couldn't be the one! He had taken the utmost care to make sure no one saw him leave the Dorms. All his tracks were covered. What had gone wrong? Could... could there be a spy involved?

Reed's mind jumped back to the first shakedown, set off by the mysterious ringer. Gabe. That night, Reed had first suspected and even doubted. But now... now...

Could it be that Gabe had turned them all in himself and was trying to shift the blame to Reed? That might explain his agitation over the past week and all his inside knowledge. He hadn't wanted Reed to be there, either; it might have thrown some sort of kink in his plans. It was a possibility—dark, but still a possibility.

Reed finally arrived back at the Hill. His clothes, which he had wrung out in the woods, were wrinkled but dry from the long walk.

Hopefully, no one would suspect where he had been.

Not a soul was in sight. It must be later than he thought, perhaps even past curfew. He neared his dorm and reached into his pocket for his ID card. It was gone.

With growing alarm, he searched his pockets. It wasn't in any of them. Now that he thought about it, it had not been on him when he squeezed out his clothes in the woods. He must have lost it in the lake. He tried the door in desperation. Locked, as expected. The new card reader flashed at him tauntingly from the door frame. Now what?

He turned his back on the door and glanced around. His eyes fell on the spruce tree growing close by the wall. He was at the dorm's back entrance. The night of the first shakedown leaped out of his memory, and he suddenly remembered Alec describing a way to climb up to the roof of the building. This tree was where he could begin. He looked up at the dark spire towering into the night sky. It appeared to be his only option.

Quickly, he pulled himself into the lower branches and clambered up through the limbs until he reached the maintenance ladder. This was where it got tricky. He licked his lips. With a hair-raising jump, he threw himself against the flat brick wall and barely caught the left side of the ladder. He swung for a moment, trying not to look down. Then, pulling his feet under him onto the bottom rung, he climbed up to the roof.

It was flat, as Alec had said, and easy to walk on. Reed crept along the edge until he saw the tree that stood outside his window, the young leaves and slender branches a shadowy tangle in the darkness. Reed stopped. Now for the worst part. He gritted his teeth. Slowly, he turned around and lowered himself off the edge into the dizzying black space. Down, down he went until he was almost out of arm length. He shut his eyes and felt desperately with his feet. There, he found the brick edging around the window. With a rush of relief, he dropped onto it. The light was on, but the room was empty.

Reed got his fingers into the corners of the window frame and pushed to open it. Nothing happened. He tried again. Still nothing. The window was locked. Reed cursed his luck and would have stamped his foot if he hadn't been so narrowly balanced. Of all the nights for Reagan to shut the always-open window! Now what?

He turned himself around slowly on the narrow edging and looked down. Past his feet, the Square yawned up at him over thirty feet below. He gulped and lifted his eyes quickly. A branch stabbed his cheek. He pushed it aside and then stopped. Right in front of him, he could see the dim trunk of the tree that shaded the window. Alec had said it was possible to jump to that tree from this window. Reed licked his lips again. There was nothing else to do. He couldn't make it back up onto the roof tonight. Gathering all the nerve he had (and a little more), he hurled himself from the window into the branches.

He found the trunk more easily than expected, perhaps too easily and a little harder on his face than he would have liked, but he was safe. Sliding down the tree, he dropped to the ground and dusted off his hands.

A sound caught his ear. He froze. Someone was coming. He slipped into the shadow of the tree and waited. A figure appeared out of the darkness. It was Alec, who was supposed to have left the island directly after Reed. He was cutting across the Square toward his dorm, passing very near the tree where Reed flattened himself.

Hope flashed upon him. Alec had promised Reed could come to him anytime for anything. Maybe he would remember that now. But then again, maybe he wouldn't. Reed had just been labeled a traitor. It was still worth a try.

"Psst!" he hissed, stepping out of the shadows. Alec tensed and spun on him in a stance that would have made the late gunner tremble in recollection.

"Whoa!" Reed held up his hands. "It's me. I lost my key and can't get in."

Alec relaxed. "Oh, sorry. Did you try the window?"

Reed nodded. "Locked."

"Shoot. Well, my card's kinda wet, but it might work on your dorm. Let's try it."

Relief washed over Reed. Alec was going to help him. They moved to the entrance of the dorm, and Alec inserted his key. The light turned green. The door swung open without a noise. It was too easy.

Reed stepped inside. "Thanks, Lick," he whispered gratefully, using Alec's nickname in the group. "I won't forget this."

"No problem," said Alec, turning to leave. "Just returning the favor. Oh, and Reed, about what Gabe said: forget it. I don't believe it for a second."

Reed's gratitude overflowed. "Thanks a lot. It wasn't me, I promise!"

Alec nodded. "I believe you. G'night."

As he climbed the stairs, Reed felt lighter than he had the entire trip back. Alec believed him. Never had three words meant so much.

CHAPTER 28

"You lost it?" Reagan stared over the screen of his computer. "You lost your ID card? How on earth did you manage that?"

"It wasn't too hard," said Reed lightly, beginning to wish he hadn't said anything about it. "I didn't even have to try really."

Reagan had asked no questions the night before when he had come in from his shower to find Reed back in the room. But the next day, between applying for a new key and washing his wrinkled clothes, Reed had been forced to do some explaining. "It's not like it's that serious," he continued, shaking out a shirt. "Michael was awesome about it, and I'm supposed to get my new one sometime tonight."

"Michael's always awesome," retorted Reagan. "I just hope nobody finds your old one and steals your identity."

Reed agreed and focused busily on his shelf space. He was busy rearranging his closet, putting his winter coats and jackets into storage to make room for warm-weather clothes. "I'll keep the blue Henley out for now," he murmured to himself, "And the green…"

"Have you seen Allie lately?" Reagan asked abruptly.

Reed stopped in his sorting, the blue Henley half-folded in his hands. "What?"

"I said, have you seen Allie lately."

"Umm… yeah, around," Reed said. "Enough to know she's all right. What brought that up?" He resumed his folding.

"Nothing." Reagan shrugged, leaning back in his chair to watch

Reed. "It's kinda my hobby to know about these things. I was just wondering. Why haven't you?"

Reed really didn't want to talk about it. He shook out the shirt in his hand, forgetting it was the same one he had just folded. "Everything's been so mixed up and crazy lately I just haven't had... well, and she's kinda busy and... you know."

"No, I don't," said Reagan, crossing his arms. "Did you break up?"

"No," Reed said quickly. "I've just been unsure about things and... thinking." He avoided Reagan's stare in the silence that followed.

"You've been talking to Elijah, haven't you?"

Reed almost dropped his load of clothes. "What? Why would you say that?"

"Come on, bro, I lived with him for months. Trust me, we had a lot of... chats. This has his fingerprints all over it. Hot girl digs you, starts making moves, and you suddenly get cold feet. There's only one explanation." Reagan leaned forward and put his folded arms on the desk. "He's trying to talk you out of it, isn't he? He probably gave you the whole spiel."

"Umm... which one?"

"The whole 'save it and be careful' one, of course! I heard that one a *lot* right before he left."

"You mean he preached at you?" Reed could hardly imagine that coming from Elijah. He righted the tumbled stack of laundry.

"Well, he didn't do all the talking. When you live the way I do and he lives the way he does, it's bound to come up."

"So you don't agree with him."

Reagan snorted. "Of course not! We couldn't be more opposite. Let me guess: he told you that what you were doing wouldn't satisfy you and you would eventually end up unhappy, looking for more?"

Reed nodded, a half-folded pair of jeans in his hands.

Reagan sat back and threw out his arms. "There's your problem! He's got the wrong idea about happiness because he thinks it's secondary. He says you shouldn't do things that make you happy just because they're not the 'best' thing, but he's got it backward. Everybody knows what's best for you is whatever makes you happy. But he doesn't get that, probably because of his background. He doesn't understand it like we do."

Reed stopped his sorting and focused all his attention on Reagan. "You mean…"

"I mean what we've seen—our families. Elijah's the type that had a perfect home growing up, sees the world as sunshine and roses, and thinks we'll all live happily ever after if we act like it's the 1950s. But that's not how life works, is it, Reed?"

Reed looked away and said nothing.

"That's what I thought." Reagan leaned back in his chair. "Elijah can preach all he wants, but me and you know life isn't a fairy tale with a perfect princess and a happy ending. We have to take what we can get when we can get it because that's all there is. There's no pie in the sky at the end of the day, so date whoever the frick you want to, Reed. If a girl makes you happy, do it."

The door opened without warning, and Michael stepped in. "Hey, guys," he said cheerfully. "How're the Rockin' Rs today?"

"Rocking, as usual," answered Reagan, suddenly occupied with his computer. "Did we do something?"

"Nope, I just came to drop off the new ID card. Here you go." The RD tossed the card to Reed. "It should be just like your old one. Try to take care of it. Director Connors was *not* happy about making a new one."

Reed gulped and nodded. "Sure. Thanks a lot."

The door opened again. This time it was Riley, the damp towel around his waist proclaiming him to be fresh from the shower. He wasn't expecting to see Michael.

"Umm… hi."

"I was just leaving." Michael grinned and eyed the towel as he moved toward the door. "I stopped in to give Reed his new ID card. You guys make sure he doesn't lose it again." He paused at the doorway. "Oh, and Riley, the Director doesn't allow spending the night in other dorms, even if it's with another male. I've let it go, but he caught wind of it and was not happy. He said it's a warning this time, but it might be worse later. Let's not find out." And he was gone.

Riley hurled his towel against the bed in disgust. "Connors! That's none of his business! Why can't people just let me do my own thing?" He scowled as he began to jerk on his clothes. "I hate judgmental people."

"You and me both," smirked Reagan. "They don't seem to leave us alone. If he knew what you were doing over there, Connors might've had something *else* to say."

"That's none of his business either," Riley retorted, slipping on his shirt. "If he ever brings that up, I'll get..."

"You need to get your mind off it," Reagan said easily. "Speaking of judgmental, we were having an interesting chat before Michael came in. I bet you remember all those long talks we used to have with 'Lijah, don't you?"

"Of course," Riley answered, dropping onto his bed, "and my view hasn't changed any."

"You didn't agree with him either?" queried Reed.

"Heck, no! He had a bunch of old-fashioned, judgmental ideas and thought everybody had to be like him or they were wrong." Riley pushed himself up onto one elbow. "It was the absolute worst. He thought people should deny who they are and what they want just to meet his standards, like his were better than anybody else's. He said it was more important to do what was 'right' than what made you happy, but everybody knows what's really best for you is whatever makes you happy."

Reagan nodded sagely. "That sounds like something a wise man would say."

"Thanks, I try," Riley returned, dropping back onto his pillow. "But what brought all this up again?"

"'Lijah's trying to talk Reed out of dating Allie."

"Not exactly," countered Reed as Riley's eyebrows shot up. "He made me think."

"Well, now you've got something to make *him* think next time you see him," Reagan said. "Maybe he'll take it better from you than from us."

Reed turned back to his neglected sorting. Last night had changed a lot of things. Alec believed in him, but he was only one out of a dozen. "I don't know if I'll be seeing him again anytime soon," he said quietly.

Maybe never again.

CHAPTER 29

✦

Reed didn't see anyone from the group for a while. Their paths didn't cross around the Dorms, and he made no effort to seek them out. Nathan, whom he would have seen around the belt at the factory, had been promoted and had left the packing room. Lucy was still the receptionist, but Reed came and went only when the crowd was thickest. He couldn't hide the truth, even from himself. He was avoiding them.

Reed, like anyone, had pride. It stung to be suspected, and it would be even worse if he went back as if nothing had happened. He wouldn't plead his innocence like a naughty child, and he certainly wouldn't live under the stain of their accusation.

But there was something else wrong, too. To be suspected by friends, to have trust broken, was a painful thing. It hurt that they would even consider him that dishonorable, as if he was capable of betrayal. What's worse, the knife cut both ways. They had opened their circle to him, taken him in, welcomed him as a friend and, as far as they were concerned, he had stabbed them in the back.

With this on his conscience, Reed threw himself into the swirl of Dorm life like never before. Nothing was too wild or overdone. Even Reagan commented on the new Reed. "Dude, you've never been so much fun! I might have to try to keep up with you!"

Reed laughed and said that wouldn't take much since Reagan had taught him everything he knew; but inside, his laughter rang hollow.

For the rest of the Hill, however, life had never looked so good.

Despite all the delays, the eagerly awaited rec center finally opened. The building was everything it had been made out to be. The highest quality volleyball, basketball, and racquetball courts; enormous weight rooms with top-of-the-line equipment; the highest climbing wall in the state; an arcade and lounge; an indoor track; a four-screen cinema; a production stage and auditorium; a full food court; and even a huge indoor swimming pool were only some of the delights it offered. For the first few days, most of the teens wandered through the maze of rooms, open-mouthed. But, as the awe wore off, it turned into a popular part of everyday life. As soon as each workday ended, the complex filled with eager teenagers who stayed late, often until curfew and the RDs pushed them out.

Reed fell in love with the new building. He discovered that he liked bowling, he was a good ice-skater, and he could outshoot anybody on his hall in Eight Ball. The center became a haven for him when he needed to get out of his room or away from his thoughts. But, even in the colossal building, he couldn't completely escape his troubles. They had a way of popping up again when he least expected them.

It was a late night in early May when Reed wandered into the gym at the heart of the complex. The room was unusually empty for that time of day—only two games of volleyball and a single basketball match with a few fans on the sidelines. The hollow thumps of pounding balls and the squeak of shoes on wood echoed through rows of empty bleachers. Reed stopped in the wide, double doorway and surveyed his options. None of the games promised to end any time soon. He took another short glance around and turned to leave. But, as he did, he came face to face with someone coming up behind him from the water fountain in the hall. It was Alec.

"Reed!" he exclaimed, his face lighting up with a delighted grin. "Where have you been? I haven't seen you in forever!"

"Oh, around," Reed answered vaguely. He fished in his pocket for something that wasn't there. "Just... really busy."

"Well, if you're not now, why don't you come in and play a game or two?" Alec invited, drying his hands on the thighs of his black soccer shorts. "Everybody's here."

Reed looked out over the court. Sure enough, one of the far

volleyball teams was made up entirely of the teens from the group. Lucy, Nathan, Gabe, and the rest were too engrossed in a play to notice the pair by the door. Cody went up for a spike that flattened the other team's defense.

"I'll pass." Reed kept his eyes on the game. "Why aren't you playing?"

"I am. I just rotated out and stopped for a drink. Oh, come on! We could use another player." Alec took his arm insistently.

"No!" Reed jerked back. "I can't. It would be… awkward."

Alec searched his face. "Reed, if this is about the whole Gabe thing, I told you, forget about it."

"Even if *I* could, he wouldn't, and you know it. I'm not going back to that. Listen, I really have to go. I've got something set up in five minutes."

It was rude, and Reed knew it. Alec stepped back at the rebuff, but there was no anger in his bright eyes, only a sad understanding.

"I see," he said quietly. "Reed, you can't hide from it that way. Having fun and getting mixed up in stuff won't help what you're feeling. It'll probably just make it worse. There's only one real way to deal with it."

"I've gotta go." Reed turned and fled down the hall.

The incident threw him into a deep dejection for the rest of the night. Seeing all his friends again, together and happy, stabbed him with a blade of mixed emotions. That familiar sensation of looking in through a closed window was back. This time, it was flavored with the hopeless and bitter taste of a shameful exile. He understood now a little of what had drawn him toward these people from the beginning. Never had they seemed so pure, so clear, and so out of reach. It was like looking toward the stars with his feet chained to the ground.

As if that weren't bad enough, seeing Alec again affected him strangely. Everything wild and crazy he'd done recently leaped into his mind when his eyes met Alec's. But it wasn't Alec accusing him; it was himself. It gave him a peculiar feeling that tightened his chest and made him bite his lip. He wished he hadn't seen Alec at all.

* * *

A day or two after the encounter, Reed still hadn't been able to shake his gloomy attitude. He trudged up the dorm stairs to his room after work. He was later getting back to the Dorms than usual, and he found the hall empty and silent. Everyone had come and gone, either down to supper or straight to the rec center. That was disappointing. He had hoped for a social evening to lift his spirits.

He shut the door to his room behind him, leaning his back against it, and ran his eyes lethargically over everything. Reagan's computer blinked a slow blue light on the desk. Riley's phone was charging by the window. A poster lay on the nightstand; he'd been planning to put it above his bed. None of it interested him.

What was wrong with him? He crossed the room to the window and leaned his forehead against the pane, staring out at the scene below drenched in late afternoon sun. All his old hobbies seemed dull tonight; nothing caught his interest. He straightened and shook himself. This was ridiculous. He had to stop moping. Everybody else would be at the rec center. He would go for a swim.

Kicking off his shoes, he began digging for his board shorts. Hanging around the pool never failed to perk him up. That was where Reagan spent most of his time now. He said the atmosphere and the sand volleyball made him think of the Florida beaches. Reed smiled. It was also the place where Reagan could best show off for the girls. Reed retrieved his cyan Hurley suit and pulled off his shirt, pausing to eye his muscles in the mirror over the sink.

Yeah, this'll definitely do it.

A few minutes later, Reed clattered down the stairs with a towel flung over his shoulder. He pushed out of the dorm's back door, his bare feet savoring the pleasant grit of the warm, dry concrete. But, as he neared the enormous complex, he began to doubt his plan. He didn't feel the growing excitement he'd expected.

He swiped his card and pushed through the glass door into the pool area. It was a gigantic room, almost too big to be called a room at all. The lofty, bubbled ceiling arched over the huge concrete patio and Olympic-size pool. On the far side, beneath a couple of fake palm trees, a two-story pyramid of fiberglass rock formed a hissing waterfall and slide, dotted with artificial ferns and mosses. The entire right wall was glass, opening onto the sand volleyball courts outside.

The pool was full. Teenagers churned the water with their constant diving, kicking, and splashing. The "shore" was even more crowded for, as Reagan said, there was a certain "beachy" atmosphere about the place. Reed moved away from the door and deeper into the crowd, looking around him. Here he was, right in the middle of it all, and he felt no different.

This couldn't be happening. The pool never failed to rouse and excite him. There must be something here to shake him out his melancholy. He ran his eyes over the busy area, and then, through the shifting crowd, he saw it.

On the left side of the room against the white cinderblock wall was a set of chrome bleachers overlooking the water. Reagan was sitting on the back row. He wore only a suit he often boasted of bringing from Florida—small, red, tailored. For all practical purposes, it wasn't much of anything at all. But he didn't seem to care; he was too caught up in his companion. A girl, known to the entire Hill for her beauty and her habit of flaunting it, lay across his lap with her arms around his neck as she leaned up to lock her lips with his. As Reed caught sight of the pair, she broke away and whispered something into Reagan's ear, running her hands up through the back of his hair. Whatever it was, he loved it. He threw back his head and began to laugh, long and loud.

A wave of unexpected revulsion swept through Reed. The sight was nothing new for him but, this time, it was as though a veil had fallen from his eyes. He saw past the steamy surface to what was actually happening. This, right in front of him, was Reagan's idea of happiness: quick, casual, and temporary. But it was his *only* idea of happiness and, in a day or two, it would be over. They would go their separate ways, looking for something new to give them their next buzz. And they would do it again and again, because they didn't have any other way to meet this need. This was exactly what Reed had been working toward since he arrived on the Hill; it was two young people so deep into temporary pleasure that they could forget the past, ignore the future, and tune out what was happening around them.

Reed turned away from the sight, a sick feeling in his stomach, but he couldn't escape it. Not only was it etched indelibly in his memory, but it was all around him. His eyes were opened to see the crowd as it was—scantily dressed boys and girls mixed together in an erotic setting, each doing whatever they pleased. It wasn't just at the pool, either; that's all the Hill was. It was a culture of teens doing whatever they wanted, trying to drown out everything else, because *that's what made them happy*. Reagan wasn't the exception; he was the norm. And this was what Reed had built his life around for months. Alec was right; it wouldn't help him. It never had, and it never would.

Slowly, Reed made his way to the door and pushed out without looking back. He didn't want to swim anymore. He turned his steps back toward his dorm to change. If he hadn't known what to do before, he certainly didn't now.

CHAPTER 30

O nce he was dressed, Reed wandered back outside. He passed through the Dorms listlessly and ended up on the sidewalk that ran down toward the city. He didn't care where he went; there was a more important issue. For months, the Dorms and their culture had been what he lived and breathed. He had let it dictate what he did and define who he was. Then, in one day, one moment, it had evaporated under his feet. He felt lost. And he didn't even know why it had happened.

What's going on? Where did this come from?

He couldn't answer his own questions.

He walked with his hands in his pockets, eyes on the ground, paying no attention to where he went. Caught up in his inner mayhem, he wound his way through the maze of Hill apartments without caring that he didn't know his way. He ignored his surroundings until he almost ran into a bench. With nothing else to do, he sat down on it and put his elbows on his knees, weary, though not from his walk. He could go no farther. He didn't care that someone else was already on the bench. Really, he didn't even notice.

"Are you okay?"

Reed jerked his head up in surprise; the voice was familiar. Snapping out of his mental haze, he found a pair of very concerned, very blue eyes on him. "Oh, Elijah." He looked down again. "Where'd you come from?"

"I was just sitting here when you wandered up; I'm out here a lot in the evenings. But you don't look yourself. Are you all right?"

The memory of the night in the woods and his unwarranted disgrace swept through Reed's mind. He had been avoiding these people; perhaps he should leave. But suddenly, he didn't care. All his stubbornness and emotions gave way, and he buried his face in his hands. "No," he answered, "I'm not."

Elijah was quiet. After a few deep breaths, Reed looked up again. "I don't even know where to start. There's today and Reagan and me and you and Allie and everything else. I don't know about any of it!"

Elijah looked at him thoughtfully. "So Reagan told you to date her because she makes you happy?"

Reed blinked. "How did you know?"

"I lived with him for months. Trust me, we had a lot of... chats."

That sounded familiar. Reed nodded and dropped his head again. "Yeah, he told me what he thinks, but that didn't really help. Now I don't know who to believe, especially after what he said about you."

"I see."

That was all. Reed waited for Elijah to ask what he meant and, when he didn't, Reed volunteered it. "He told me you were really judgmental to him and Riley, and you preached at them all the time because everything had to be your way. Why did you do that?" This was a question that irked him. Something didn't add up.

Elijah was silent for a moment, staring out at the view. Their bench commanded the view of an entire park, laid out on gentle slopes before them. Except for a jogger or two on the trails and a pair of tennis players on the far-away courts, it was deserted. The lonely trees soaked up golden rays as the sun set above the city below, and a few cicadas sang lazily, echoing each other in the warm evening stillness.

Elijah finally spoke. "I'm not surprised he would say that." He sighed. "So you want to know why I did all that? Well, I actually didn't. He says I preached at him, but I never did. I only answered the questions he asked, even when they were rude and meant to mock me. He couldn't get over the fact that I disagreed with him. He accused me of being a hater and a legalist, trying to stop everybody else from enjoying life. He took all my answers as personal criticisms that targeted his character, which wasn't it at all."

Elijah took his hand off the back of the bench and slowly rubbed it back and forth on his knee. "See, Reagan's the type that loves doing his own thing in life and, if you don't agree with it, he takes that as something against him. People are like that, especially when they're doing things they shouldn't be. They don't want tolerance; they want unconditional agreement and acceptance. Did I hate him? Never. I loved Reagan, and I still do. I just didn't like the things he was doing."

Reed kept his eyes fixed in the distance, listening as Elijah continued. "You know what I'm talking about: the girls. It was mild at first, but it got worse as he got more popular. I knew what was going on, and I tried to stay out of it. I finally had to put my foot down when he started trying to sneak them into our room, sometimes several in one night. That didn't stop him, though." He hesitated. "He just sneaked into their rooms instead."

Reed said nothing. Elijah went on. "Riley—he's a different story. You live with him; I'm sure you know what I mean. He was very private about it when he first moved to the Hill, but he got comfortable quickly when he saw how tolerant the culture was. After he officially came out, he got bolder and even a little hostile. I just wish he'd given me a chance. Instead, he assumed I would be cruel to him because of my faith, so he refused to even talk to me about it. He had a lot of anger built up from his past, and I got the brunt of it. I could handle it, though, all of it—the way both of them treated me, acted around me, talked about me. I could put up with a lot of the other stuff they did, too, but I couldn't live in the same room with them if it was going to ruin our relationship. If we couldn't talk about our differences like adults and establish mutual respect, we would all end up angry, frustrated, and bitter."

"That's why you left," said Reed softly.

Elijah nodded. "It is. I don't know if it's still like that, but you can imagine."

Reed looked down. "Yeah, I can. I've seen it all, and… I liked it, too." He kept his eyes fixed on the ground. "But it's different now. I always agreed with Reagan 'cause I liked the way he did life, but then I saw something today and, I don't know why, but…"

He poured out the story of the scene at the pool and his

inexplicable reaction. "And I don't know what's come over me!" he finished. "That was nothing compared to other things that go on all the time. They've never bothered me before. Why are they so strange to me now?"

Elijah was leaning forward, elbows on his knees and hands together, listening and staring into the west. He didn't answer right away. He seemed to collect his thoughts and choose his words carefully. "Reed, I think there's more going on here than you'd believe." He tapped his thumbs together. "You said you'd felt listless and confused all day, right? There's something to that. Do you think it could all be traced back to the shooting?"

Reed thought. True, that had shaken him badly at first, but he had gotten over it... or had he? He shrugged. "I don't know. Why?"

"Because big things like that usually have a deeper effect on us than we realize. What if that shock and trauma set you up for this? Perhaps it was meant to bring you to this point."

Reed realized, the shooting marked the day when something had changed. He had never been able to truly go back to his carefree mindset afterwards. There was doubt now. He had seen that, despite everything, the system was frail like Elijah said. Perhaps it *had* been... wait.

"Bring me to this point? What do you mean?"

Elijah turned and looked at him steadily. "Reed, the Hill is a materialized delusion and nothing more. Like I tried to tell you before, it's fake. The whole thing is a fantasy world built on being young and all the things that go with that. Being our age is wonderful, but it's temporary. The Hill is an attempt to make it last longer than it's supposed to, and it's doomed to failure. It's so unrealistic that, when real life hits, it'll all come crashing down."

Reed wasn't sure what to think about that. "So what's that got to do with what we were talking about?"

"The shooting showed you that. It was like you and everybody else got a horrible slap in the face from reality. You have to see now that the system's not strong enough. You can't wrap your life around it like they tell you to. A crisis could turn it all to dust in a second. You've been called out, Reed—warned, before it's too late."

"Too late? What do you mean? Nothing's happened."

"No, not yet. But anybody can see it's getting close. The government has built itself into a huge complex set up on empty credit and promises. It can't last forever, and when it gives out, the Organization will vaporize. Then what'll happen to the Hill? The shooting had a purpose: it was the last warning to get off the sinking ship and onto something better before it's too late."

"Whoa." Reed held up his hands. "The shooting was on purpose to get me into 'something better?' On purpose? Something better? You mean your God." His voice rose in anger. "So your God allowed sixty-seven kids to get mown down by a maniac on *purpose*? Some God! Did it ever occur to Him that those were my friends? Did He ever *think* it would hurt people?"

Elijah's voice never changed from its kind, soft tone. "Reed, God was just as heartbroken about what happened as anyone. He didn't want it to be that way. Why didn't He stop it? Nobody knows the mind of God, but I do know one thing. God can take the horrible and heartbreaking and draw something good—even beautiful—out of it. Pain can be His best tool."

"Pain!" Reed shot out bitterly. "What would you know about that? Do you know what I grew up with? My parents divorced when I was eight. They didn't care how me or my sister felt; they just did it. My dad got custody of me, but my mom tried to take my sister so Dad couldn't have both of us. They dragged us through court for months before Mom finally got her way, and they split us up. I lived with Dad in L.A., but he didn't care about me. I was just a pawn for him to use against Mom. He was too busy with the girlfriends he brought to live with us. I hated every one of them. He hardly paid me any attention, ever. I grew up on my own. My soccer coach taught me how to shave."

Reed clenched his teeth for a second, staring at the ground before he went on. "Mom wasn't any better. I had to visit her because the court said I did, but I didn't want to. The divorce was all her fault; she walked out and left us for a CPA. She married him, too. He already had a son who was an absolute *jerk*. Of course, they tried to make us get along because we were 'step-brothers,' but I'm no more related to him than to... to Darth Vader. My sister had to live with him, and she said he was awful. She's the only one in my family I even remotely cared for, but I haven't heard from her since we got shipped off. I have no idea where she is now.

"*That's* pain, and you have no idea what it's like! You grew up in a perfect family and lived a dream all your life. You can't understand." Reed turned away abruptly, his emotions getting the best of him, and worked to bring himself under control.

Silence hung in the air for a moment, interrupted only by a cicada singing in the distance. Elijah sighed. "That is pain, Reed. Terrible pain. But..." he paused. His voice sounded strangely tired and sad. "But I'm not like you think. I don't like to tell people this, but there's something you need to know. It's a long story; maybe it will help you understand."

CHAPTER 31

✦

"You're right," Elijah began. "I did grow up in a wonderful family. We didn't have everything perfect, but it was about as close as you can get. There were five of us kids—three girls and two boys. My parents were strong Christians who taught us to love Jesus and love people. Their goal was to give us a stable, Godly home to grow up in, and they did an amazing job. We had a gorgeous place out in the Texas hill country with acres of woods and pastures and a beautiful house. Growing up was fantastic.

"One summer, my oldest sister and brother were invited on a mission trip down into Mexico. Mom and Dad thought it might be dangerous but agreed to let them go because they thought it would be a good experience. Everybody was so excited about it. They went to the city of Juarez, just south of the border. On their third day there, their group got caught in the crossfire of a gang shootout. They died at the scene."

Elijah tightened his lips for a moment, keeping his eyes fixed on the horizon. "We'd known there would be risk involved if they went, but still… we weren't prepared at *all*. Burying two of your siblings is painful beyond words. I was heartbroken. As I stood in the rain at the funeral, I didn't think anything could ever hurt that badly again." He swallowed and looked down. "I was wrong. That fall, my mother was diagnosed with terminal cancer. It was already in stage four when they found it, and there was nothing they could do. She died within two months, at Christmas. We buried her next to the other two before the grass had even grown over their graves."

He took a shaky breath and rubbed his hands over his eyes. "It was so sudden. Two months isn't long when it's all you've got. We tried to adjust, but it was so empty, so lonely trying to put the pieces back together and find some kind of normal. That winter was hard, very hard. We tried to stay busy, but it just didn't seem like there *was* a normal anymore."

He heaved a deep sigh and dropped his hands. "Spring came, and things started to get a little better. Spring's always beautiful in the hill country. I was still in school, but I got a job. It helped keep me busy. My sisters were starting to feel better, too, but it was harder for Dad. The months after Mom died wore on him brutally. Still, he felt sorry for the girls. They were working their hearts out around the house most of the time, trying to take Mom's place. He decided they needed a break.

"One day, he announced he was going to take us down to San Antonio for the weekend on a mini-vacation. The girls were more excited than I'd seen them in months. I just couldn't make it work with my job schedule. They wanted to put it off until another time, but I told them to go on without me. I didn't want to make them wait.

"They left around six-thirty on a Friday night—Dad and both girls. I was working the late shift that night. I got the call just before seven. They had been on an overpass on their way out of town when a drunk driver hit them. The car flipped off the bridge and landed upside-down on the freeway underneath. My second sister was the only survivor."

Elijah's voice nearly broke. He pressed his fists together and swallowed hard before he went on. "I got to the hospital as soon as I could. I had no idea what to expect. I knew it wasn't going to be good, but... it turned out worse than anything I'd imagined. They let me in to be with her, but they told me right away she didn't have much of a chance. Not long after I got there, she slipped away while I was holding her hand."

Reed listened in stunned silence. Elijah put his hands over his face for a moment and drew a long, deep breath. "That night in the hospital, I felt the full weight of complete, crushing grief. In less than a year, I had gone from one of five children to the last survivor of my family. In the hall outside her room, I put my back against the wall and slid down to the floor, overwhelmed. I had lost it all—everything that had been my life was gone."

He swallowed again and wiped his arm across his eyes. "But, as I sat there, somewhere in the back of my mind, I heard a voice—a small, quiet voice telling me everything was not lost. There was something more, something greater, and I was still incredibly blessed."

Reed lifted his head for the first time and stared at him.

Elijah was gazing down the slope at nothing. "I grew up in a Christian home, saved at a young age and taught the Bible as long as I could remember. I knew everything was supposed to work out for the good of those who love God. I knew I was supposed to trust Him; I was supposed to have faith. I *knew* that. But now, when all that teaching turned to real life, it was too hard. My life was in pieces all around me; I couldn't even stand on my own feet. With everything gone that I loved, there was a hand reaching out to help me, but I didn't have the strength to take it. I knew I needed to—I wanted to—but I was too broken. I couldn't—*I just couldn't.*"

Elijah gripped his hands together tightly. "As I sat on the floor with my face in my hands and all this in my mind, I cried out to God from an absolutely broken heart. He was all I had left; He was what I needed. I wanted Him *so* badly! 'God!' I cried. 'Give me strength. I don't know what You're doing. Show me something. Help me understand!'

"Someone touched me on the shoulder. I looked up and saw a man I didn't know kneeling down next to me. He had tears in his eyes, and he said the nurses had told him what happened. He told me he had something for me and he knew I would understand it. Then he put something in my hand and walked away. I'd never seen him before and I never saw him again, but I know God sent him. What he gave me was this."

Reed sucked in his breath. Elijah, reaching into his shirt, drew out by its silver chain the mysterious pendant. It lifted out of his collar, spinning slowly, and he laid it in his open hand.

It was unlike any piece of jewelry Reed had ever seen. Part of it was a cross, about an inch long, made of some kind of metal—steel perhaps—unrefined and rough. Mounted on top of this, however, was a jeweler's masterpiece. It was a long, T-shaped leaf crafted from some kind of deep green gemstone of perfect beauty, outlined with an edging of silver. Delicate silver veins branched from the base of the stem where the chain ran through. The entire leaf, set where the two crosspieces intercepted, was shorter than the cross, but it almost could have grown there. Delicate silver tendrils from the stem twined their way about the rough metal bars as if alive. It was truly beautiful.

Elijah gazed at it in his palm. "The man was right. I did know what it meant. As I looked at it, I realized it was a picture of what was happening to me. The cross, like this one, is a symbol of pain, death, and sacrifice, a sign of suffering. But out of that suffering comes something else, like this leaf, pure and beautiful. This pendant said it all perfectly. For me, there was terrible suffering that I couldn't understand, but God was using it for a purpose: He was going to bring beauty and goodness out of it. I could trust that His plan was good, even if it hurt me. He gave me a picture to help me understand that, a picture of the greatest thing I had left—hope."

Hope. The word was like a shaft of light, breaking through a dismal darkness and streaming down to Reed. Hope—a fresh word, a strange word—a word that awakened a longing in his heart and answered the cry of his soul.

Elijah went on. "As I held it, I understood—not in my head but in my heart—that I *hadn't* lost everything. Most of the dearest things in my life had been taken away, but I could still find the courage to get up and live another day because I had a reason for living. So many people never have that. But I did. I had a God Who gave me purpose and meaning. A God Who gave me a base to rebuild my life on. A God Whose heart broke with mine and Who would carry me in His strong arms, no matter what happened."

Elijah gently touched the jewel with the thumb of his open hand. "That night in the hall, God gave me the strength to take His hand and go on—through the funerals, the loneliness, the heartache, and the healing. Ever since that night, I've worn this pendant constantly. It's a weight I carry for His sake. It represents the sorrow and pain of losing my family."

Reed recalled Elijah's whispered words to Ethan weeks before at the Shellys' farm. *I hope you never have to, Ethan. Never.*

Elijah continued. "But it also stands for something else. When I put it on, I accepted God's will for me, no matter how painful or confusing it might be. It's like a symbol of trust and a reminder of the cost at the same time."

Elijah released the gem and let it fall back onto his chest. "See, Reed, I *do* know what pain is. I know what it's like to have everything fall apart around you. I know that life can seem so good one minute and then knock the breath out of you the next. I know how insecure it is. But I found *real* security. There's only one thing strong enough to build your whole life on. It's Jesus, Reed, Jesus! People will let you down, popularity changes, looks fade, styles get old. They're all flimsy and shallow and trivial. You've seen that now; I know you have. But what I found isn't like that. It outlasts everything else and gives me an established identity in Christ. Does that make sense?"

Reed stared at the ground in inner turmoil. Elijah's words stirred his heart and made it yearn for exactly what he was talking about. This was what had been evading him his whole life—this, right here. But something held him back. "Yeah, I see," he said at length. "But there's a catch. I've heard you guys talk about this before. You said you have to sign over your whole life to God and be His slave. I ain't *nobody's* slave. I can take care of myself without anybody telling me what to do." He tried to sound calmer than he felt, but his grammar betrayed him.

Elijah looked at him strangely. "Do you really think so?"

"Of course! I'm pretty independent."

Elijah shook his head and leaned his elbows on his knees again. "Don't take this wrong," he said softly, "but you're really not."

"What do you mean, I'm not?" Reed retorted. "Wouldn't I know?"

Elijah sighed. "It's like I said at the beginning. There's more happening here than you think." He clasped his hands together. "See, Reed, there's a war going on over our world. Two sides are fighting to the death over every single person on the planet, but most of us are completely oblivious. But even if we don't have a clue about what's going on, we're all on one of those two sides. Reed, *there's no such thing as the middle*. You're either on one side or the other.

"I've just been telling you about one side: God and His Son. But there's more to it than that. There are powers of darkness, evil that only wants to destroy us. When we think we're living for ourselves, we're not. We think we're doing whatever we want, but the power of darkness is using us for its purposes. Evil's tricky like that; it always betrays."

Reed cocked one eyebrow. "Do you really expect me to believe that?"

"Why not? You're literally surrounded by it every day."

"What are you talking about?"

"The Hill—it's a giant trap built by evil to keep you from being all you can be. Reed, you're literally a prisoner. You're not free to do what you want, to be your own person. You're ruled by what everyone else says, by popular opinion, by rules, the government, the Council, and by the force behind it. And, what's really crazy, you don't care. You used to, but they've used all the glitz and glamor to blind you to what's really going on. They know how to make it look good."

Elijah turned his eyes toward the distant hills. "Take Michael, for instance. He's awesome, right? That's why they picked him. He's a mask for what's really behind it all—the darkness, the fear, the evil. They pay him to make them look good so you let down your guard and they can get in. They're brainwashing you."

It rose in Reed's mind like the memory of a dream that he *had* been angry when he first got here. He had seethed against the government, against GRO, and even the Hill. *Never forget and never let go,* he had said. Now, of course, he still grumbled about the Council and its rules, but... he wasn't angry anymore. He liked what they had done. He was *glad* he had been brought here. What had happened?

"It's what darkness does," Elijah answered his unspoken question. "You're right in the middle of its most effective scheme on the planet. But it's not the only power out there. What you've been telling me shows that you're being drawn out of the darkness and into the light. God has used all sorts of things to point you in the right direction—curiosity, loneliness, even rebellion. He can turn them all into His tools. Everybody feels a desire to get more out of life at some point, but you, you're feeling God's special call firsthand. He's chosen you, Reed. We've all known it from the beginning."

"What do you mean?"

"The first day Nathan met you at the factory, he knew you were different; there was something about you. That's why we let you come to our meetings." Elijah looked over at him. "We wouldn't take that kind of risk unless we felt God wanted us to. The first night we met you was a confirmation. I could even see it in your eyes. God was trying to draw you to Himself, but the devil was fighting tooth and nail to keep you. You felt it, didn't you—a struggle you didn't fully understand?"

Reed said nothing. He could feel his skepticism melting out from under him.

"Reed, you've been given an amazing chance! Don't you see how God worked all this out? He placed you next to Nathan in the factory out of all people in the entire city *and* in the same room as Reagan, of all people. You've gotten to taste the very best of life on both sides so you could make a choice. And now, He's opening your eyes so you can see the truth. That's what you're feeling! That's what happened to you today at the pool, and that's what I meant when I said God had a purpose in the shooting. He used it to show you that the Hill's not enough for you anymore. That's how the good is coming out of the pain. There *is* something more, Reed! You see that now."

"But..." Reed suddenly became aware that, even though his anger and hatred had been anesthetized, the greater, colder force—the gripping fear—had not. "But I can't just change," he breathed in a low voice. "That would... would..."

"Yes, it would. All of us paid a price for being different. They make us pay it every day on the Hill. We all have to give up something, Reed. I did. It can cost a lot, but it's worth it—every bit worth it! The scorn, hate, pain, sorrow—it's nothing compared to what God can offer. Just think about it."

Reed didn't answer, and they sat in silence. As they talked, the sun had sunk out of sight behind the mountains, and the last of its golden gleams vanished from the sky. Lights twinkled in the city below, and a soft green glow lit up the west, rising from the horizon and fading into a deeper blue above. Just where this last bit of fleeing day met the oncoming night, the first star appeared, large and bright in the evening sky.

Elijah gazed at it for a moment. Softly, he said, "You know how some people think it's comforting to look at the hills when they're tired or lonely? I've always looked to the night sky. The stars are so beautiful, and they're like... a promise. God says He knows every single star and names them, so why would He ever forget about me? I can't count how many times when I was lonely or hurting that I've looked up and seen this same star in the west. It was always there, always bright, and it was comforting to know that the same God Who made it made me, too. Maybe it's dumb, but I claimed it for my own a long time ago. And ever since, whenever I look at it, I always think of God and feel closer to Him."

Reed turned to look at him wonderingly. Elijah's eyes had never been a purer, more blazing blue than they were in the fading twilight as he gazed up into the sky. They were beautiful, stunningly beautiful, and Reed suddenly understood a little more about them. They always held a kind of life and sparkle, but there was more to them than that—there was the depth Reed had marveled at from the beginning. Only now did he understand it. It was the depth caused by the crushing weight of great sorrow and pain and by the strength that grows from enduring and overcoming. Elijah had survived, risen above, come through into a higher nature. It was the refined beauty that suffering produces.

"No," said Reed. "I don't think it's dumb at all."

Elijah smiled and stood up, slipping the pendant back inside his shirt. "Cody's probably wondering where I am. I should go. But don't forget this, Reed. Think about it. Really think about it. You've heard us talk about what to do—praying, salvation, the Christian life—but it's your choice. Maybe God will show you the love of Jesus for yourself in a way you can really understand." He put his hand on Reed's shoulder for an instant. "I'll pray for you."

He walked away, whistling softly, and disappeared into the gathering dusk. Reed stared after him, dazed. There was so much at once, so much to put together. He rose to his feet. Perhaps it would be made clearer for him like Elijah said. He was torn, mixed up, and... well, stubborn. But he couldn't stand here all night. With his heart and mind full, Reed turned and began his walk back to the Dorms.

CHAPTER 32

*

The next morning was the typical beginning to a typical day on the Hill. Everyone got up, had breakfast, and left for work as usual. The morning rush was crowded, loud, and much too early, as usual. In fact, the only thing that wasn't as usual was Reed. He was tired, thoughtful, and silent as though he hadn't slept well or hadn't even slept at all.

He ran into Hunter at breakfast, who wondered aloud what was wrong with him. Reed explained grudgingly as he poured a cup of coffee that he had missed supper the night before and didn't sleep well with an empty stomach and a full head.

Hunter was sympathetic; he, too, had missed supper and hadn't slept much. He had been working on a special assignment the night before and would be doing the same most of the day.

"But, hey," he shrugged, reaching for a Styrofoam cup, "you do what you've got to do when you're on your own. One day it'll pay off."

Reed didn't see Hunter as being truly "on his own," but he said nothing.

The rest of the day was no different from the morning. Everything seemed completely normal to everyone but Reed. A thousand tiny fragments of what he had heard last night orbited his mind like asteroids around a spinning planet. He couldn't focus on his work, he couldn't remember what he'd had for lunch, and he ate supper by himself. He felt distanced from everything else in the world, like he was watching the rest of the Hill go on around him from behind a glass wall. Part of him longed to return to his old, normal life but, in a way, he didn't want to go back to the way things had been. Something needed to change. He yearned for it, but he dreaded it.

He was still struggling with the feeling toward the end of the day as he sat on the edge of a flowerbed on the Square, watching a game of foursquare. It was a warm evening. A mesh of streaking clouds, orange and red, stretched over the western horizon like a flaming fisherman's net. Occasional laughter echoed off the walls of the surrounding dorms and drifted away in the still air. The Square was overhung with the exotic sweetness of late Japanese cherry blossoms, wafting from the bloom-laden tree at the corner of Dorm Three. Reed was alone.

The sun had not yet set behind the ring of misty purple hills when he felt a quick tap on his shoulder. Turning, he was surprised to find Alec fidgeting by his side. The other boy wasted no time with formalities.

"When you saw 'Lijah last night, were you two by yourselves?"

Reed blinked. "What?"

"When you met with Elijah last night, did you see anyone else around?" Alec repeated. He was not smiling, and he jerkily shifted his weight from one foot to the other and back.

"How did you…"

Alec shook his head. "Never mind how I know! Did you?"

"Well, yes," Reed said slowly. "There were a couple of joggers and some tennis players."

"So you were at the park on Harvard Street?"

"Yeah, it was a park, but I don't know where."

"You don't know?" Alec asked.

"No! Now what's this all about?"

Alec calmed somewhat and fixed his eyes on Reed deliberately. "Early this morning, before Cody and Elijah left for work, Cody went out to pick up breakfast. When he came back, he found their apartment had been broken into and the living room completely ransacked. Elijah's gone. The Council took him."

Reed felt like someone had punched him in the gut.

Alec went on. "If Cody had come back a few minutes earlier, they would've gotten him, too. He's left the city to hide out in the woods. He only stopped long enough to tell Sarah what happened on his way out of town, and she got word to me and Gabe. He told her you might know something since Elijah had seen you sometime last night."

"No! Just what I told you," breathed Reed, still in shock. "I wasn't paying any attention to anybody when I ran into him. But what will they…"

"I don't know. I just found out, and I'm headed over to the apartment."

"I'm coming, too." Reed stood up quickly. "But you'll have to show me the way."

A few minutes later, they reached the quiet street where the green-shuttered apartment stood. As they neared the door, Reed saw that it had been kicked in and still hung slightly ajar.

Alec examined the doorframe. "They didn't even bother turning the handle," he muttered, running his fingers along the broken wood.

Reed pushed past him into the dim interior. It was hard to believe this was the same room where he'd waited for Cody only a few weeks before. The leather recliners lay like lifeless animals, their arms and backs torn open and the handles snapped off their sides. The loveseat was tipped upside down and its bottom crushed in. The couch was still right-side up, but its cushions were scattered across the floor. A thick layer of sheetrock dust had settled across its once-brown leather surface. The huge metal star had fallen from the wall and buried itself deep in the couch's back, still lifting two of its points in defiance.

Reed could only stare. Everywhere he looked, the room had been mutilated. All the chests and bookshelves were overturned and broken. One of the floor lamps, its metal post bent into a crescent, lay almost at his feet. The sturdy coffee table alone seemed to have retained its shape, though the carpet was covered in a layer of broken glass.

Reed touched the torn arm of the couch where he had sat on his last visit and clenched his fists in sudden anger. "They had no right!" he seethed. "Council or not, they had *no right!*"

Alec joined him. "No, they didn't," he agreed, stepping over the shattered glass to examine the table. "But they don't care about rights."

"Why?" Reed exclaimed. "Did they wreck this whole place just out of spite? Of all the…" his last words were inaudible.

Alec didn't answer. He dropped down and studied the floor. "No," he said suddenly. "No, it wasn't for spite. God bless him, he gave them the fight of their lives! Look." He pointed to the floor beneath the bent lamp. A dark, crimson stain dyed the beige carpet. Blood.

Reed eyed it. "Yeah, but is it his or theirs?"

"Theirs, of course. I know him. Believe me, you don't mess with 'Lijah. Whoever tried here has the biggest headache of his life. That's what bent the lamp!" Alec straightened up and surveyed the room. "That's what happened to all the furniture! They were fighting all over the room. Boy, he must've really given it to them! Those holes in the wall came from fists and heads. Sweet, he even flipped one over his back!"

"How do you know?" Reed was baffled.

"Look." Alec jumped over the broken glass to the loveseat. Sure enough, the crushed bottom was broken in the size and shape of the posterior end of a large person. "That was a special trick he had. Dude, that must've been awesome!"

"But they took him anyway," Reed said softly.

Alec stopped in his excited investigation. "Yes, they did." He looked at Reed. "I wonder how. I'm afraid they'll make him pay for everything he gave them."

There was nothing else to see here. They left the room just as they found it and locked the front door's deadbolt, still intact, with a key under the mat. They hurried away from the site and out of the quiet street. They had put a few blocks behind them before either of them felt like speaking.

"I've got to go break the news to the others." Alec shoved his hands into his pockets. "You can go back to the Dorms."

"Alec," Reed said, a sudden thought breaking on him, "I'm going to get blamed for this, aren't I? I saw him last night. You have to tell them it wasn't me."

"I will," Alec assured him, shaking his head. "All the same, you'd better keep out of Gabe's way for a while."

When Reed arrived back at the Dorms, he found the news of the arrest had already gotten out. Nothing like it had ever happened on the Hill before, and Elijah's name was on everyone's lips. He found the Hill buzzing with anger and resentment.

"How *dare* they?" and "Who do they think they are?" were the questions that flew back and forth. Behind the closed doors of their halls and rooms, teens swore against the police, muttered about the government, and even talked of starting a petition for Elijah's release. Reed was shocked. He knew Elijah had once been popular, but he never would have expected this kind of reaction. Everyone seemed to be up in arms over the arrest. *Why?* he wondered. *Why do they care?*

It wasn't until later that night, when he ran into Lucy out on the Square, that he began to understand. They hadn't seen one another since the ill-fated night in the woods, but neither of them seemed to remember that now.

"Oh, Reed!" Lucy moaned as soon as they met in the crowd. "What'll they do to him? It's awful to think about!"

He had to agree, but he comforted her with what he'd learned of the general opinion. "They'll have to take that into consideration," he consoled her as they moved over to a flowerbed and sat down on its stone edging. "Everybody's against it; I just don't understand why. Why does the Hill care what happens to him?"

Lucy looked up from rubbing her face with both hands. "Why? Because, even if they don't understand him, that doesn't mean they don't respect or even like him. Elijah was the way he was and wasn't ashamed of it. He never got in anybody's face about anything, but he stuck to what he believed with a quiet resolve that very few people have. He was brave. It showed strength people respected, even if they didn't like what it meant. Not everybody can do that. Take Sam, for instance."

Reed smirked. Lucy held up a finger. "Hold on. I just mean he's different from a lot of people here, but he doesn't even respect himself for that. You know as well as I do that he sells out to the highest bidder. He's constantly molding to fit in with whatever's popular because he's too weak to stand out."

She looked away. "People are quick to spot a jelly backbone, and they don't like it. They despise it. Sam wants to be liked and accepted, and he tries to get that by 'fitting in.' But he's not getting the thing he's trying to get because he's trying to get it that way."

Reed had to think about that one for a moment.

Lucy dropped her hands and sighed. "He doesn't understand. He's just a lonely little boy in a big, crowded world. Reed, people like him need help more than anything. That's why Elijah's always been so nice to him, even though they were complete opposites."

She watched her fingers twining and untwining in her lap. "'Lijah never tried to hide his differences like that. He's a nice, easygoing, likable guy, but he won't budge on his faith. People respect his strength. When he left the Dorms, it showed everybody how serious he was about living out his faith in a practical way. That's why they didn't just forget about him. He's not like Sam because he's got a... a..."

"An identity," finished Reed, staring across the darkened Square.

Lucy looked at him curiously. "Yeah, that."

He gave her a slight smile in return. "I think you answered my question. I guess now we just have to wait to see how everything turns out."

She sighed and rose. "Yeah, I guess. Wilson said the trial's set for tomorrow afternoon."

"The what?"

"The trial. They're not wasting any time. They're putting him before the Chairman, the head of the Council himself. They picked tomorrow afternoon 'cause it's a Saturday, and everybody's 'invited.' They've never done that before; it probably means they want to make an example of him. I don't like the way it sounds."

"Me, neither, but I'm going." Reed stood up grimly. "Somebody's got to show up for support. Are you?"

She let out a shaky breath. "I don't know if I could stand it."

"Then maybe I'll see you tomorrow." He patted her shoulder awkwardly. "Just go to bed and try not to think about it."

"Thanks, Reed," she said, smiling and wiping her eyes. "I feel a little better just having talked it through. But I've got some praying to do before I go to bed. Good night."

But Reed did not have a good night. The shadow of what was to happen the following day hung over him with a deep-seated dread that haunted his thoughts until the early, gray hours of the morning.

CHAPTER 33

The trial was to be held in the city courthouse downtown which, in reality, was no longer the city's. It had become the Council's headquarters, and it belonged to them. Reed couldn't shake feelings of fear and awe as he entered the great building. He crept through the silent, lofty halls, his pulse pounding in his ears. The marble floor echoed his footsteps back like cannon shots. All the forces that held the Hill in place and kept it in submission seeped out of these dim, wood-paneled corridors: fear, force, mystery.

Reed swallowed and turned down the third hallway to the right like the secretary had told him. Great doorways of carved oak frowned down on either side of him. A mahogany side table and empty, claw-footed chairs glinted in the dim light. He had the uncanny feeling he was being watched. An invisible presence pervaded the atmosphere, just like the night Reagan first told him about the Council. He felt the same chill that had shot up his spine when he saw the two officers in the dark alleyways of the apartments or when the eyes of the factory overseer fixed on the back of his skull.

Whatever it was, it hung over him, menacing and cold, like the threat in the eye of a coiled snake. He shivered as he climbed the stairs to the gallery and stepped through the great, mouth-like door. *Man, I hope I'm not the only one here.*

He wasn't. As soon as he stepped in, he saw that the large room was packed. Hill residents overflowed the gallery and spilled down into the floor-level seating. But it was quiet—deathly quiet. The only sounds were the subdued hiss of hushed whispers and the rustle of people trying to settle themselves in their seats.

The gallery ran along three walls of the room, leaving the wall opposite the door open for the judge's stand. Reed squeezed through the crowd to the far end that would be on the judge's right. He would be able to see faces from this point. He sat in the front corner of the balcony and looked around.

The judge's bench at the front of the room was set high above the pale wooden floor where the defendant, given no dock, was to stand. Black curtains draped around the seal of the city, gleaming dully behind the judge's straight back chair. Both the tall desk and the wall behind it were of dark, heavy paneling that brooded over the rest of the room. Even the rows of seats on the floor shrank back from it, cowering behind their balustrade. There were no windows. Reed swallowed. It was intimidating. Worse, it was oppressive.

A bailiff entered the room. "All rise." The sepulchral tone was chilling.

The command was almost unnecessary. The few teens who managed to get seats rose, but it was practically standing room only. No one sat back down. The whispers dropped away like the fading patter at the end of a rain shower.

A door in the paneling opened. Out of a darkened hallway stepped a tall man in the black robe of judicial office. All noise of any sort ceased as the room held its breath. It was the Chairman of the Council. A shadow fell over the room in his presence, like a cloud that blots out the sky or a heavy fog seeping into a valley. The very air seemed heavy and cold. His slow, measured steps reverberated on the wooden floor as the door swung noiselessly shut behind him. Every eye in the room fixed on him.

The Chairman mounted the judge's bench with a sweeping hiss of his long robe. He sat stiffly in the high-backed chair and brought his gavel down with a bang that echoed through the silent courtroom. The packed galleries waited.

The drum of approaching feet broke the hush. Several officers in uniform led by a man in a black suit entered the room, a prisoner in their midst. Not a soul in the crowd stirred. The man in the suit and two of the guards led the figure to the center of the floor and left him there alone, the two guards taking a few steps back and the leader moving directly in front of the judge's stand. He snapped his hands behind him and turned to face the crowd. Vonhauser. Reed recognized the stony face of the Council's head of police from months before in the Mushroom. Perhaps that explained a little more about the brutal scene at the apartment.

He tore his eyes away from the officer and turned quickly to the prisoner. He immediately hoped Lucy was not in the crowd. Elijah looked terrible. Even from a distance, he looked like he hadn't slept all night. His arms were jerked tightly behind him, tied or handcuffed, and his shirt was stained and ripped across the chest and shoulders. Reed could only see half his face. A narrow bruise showed black against the left side of his jaw, and a streak of dried blood etched down his cheek. But there was no defeat in his tired posture.

The trial began with a reading of the charges. They were written in legal terminology no one could understand, but they sounded very serious. After that, several witnesses were called. None of them were from the Hill, and their testimonies made even less sense than the charges. The Chairman seemed satisfied by their words all the same. A few more legal procedures that Reed did not understand were enacted before the Chairman finally looked down to Elijah over his glasses.

"You stand so accused." He spoke coldly, and there was no emotion on his clean-shaven face. "These charges have been drawn from the testimonies of reliable eyewitnesses and augmented by your hearing before the Council last night."

Reed shuddered. *That must have been terrifying.*

"Your role in plotting insurrections and civil disturbances, and your direct violation of the law laid down by the aforementioned body, is indisputable. However…" he removed his glasses, "in the view of justice, I must ask: have you anything to say?"

Elijah raised his head to look at the Chairman. The blue of his eyes seemed to light up the gray gloom around him, lifting Reed's heart like a streak of rising dawn.

"I have, Your Honor." His voice was clear, carrying through the entire room. "Your Honor is mistaken. These charges are completely erroneous, having no basis in fact and making them unsuitable for further deliberation in this court."

Good grief, thought Reed, *he's making legal baloney out of the judge's little speech.*

"Secondly, Your Honor, I would like to inquire as to the nature of these charges; namely, what insurrection have I had any role in plotting and what civil disturbances have I led?"

The Chairman had apparently not expected such an answer. He glared at Elijah in silence for a moment before replying. "Do you deny, then, that you do not support the nation, the government, and its provisions made for the betterment of its citizens?"

"Sir, no one is more loyal to the United States of America than I am. I completely support any steps that better its people. But, sir, when it comes down to measures taken to seduce and cripple Americans, especially young Americans who don't know any better, by an oversized and tyrannical governing body, then I do *not* support such movements. But since when, Your Honor, is peaceable disagreement worthy of the title 'insurrection?'"

There was a stir, ever so slight, in the crowd. "Geez," whispered a boy next to Reed, "did this kid go to law school or what?"

The Chairman waited until the stir subsided. "You have just confessed with your own mouth that you disagree strongly with the government's policies." He sounded exultant. "Such an admission is highly questionable when put in consideration with your behavior. You cannot deny that you left the government-provided accommodations known as the Dorms with little explanation and that, prior to your move, your presence caused unrest in the remaining residents. With your opinions, it is obvious that you were endeavoring to stir up discontent against the Council and incite rebellion."

"I'm afraid Your Honor is mistaken again," said Elijah. Reed wished he wouldn't be so polite. "The people of the Dorms are certainly unhappy and dissatisfied, but it's not because of anything I have done. They're restless because what they find in this contrived bubble you've set up isn't enough. They want stability and reality, but they can't find it. They are left precariously balanced. As a fair warning to you, sir, the government has underestimated this generation; you are playing with fire. You've tried to be something to them that you cannot be and, if you fail them, they will make you feel their anger."

The Chairman stared down at him coldly. "We are not here for a philosophical discussion. You may try to deny these other charges, but you cannot deny that, in direct violation of the law laid out by our sovereign body, you took part in and hosted illegal religious activities. What do you say to *that*?"

"I do not deny it, Your Honor." A low murmur filled the room, but a bang from the Chairman's gavel silenced it.

Elijah hadn't finished. "I did take part in those activities; it was against the Council's rules. The question is, sir, which is more illegal?"

Stunned silence.

"The Constitution of the United States explicitly allows for the complete freedom of religion; your law goes directly against that and is clearly not within the government's legal power. It is plainly an attempt to set the government up as a god which, sir, is more unlawful than anything I have done."

The Chairman slammed his hand on the stand like a thunderclap and leaned forward. "*We* are the absolute authority here," he snarled, "and we hold your life in our hands. We have declared this to be law, and there is no other!"

"The government is not the absolute authority, Your Honor. There is One higher."

"Will you or will you not obey it?" the Chairman bellowed, disregarding this last comment.

Elijah looked him straight in the eye. "I must obey God rather than men."

The Chairman remained leaning forward, staring at him for a moment. Reed was staring, too. He was stunned, awed. The Chairman, in his wrath, had overshadowed the entire room, huge and black like a dragon spreading its wings against the sky. Everyone shrank back, terrified—everyone, that is, but one. Elijah remained unmoved and calm in the center of the floor. He was so steady, Reed thought, even with the Hill's greatest fear looming over him. He was almost like... a star, shining clear and strong beneath a bank of roiling, black clouds.

The Chairman seemed disinclined to say anything for a moment. In the hanging silence, Elijah spoke again. "Your Honor, we both know why I'm really here. If you want me to answer for *that* charge, I will. If it is a crime to live a peaceful, productive, happy life of freedom, I admit to my crime. If it is wrong to find a deeper meaning to existence and bring comfort to others in a dying world, then I am guilty. And, if you bring the charge against me of being a Christian, then so be it, for that I am, and that I will stay."

The Chairman leaned back, keeping his eyes fixed on the young man. "Very well," he said slowly. There was an odd tone in his voice that sent shivers through Reed. "So you choose. Before the court issues a verdict, there is one final question. Keep in mind that your cooperation *might* influence the decision. Who are the others in your little faction?"

Oh, brother, thought Reed. *They always want to know that.*

Elijah never hesitated. "You'll have to find that out on your own, Mr. Chairman. I don't betray my friends."

"Indeed," said the Chairman. A leer crept over his face, visible even from the balcony. "It's too bad they're not so loyal to you. It might interest you to know we didn't find you on our own. We had a little help from someone the night before last, one of your precious 'friends.' I think you know who I mean."

Whispers began in the crowd. Reed's mouth went dry. Night before last? But that was the night he and Elijah had... No. No! It couldn't have been... *him*! They would've had to follow him. That was the only way, and even he hadn't known where he was going when he left the Dorms. Even as he fought the idea, it sank slowly into his mind and left him feeling sick. The Chairman had said it himself. How else would they have known?

The Chairman went on, gloating. "Yes, you know him. He came to us that night not long after he saw you and told us everything on condition of his own safety. We know it all."

Reed snapped his head up. He hadn't done that; he *never* would have done that. Could it be... the Chairman was bluffing? Of course! He wanted to make Elijah feel betrayed so he would turn on the others.

"Mr. Chairman." Elijah's voice was completely calm, "even if one of my friends did come to you, it would make no difference. I still wouldn't turn him or the others in for the world. I love them all too much, even if they don't care for me the same way."

Reed felt like someone had stabbed him through the chest. He knew his innocence; Elijah did not, and he was still saying this about Reed.

"But," Elijah went on, "that is only *if.* I have to doubt your story, sir. If what you say is true and he did tell you *everything*, why do you need me to tell you *anything*?"

There was a moment of silence. Then, from the far gallery, there was a snicker—single, loud, and pointed.

The Chairman stiffened at the sound, glaring at the crowd. Reed could see the muscles in his jaw knotting as he searched the sea of faces. Leaning over to Vonhauser, the Chairman snapped coldly, "Hit him."

The faint titter stopped immediately. The officer stepped toward Elijah and pulled back the heavy, black police club in his hand. Reed couldn't watch. He jerked his head away and closed his eyes, but the thud that followed sickened him. When he dared to look back, Vonhauser had returned to his place. Elijah remained standing, but there was a trickle of fresh blood down his temple. The Chairman's face was like granite.

"The decision of the court will be announced at a later time," he clipped. "Until then, remove the prisoner. This court is adjourned."

Slam! The sound of the gavel echoed in Reed's ears even after he left the building and downtown far behind him. That gavel would fall again and decide Elijah's fate, whatever that might be. In his head, the sound changed to the heavy *thud* of a blow, and he cringed. He was right. Changing sides would hurt. Was it really worth it?

CHAPTER 34

The rest of the day passed uneventfully, like most Saturdays on the Hill. The report of what happened at the trial trickled through the Dorms. No one knew if there was a future date for the conclusion of the affair. The Council issued no announcements.

Reed made a point to personally tell Lucy about the hearing. He was forced at her insistence to reveal how Elijah appeared to have been treated during his imprisonment, and the horror in her eyes made him want to punch somebody. He did not tell her how the Chairman had ended the interview.

Even though the case hung open-ended, Dorm life went on. The initial reaction after the arrest subsided once it was clear nothing more would happen in the near future. It was as though the Hill had paused, shrugged sympathetically, and gone back to its wild business. Reed couldn't bring himself to go on like everything was normal.

That evening, he sat alone in his room, listening to the sounds of carousing coming from the hall and up through his open window. It was Saturday night and spirits were high, but he couldn't—wouldn't—join in.

He hadn't been by himself very long when the door opened and Reagan breezed in. He stopped when he saw Reed sitting on the nightstand, staring out the window. "Yo, dude, what are you doing? Everybody's looking for you. Come on!"

"Don't wanna," Reed replied gloomily without turning his head.

Reagan was shocked into momentary silence. He came around

the desks and stood in front of Reed, incredulous. "What did you say?"

"I said I don't wanna," repeated Reed, still not moving.

"You don't wanna? Why, are you in *mourning*? Come on, it's Saturday night! The pool's hopping. Don't you want to have some fun?"

Reed turned from the window abruptly. "Fun? Your kind of fun? How could you? I *saw* you the other day, Reagan. That was gross, dude, really gross."

Reagan blinked. "What?"

"You and Taylor at the pool day before yesterday—I saw it. Why would you *do* that?"

Reagan, actually serious for once, furrowed his brow. "What do you mean? Do you mean when we... but I've always done stuff like that. You've seen it before, and you thought it was great." He searched Reed's face. "What's wrong with you, Reed? This is the way I've always been. I haven't changed, but you... you have. What happened?"

Reed looked back out the window. He couldn't deny something had changed, but he wouldn't admit it, either. He pulled at his ear. "I just don't think it's... I mean, you shouldn't... Don't you even care that your roommate's in jail?"

Understanding swept Reagan's face. "So that's it." He pulled up a chair and plunked down directly in front of Reed. "Do I care? Well, I guess I do, sorta. But I don't see what that's got to do with us. Elijah made a choice that got him where he is now, and that's his problem. Why should it affect me? Life's good right now; why not enjoy it? I chose to be where I am, too. I'm getting what I want, and he... well, he thinks he will later on. We all have a choice, Reed."

"But what if..." Reed's voice almost dropped to a whisper, "what if he's right?" He swung around and stared at Reagan. "What then?"

Reagan leaned back in his chair slowly. "Careful, Reed. That's the kind of thinking that got Elijah where he is now. It could change your whole life *forever*. Think about that. Is it worth it?"

"Believe me, I am thinking about it." Reed turned back to the window. "I'm thinking, but... I don't know what to think."

"Yeah," Reagan agreed, rubbing his chin. "It did that to me, too, after he talked to me about it the first time. I didn't know what to think, but... I got over it. You will, too." He stood up and stretched. "But right now, I'm going swimming. The girls await."

He moved over to his shelves, whistling as he kicked off his clothes and tossed them into a pile on his bed. Once he was ready, he moved over to the door, towel around his neck, and opened it. "Come down whenever you're ready," he said. "There's plenty to go around."

The door slammed, but Reed remained staring out the window at the darkening sky. His mind was too full to answer.

By the next morning, he still hadn't gotten anywhere. Though nothing else filled his mind for hours on end, it was no use. Processing it all on his own was like trying to put together a puzzle with a missing piece. The sensation left him feeling restless and moody until he was knocked breathless by an event that set the whole Hill buzzing.

It first struck him when he was on his way to a late breakfast at the Mushroom. The air was electric, tingling around his ears as he walked along the sidewalk. Something had happened; he could feel it. The sensation grew stronger and stronger until he thought he couldn't stand it another minute. He was just about to ask the next random person what was going on when he met Lucy at the bottom of the North Stairs. She grabbed him by the elbow without so much as a "good morning."

"Did you hear what happened last night?"

"No, I haven't heard a thing. What?"

She looked around and lowered her voice. "Early this morning, Director Connors got a call from the Council. They are furious! Nothing like this has ever happened before, and they don't even know *how* it happened."

"*What?*"

She took a breath and pronounced each word impressively. "Reed, sometime last night, nobody knows when, Elijah escaped from prison."

"What?" Reed grabbed her arm. "How?"

"Nobody knows! They didn't even realize he was gone till they went to get him out of his cell this morning."

"But…" Reed stuttered, "how? I mean, now what? Won't they have every cop out looking for him?"

"I'm sure they will, but I bet they'll be quiet about it." Lucy tossed her hair. "This doesn't make them look good. Besides, if God got him out of jail, He can keep him that way. Isn't it wonderful?"

"Do you know where he is? Have you seen him?"

"Shh! No," she whispered, looking around again. "I haven't, and I don't think I will. He probably won't contact us for our own safety, even if he's still around here. *They* are going to be watching us closer than ever. We'll have to be extra careful now."

Reed hadn't thought of that. However the Council managed to track down Elijah could work just as well for the rest of them.

He lived the next several days in extreme caution. By mutual consent, none of the group saw each other except on chance encounters around the Dorms. Reed didn't venture near the apartments and did his best to blend in with the crowd.

The search for the escapee was, as Lucy predicted, kept low key. Not a word came from the Council or Director Connors concerning it. Still, news of the escape had already swept through the Dorms, and everyone knew a search was in progress. But Elijah had disappeared. As time passed and no new leads surfaced, the people of the Dorms began to whisper that he had escaped completely, perhaps even leaving the country. The excitement lapsed as the hours turned to days and, gradually, it subsided and was forgotten.

Reed couldn't help but wonder what had happened to Elijah. He doubted he would ever see him again. It was unlikely, even impossible. Even if he never did, he wouldn't forget him. Reed was stirred in a way that could not be undone, and his searching hunger had redoubled to a yearning that cried for fulfillment. He could only hope that things would be made clear to him like Elijah had said.

Even after the excitement ebbed on the Hill, Reed remained wary. The Council's silence worried him. What were they up to? He guessed their next move would be quick and relentless, like a lightning bolt, and no one would see it coming.

One warm evening nearly a week after the escape, Reed was on his way down to the city. He'd gotten a message from a few of his friends earlier, asking him to come down to the Boulevard to "hang out." Having nothing else to do, he agreed and started out not long after supper. It had been a long day; he was ready to relax.

The sun had already set as he made his way along the now-familiar route. Dusk was gathering in little pools between the buildings and trickling into street corners. Sparrows flitted across the glowing sky like late children hurrying home for dinner. The streetlights had not yet turned on. It made Reed nervous to be out alone this time of day, but he couldn't spend his life locked in his room. Besides, he could look out for himself.

As he turned down a cut-through to the next street, an odd feeling leapt into the pit of his stomach. It was something he had experienced months ago on the night when the boy from the Dorms was beaten in this same area. It was an uneasy, almost sick sensation. All his senses snapped on alert, but it was too late.

A figure appeared right in front of him, blocking the narrow alley. Reed nearly jumped out of his skin and took a step back. It was an older boy, much larger than Reed, with a dirty white tank top, scruffy face, and bulging, brawny arms. Reed eyed him, fighting panic, and wondered how fast he could run.

The boy spoke. "Goin' somewhere?"

Reed forced himself to sound calmer than he felt. "Yeah, back that way, actually. If you don't mind, I think I'll be leaving."

"Suppose I do?" The voice was behind him. Reed spun around and saw another hulk blocking the alley in that direction. Trapped.

"What do you want?" he demanded, doing his best to keep an eye on both at the same time.

"Us?" said the first boy. "Nothin'. But somebody else wants *you*."

"Me? Well, tell 'em I'm flattered but no thanks. I've got friends waiting for me."

"Do ya?" said the second boy, moving a step closer. "Funny, I don't think so. Ya know, *we* sent that message. Your little friends aren't waiting for you. They have no idea where you are. Somebody else wants you, and they don't take no for an answer. You're coming with us."

"Oh, really? Well, whoever this is, they should find better staff than two sasquatches that don't wear deodorant. I'm not going anywhere with you creeps."

The first boy narrowed his eyes. "Listen, kid, we're talking about the Council here. Whatever they say goes."

"I don't care who we're talking about. You're not taking me anywhere."

"I'm warning you, kid. We have orders to bring you by 'any means necessary.'"

Reed got his back against the alley wall and braced himself. "Come and take me then," he shot back.

It was an invitation. The first boy lunged at him with surprising speed. Reed was quicker. He shot out a strong kick that met the stomach of the oncoming crook and sent him reeling backward, gasping. The second one was on him in an instant but also fell back, deterred by a well-aimed fist that connected firmly with his jaw. Reed kissed his throbbing knuckles. "Frick," he muttered, "it looks a lot easier in the movies."

The first boy tried again. Reed beat him off once more, but not without having a little of his own blood drawn. He scarcely had a second to wipe it from his lip before the other boy was on him. He met with less success than his companion.

Again, they each tried, but Reed drove them off once more, fighting for all he was worth. After a few more attempts, both assailants withdrew to consider their options. Apparently, this wasn't going the way they had anticipated.

Reed wiped a trickle of blood from his chin and gingerly touched his throbbing eye. He couldn't hold them off forever. They weren't very bright, but they would catch on soon enough and attack him simultaneously. There would be nothing he could do then except make them pay dearly for their prize. He gritted his teeth as the two separated and moved into position on either side of him.

Without warning, a broad figure dropped from the building above Reed's head and crashed onto one of the attackers, throwing him to the ground. In the same instant, another swung off the roof and slammed into the remaining brute feet first. The force caught the boy full in the chest and threw him against the alley wall. Before he could recover, the new arrival landed in front of him and socked him in the jaw with each fist. The first thug picked himself up from the street, but the broad attacker was already raining punches on him.

In the skirmish that followed, Reed remained where he was, astonished. He offered no help in the melee, but it didn't seem like his help was needed. The two ruffians were getting the worst end of the deal. Reed had never seen such fighting, if it could be called that. His mysterious rescuers laid into the other two so relentlessly that there was barely any resistance. It ceased to be much of a fight and became more of a pounding.

At last, the first assailant slammed his opponent in the gut with a breathtaking roundhouse kick and, as the thug doubled over, caught his head between his hands and cracked it on his knee. The ruffian collapsed without a sound. At the same time, the slighter figure caught his adversary by the forearm and, with a peculiar twist, flipped him easily over his back. Something clicked in Reed's mind. That trick seemed familiar somehow.

The mugger hurtled through the air and landed heavily on his back in the street. In an instant, he was on his feet again but turned to run, vanishing into the gloom.

The two victors did not follow. Dusting their hands on their jeans, they turned back to where Reed leaned against the wall, struggling to think clearly and doubting his senses. The slighter one looked him up and down. "You all right?"

The voice was unmistakable. Reed's knees gave out and he slid down the wall to the ground. He tried to speak but found his mouth was full of blood from his busted lip. He spit it out and gasped, "Elijah?"

CHAPTER 35

E lijah dropped down next to Reed. "Yeah, it's me and Cody. Are you okay?"

"Me? Sure, it's just my lip. But how—where—what are you doing here? How did you get out of jail?"

"How?" Elijah grinned. "It was a miracle; that's really all that matters. Why am I here? Long story, but we can't stay. Cody and I were on our way back from paying Wilson a visit over the roofs when we found you. God seems to have a way of throwing us together, doesn't He? What were those guys up to?"

"I don't know. They lured me here with a phony message and then said the Council wanted me for something."

Elijah glanced up at Cody. "Ah, then you can bet that punk's making tracks for downtown. But why did they want you?"

"I don't know. Lucy says they've been watching us closer since you escaped."

Elijah mulled this over for a second. "That means they somehow know you're connected with us." He turned to Reed. "Whether you're one of us or not, you're in trouble."

"Swell. What do I do?"

Elijah straightened. "Go back to the Dorms. If you make a big deal out of this and spread the story around, they'll have to leave you alone for a while. Try to stick with the crowds. We've gotta get out of here now, but come to the Shellys' tomorrow night. We'll figure out what happens next."

"Tell some of the others to come, too, if you can," added Cody.

Reed wiped his lip and grinned. "I'll make sure Katy's there."

With the help of a handy dumpster, Cody and Elijah hoisted themselves back onto the roof. Reed, watching them disappear, had a sudden thought.

"Elijah!" he hissed.

A silhouette appeared over the edge of the roof.

"The Chairman was lying at the trial. It wasn't me that turned you in. Really!"

Elijah leaned over the edge. "I know. Don't worry about it."

"But I need to talk to you! There's so much..."

"I know, Reed. God will make it all clear in His time. We'll talk as soon as we can, but I'll keep praying for you. See ya later."

And Reed was left alone in the dusky alley with an unconscious thug.

That night and the next day, Reed followed Elijah's advice, spreading the report of what had befallen him all over the Hill. Reed was smart; he saw the wisdom of the plan. The Council now knew their scheme was exposed and, if anything further happened to Reed, they would get the blame. They would have to leave him alone or the entire Hill would call them out as kidnappers. Reed didn't dare accuse them openly, but he made it clear the muggers had "professed" to be acting under the Council's authority. It served the same purpose. Besides, he couldn't give the full story anyway. No one must know how he'd been rescued—almost no one.

Lucy and Alec were the only ones he told the whole truth. Their concern for what happened was nearly eclipsed by their joy over Elijah's return. Wilson had been his first contact; none of the others had heard from him since his escape. Both planned to go to the Shellys' the following night and agreed to spread the word to the rest.

The next day after work, the three of them slipped out of the city one by one, making their way to the farm. Reed was last in the sequence and arrived after night had fallen. Everyone else was already in the cozy kitchen of the Shellys' little house when he arrived—Alec and Lucy, Katy, Cody, Wilson, Sarah, Krista, Kara, Nathan, Courtney, even Gabe. Reed hadn't seen most of them since that fateful night in the woods. They were scattered into the most comfortable places they could find around the dim little kitchen. The shades were drawn, and a single lamp lit the room from the center of the red-checked tablecloth. All the little Shellys were there, remarkably still and quiet. Mrs. Shelly alternated between the table and a corner cabinet where she busied herself.

Reed's eyes sought out Elijah. He was there, pushed back from the kitchen table in a chair, the golden lamplight falling steadily on his face. Ethan, nestled in his lap, leaned back in his arms like an enraptured cherub, his little hands locked behind the older boy's neck. Nearby, Cody sat on the floor next to Katy's chair. Lucy was near the door, stroking Lizzy's hair as the little girl leaned against her shoulder. Alec sat on the kitchen counter with Luke. It was a warm, homey scene Reed never forgot.

He hadn't missed much by his delayed arrival. When he entered, the conversation was low and serious, centered around the developments with Reed and Elijah. "It's all up now," Wilson was saying. "They know we're here, and they know how to find us. They caught 'Lijah; they can catch the rest of us, too."

Nathan nodded. "Yes, they *could* catch us, but will they? Surely they can't come up with enough legal excuses for all of us. How would they get away with it?"

"You'd be surprised." Wilson tapped his fingers on the table. "Look what happened to Reed; it's obvious they don't need legal excuses anymore. They can get away with anything they want against us, and they will, too. It's only a matter of time."

"Then you think we should go through with it?" asked Katy quietly.

Apparently, Reed had missed something after all.

Wilson sighed heavily. "We don't seem to have any other choice."

They were all silent for a moment, Reed not daring to ask what "it" was.

Lucy looked up. "Mrs. Shelly, you're an adult and much wiser than us. What do you think?"

The woman moved over to the table, drying her worn hands on a blue-and-white towel. "Well," she said slowly, "it doesn't matter what I say, but what God says. Does He want you to do this?" She looked around at them one by one. Her eyes were a soft and gentle brown; Reed hadn't noticed that before.

"It would be a huge step," she went on. "You'd have to burn all your bridges behind you, but," and she sighed, "you don't seem to have any other choice. Elijah's life is in danger. I'm sure the Council has figured out that he's still here after last night. They'll know who that was in the alley; he's beaten up their henchmen before. He's a marked man. Cody, too. And Wilson's right; it's only a matter of time before the rest of you are. I'd hate to see it happen, but I don't think the Hill can hold you anymore."

"Then we have to leave," said Sarah softly.

Leave the Hill? Reed was bewildered. The possibility had never entered his mind. That was so final, so drastic.

"She's right," Cody said. "You can't hide Elijah around here."

"Maybe a disguise would work," suggested Lucy. "Could you, like, grow a beard or something?"

"'Fraid not." Elijah rubbed his smooth jaw. "I couldn't if I tried."

"You couldn't possibly hide his eyes, either," Wilson pointed out. "No, we'd be a danger to the Shellys and to the whole church if we stayed. I hate thinking about it, but it seems to be safest for everyone if we leave. We just need to figure out how."

Regretfully, the others agreed, all except Reed. He was still trying to grasp the situation. "But... but where would you go?"

They all turned to look at him. "You mean where would *we* go," corrected Nathan. "You can't stay here either."

"Me? Leave? But I..."

"You have to, Reed," said Lucy gently. "The Council knows you have ties with us. They'll hunt you down just like they would Elijah or Cody. I'm afraid you'll have to pay the price like the rest of us."

Reed, fighting the idea, glanced around the room and caught Elijah's gaze. The steady look calmed him somewhat but confirmed Lucy's words. Reed would have to leave the Hill and everything he'd grown to love about it—the city, his friends, all that had been his life. It was a thought that would take a while to sink in, but it wasn't quite as numbing as he would have expected.

Once it was settled they would have to flee, the group began arranging how it was to be done. Calling on the wisdom of Mrs. Shelly, they made a plan.

They needed to leave as soon as possible and with the greatest secrecy. Today was Friday. Saturday would require only half a day of work, and then the rest of the weekend would be free. If everything went well, their disappearance wouldn't be reported until Monday when none of them showed up for work.

"Besides," put in Alec, "even if a rumor got to the authorities before then, they'd be too busy to give it any thought. There've been some issues with the National Treasury this week that have the whole bureaucracy's attention."

Still, they decided that leaving tomorrow morning would be optimal if they could work out a plausible way to get Saturday morning off work. After a few minutes of silent contemplation, Lucy volunteered a strange solution. She would stay behind and go to work as usual. "I'm the HR manager for the Red district, so I've got enough connections through the office to get the morning off for everybody in Red and Blue factories," she explained. "If I stay, I could make the calls, and everybody else could get away sooner."

"And leave you behind?" Gabe sat up in his chair. "You have to get out of here, too!"

"Oh, I would. I'd just leave at lunch and catch up with you guys later. It's no big deal."

Gabe shook his head. "I will *not* let you stay by yourself."

"You're sweet, Gabe," she said, smiling, "but I wouldn't have to be by myself. Reed could stay, too."

Everyone looked at her, surprised. Lucy hurried to explain. "You can't just whisk *him* away all of a sudden. Everybody in the Dorms knows him, and they would notice if he vanished before breakfast. But if he left with me at lunch, it wouldn't be so obvious. They might think he'd gone into the city for the day or something."

They all pondered the suggestion. Nathan spoke first. "She's got a point. If Reed disappeared, everybody might think the Council kidnapped him and start a big racket."

Wilson nodded. "True. Everybody's heard about his incident by now. But I'd feel awful leaving Lucy behind in a place we're literally running away from."

"Never mind that," she assured him. "I volunteered for it, and it's only one morning. I'm more worried how Reed and I would find you guys later. I'm no guide."

Elijah spoke for the first time. "If you want," he said, "I can wait for you outside the city. I've learned my way through the woods. If I know where the others are going, I can get you there."

Gabe objected strongly to this suggestion, saying it was ridiculous and put extra risk on Elijah, who needed it least of all people. Lucy and Reed, however, welcomed the offer, and Elijah assured Gabe it would be fine. Reed, deeply grateful, wondered if Elijah wasn't trying to make an opportunity for the two of them to talk at last. That was like something he would do. In the end, after much discussion, the plan was adopted.

Gabe was still uneasy. "I don't like walking off and leaving you guys here by yourselves," he declared, crossing his arms. "I have a bad feeling about it. I should stay, too, and make sure you're all okay."

This started yet another discussion. Things were getting ridiculous; they might as well all stay at this rate. But Gabe persisted and pointed out that Lucy was only able to cover for those employed in the Red and Blue districts. He, on the other hand, could take care of anyone working in the Green district or with the private company downtown. It was this argument and the faith the others had in his invaluable protection skills that finally swayed them toward his plan. He won his point.

In the end, they decided that Lucy, Reed, and Gabe would stay in the city and, when their work there was done, they'd meet Elijah in the woods. They would all travel together to rejoin the rest of the group.

The more Reed thought about the arrangement, the stranger it sounded to him. There was absolutely no reason for Elijah to stay behind. Gabe could guide Reed and Lucy just as well and with less risk. Elijah must have something else in mind. Reed was positive now; Elijah was only staying for his sake.

Next, they had to decide upon a rendezvous point outside the city. They chose the woodland landmark of the Gorge, mostly because Reed knew how to find it.

"I'll wait there until everybody shows up," Elijah said. "Try to get there as soon as possible. *They* know where the Gorge is, too, and we'll need to get out of there as quick as we can."

Ethan had been listening quietly in Elijah's lap. As the plan un-
folded, the little boy began to shift uneasily and dart glances from
face to face. At last, he could take it no more. He sat up like a jack-
in-the-box. "But I don't wants you to go 'way, Yijah!" He turned his
distressed face up to the older boy's and searched it earnestly. "You...
you *tan't*."

"Sweetheart, he has to," said Marielle gently. "He might get hurt
if he stays."

The little boy blinked, his brown eyes filling with tears. "But...
but then I wouldn't *see* you anymore." With a sob, he buried his face
in Elijah's chest.

Without a word, Elijah gathered the boy up and carried him out
of the room. The others looked at each other, not sure whether to
smile or cry.

"Poor Ethan," Sarah murmured, blinking her own eyes. "I wonder if they will ever see each other again."

Now that the plan was complete, there wasn't much left to dis-
cuss. Those who were leaving first thing in the morning made their
own plans for meeting up and agreed upon a destination to reach by
nightfall. It was not a place Reed had heard of. He was glad Elijah
would be there to get them where they needed to go.

When the last detail was settled, silence settled over the kitchen.
The lamp glowed on the table; the crickets sang outside the shuttered
windows. A clock struck nine-thirty somewhere in the house.

They all looked at one another; it could be put off no longer.
Reluctantly, they stood up and prepared to leave. It was not like their
normal partings; they all knew it meant a final farewell to the Shellys.
It went better than Reed expected, however. There were few tears, no
fears, nothing dark or melancholy.

One by one, the teens from the Hill said their goodbyes to the
children, had a final hug and a word from Mrs. Shelly at the door,
and then vanished into the dark night. Most of them said something
to Reed before they left as well. Katy and Sarah both urged him to
be careful and to take good care of Lucy. Nathan shook his hand and
said he was glad Reed was coming with them. The genuine pleasure
in his eyes and his firm grip made Reed suddenly glad, as well.

Before she left, Lucy confided that she hoped he didn't mind her volunteering him to stay behind. "I'm sorry. It was the only thing I could think of at the moment. You're not mad, are you?"

"No, not really. I mean, of course I'm not. Like, at all."

She smiled sweetly. "I'll see you tomorrow."

Besides Cody, who was waiting for Elijah, Alec was the last to leave. He gave Reed a bit of advice. "Watch out for the ringer tomorrow," he cautioned. "The Council's being so quiet that I'm worried. Something's not right. The ringer's probably going to be on high alert, looking for any info he can get. He could strike anytime, and you're on the list now."

Reed shrugged. "Well, what better list to be on?" His own words surprised him. "I mean," he added, "if they come after us, we'll make a good pair. You can beat the fire out of them while I can make tracks to Mexico. But seriously, I'll be careful."

Alec flashed a grin, his blue-green eyes twinkling in a way only his could. "You make tracks, huh? We'll see about that. Take care, bro." He slapped Reed on the back and disappeared out the door. Reed liked Alec alot.

Reed himself was about to leave and had stepped into the doorway when Elijah reentered the kitchen alone. "Hey, Reed! Hold up a sec."

Cody tactfully slipped outside as Elijah joined Reed by the door.

"I know you don't want to leave yet," he said, leaning one hand against the door frame, "but you have to see what we mean."

Reed nodded. "I do. And, thinking about it, it's not as awful as I would've expected."

Elijah's face lit with a reassuring smile that made Reed feel everything was going to come out right somehow. "That's good! I know you still want to talk, and I'm doing my best to make it happen. But I have a feeling God's going to bring things together tomorrow. I might not need to say a word."

"I hope so," said Reed. "Anyhow, I'll see you tomorrow."

"See you, Reed. I'm still praying for you."

With a grateful nod, Reed turned and stepped into the night. A soft breeze greeted him, sweeping across his face with the sweet breath of night—fresh cut grass and lingering flowers and sleeping fields in the darkness. The sky was filled with stars, burning clear and bright. He took a deep breath and let it out slowly. He didn't know what tomorrow held, but tonight was lovely. He wanted to soak it all up in case it was never so beautiful again. He cast a glance over his shoulder toward the open kitchen door, but it was empty.

CHAPTER 36

The next morning found Reed up earlier than usual. He had the room to himself for, despite Michael's warning, both Reagan and Riley spent the night somewhere else.

Reed was at his shelves, going through his clothes and tossing an occasional item in his backpack. He was packing to leave. It felt so strange and final, like going through the yearbook at the end of school. Each shirt had a recollection attached to it—where he had bought it, when he had worn it, who had liked it—and, as ridiculously sentimental as it sounded, each felt like an old friend. Still, he took only what he needed or couldn't bear to part with.

He'd almost finished his task when the door opened softly, and Reagan tiptoed into the room. He stopped when he caught sight of Reed. "What are you doing?" he whispered, closing the door. "I thought you'd still be asleep."

"Just... cleaning out my closet." Reed went on with his task, forcing himself to sound casual. He had not anticipated Reagan returning so soon.

"At this time of the morning?" Reagan sounded doubtful.

Reed opened a drawer. "Sure, why not?" He did not look up from his work.

Reagan moved over to his bed and sat down, watching him in silence. "You're leaving, aren't you?"

Reed stopped. "What?"

"You're leaving the Hill. Don't try to hide it. I can tell."

Reed forced himself calm. "What makes you say that?"

"You," Reagan said. "I've been watching you lately. You're different. You've been hanging out with Elijah's group. They're changing you, Reed. Everybody sees it."

"They say I'm... different?"

"Yeah. People notice, dude."

There was a pause. "So what's that got to do with my closet?" Reed said, still hedging.

"Come on, Reed! You hang out with Elijah, who gets thrown in jail; you're in deep depression till he mysteriously escapes; you get mugged a week later and don't explain how you get away; and now you're packing. It's not that hard. You're leaving with him, aren't you? Why?"

Reed deliberately zipped his pack shut. He stood and faced Reagan. "You're right: I am leaving. I have to. For one thing, the Council's after me, and it's not safe for me here. But it's more than that; this place isn't enough anymore. I know there's something better out there! I'm not going to find anything in this place. It's not... not... well, it's not what I thought it was."

Reagan stared at him with an expression Reed could not interpret. "And you think they've got what you're looking for?"

Reed hesitated. "Yes," he said, "I think they do. I know they've got something. I'm not getting any answers around here."

"Where will you go?"

"I don't know, but I've gotta leave now." He shouldered his pack and stuck out his hand. "Thanks for everything, Reagan. You've been an awesome roommate."

Reagan reached out and shook it, still staring at him. "You do realize nobody can help you if you get caught. You'll be on your own."

Reed returned his look. "I know. I've thought about it, but I figure it's worth the risk. G'bye, Reagan."

He turned and opened the door.

"Reed."

Reagan's voice stopped him half-way out. He turned. Reagan stood in the middle of the dorm room, looking tired and small. The usual airy spiritedness was gone and left him an ordinary, dejected kid.

"Reed, if... if you do find what you're looking for, I wish... would you... could you find some way—any way—to come back and tell me how?"

"I will, Reagan. If it's at all possible, I will. See ya, bro." He shut the door.

Half an hour later, when he arrived at the factory, Reed found Lucy already behind her desk, alone in the lobby. She smiled as he entered. "They're gone," she said.

He nodded. "Good, I guess. What about us?"

"Gabe said we should meet at the Dorms after work and go to the Gorge together. He's still really worried about us."

Personally, Reed doubted Gabe was very worried about him, but he didn't say so.

"That's fine," he replied. "Whoever gets back to the Hill first should wait for the others outside your dorm. It'll be easier to find each other."

She agreed, and they parted.

The rest of the morning was a typical Saturday at the factory. The other workers complained about working weekends, took a poll on how bad breakfast at the Mushroom had been, and argued about the movie premiere the night before. Reed didn't enter into the conversation. He contemplated how different things would be this time tomorrow.

The morning dragged on. Reed began to feel nervous and wondered if noon would ever come. Noon came. But the whistle did not sound nor did the belts stop promptly on the hour. The teens mumbled about paid overtime but continued their work.

Twelve-thirty approached and passed. Still the belts rolled on. The mumbling changed to louder grumbling. Reed began to worry.

One o'clock came and passed. Nothing changed. The grumbling turned into angry outbursts and dark looks toward the door. "What do they think we are, slaves?" some began to growl. Reed sweated and tried to stay calm.

One-thirty... two... two-thirty... three. Everyone was furious by now. Several tried the door into the hall, but it was locked like it usually was during working hours. Reed chewed the inside of his cheek until he tasted blood.

At last, when the time neared three-thirty, the parts stopped spilling down the belts. The workers bolted out of the room in a mass exodus. Reed was the first to toss his backpack over his shoulder and dart up the steps and out the door into the lobby. Lucy's desk was empty.

With a groan, he dashed out the double glass doors and down the road to the park's entrance. When he arrived at the gate, breathless, he found that his company had not been the only one to keep its workers overtime. Young people were still streaming down from the other factory and pooling by the road. That was a relief; Gabe and Lucy must have been delayed as well. But the crowd was not waiting on the curb as usual. A growing line stretched down the sidewalk into the city. Reed, confused and out of breath, stopped a passing girl.

"What's going on?" he panted.

The girl scowled. "The shuttles aren't here, and they're not coming. We have to walk back to the Hill."

Reed's shoulders slumped. That was a long way on foot, but there was nothing else to do. Cursing under his breath, he started down the street at a brisk walk.

He hadn't gotten far when he became aware that someone was walking beside him. He glanced over and saw Hunter, keeping pace and eyeing him curiously.

"I wondered how long it would take you to notice." The other boy grinned when Reed caught his eye. "You look like you're in a hurry. Goin' somewhere?"

"Yeah, back to the Dorms like everybody else." Reed turned his eyes back in front of him. "I just don't like being three-and-a-half hours late."

"Late for anything in particular?"

"Nope. Just in general."

"So... you don't have anywhere to be or anyone to meet?"

Reed shot him a sideways glance. "Why should I?"

"Aw, come on, Reed!" Hunter exclaimed. "Everybody knows you're the life of the party. What ya got planned? I know there's something."

"Nothing," Reed shrugged. "Why?"

"Oh, it's just my business to know things. I know all about everything."

Reed had to smile at the boast. "Everything? Then tell me about these supposed plans I have tonight. I'd love to find out about them."

Hunter snorted. "Don't get smart, Reed. I know what I'm talking about."

Reed glanced at him, half-annoyed, half-amused. "You know, you're kinda creepy sometimes. Why do you make it your business to know all about everything and everybody? Does somebody pay you?"

"Who would do that?"

"Oh, I don't know. The Council pays the ringer. Maybe they'd pay…" Reed's grin faded, and he broke off as if struck by a lightning bolt.

Hunter's eyes snapped to his face and burned there with a terrifying intensity. Reed looked back at him, stunned. Any doubts about his sudden flash died at what he read in those steely gray eyes. It fit like a long-sought piece into a puzzle.

"You," he finished in a whisper. "You? You're the… *ringer!*"

Hunter's face had lost all teasing, like paint melting from iron. It was hard and sharp with a dangerous glitter in the eyes. Nothing he said could deny what was written on that face, and they both knew it.

"How?" breathed Reed, "How could you? You always *hated* the government."

"I do," Hunter shot back. "I always told you I was in it for myself. I walk the line, work the system to get what I want. If the government pays me, fine, I'll do that. But I'm not loyal to them. I get what I want from them, but I hate them."

"You mean they give you benefits for being a…?"

"They do. They pay me, give me bonuses for 'special assignments,' extend my rules, you name it. They hired me before I even got here and gave me top-of-the-line training for any kind of situation. But I took that a little further than they think. I do more than they know when it serves me. Right now, with what they taught me and what I've taught myself, I could go superhero or turn terrorist. I've got anything and everything I want. Oh, yeah, they pass me on shakedowns, too, so my room's frickin' stacked. There's a whole arsenal in there they don't know about. I was the one who armed the gunner at the street fair. He bought that stuff from me."

Reed could scarcely breathe. "You killed sixty-seven kids? You turned in the potheads and set off the first shakedown? You were the one who turned in *Elijah*?"

"I was." Hunter sounded proud of himself. "And much more. But I had a little help on the Elijah thing, from *you*."

"Me? Never!"

"Maybe not that you know about, but yes, it was you. The first day I met you on the bus, I could tell there was something about you. I decided to stick with you 'cause you might be useful. I was right. You got famous, and you were invaluable. Not long after we got here, I thought I was on the trail of this Christian group the Council wanted, then you started disappearing at nights. You were *very* clever, all of you; I never could find out names. It took months, but I got closer and closer. We almost got you that night in the woods. Finally, it all came together when you let your guard down for the first time and led me straight to a bright-eyed, pretty-faced kid on a park bench. The next morning, they arrested Elijah on my say so. No, you didn't know it, but you were *very* useful."

Reed went numb. So he had done it. *Him.* It was his fault all along. He pushed the painful thought aside to make way for another.

"You mean all that time, you were just *using* me? You didn't care for me as… a friend?"

The cold steel of Hunter's face never changed. "Why should I? I look out for myself, not anybody else."

Horror, fury, and disgust filled Reed's soul in a rush. "You *traitor!*"

"Chill." Hunter cut him off icily. "If you care for your life, you'll keep your mouth shut, now and permanently." His gray eyes, somehow wolf-like, sent shivers down Reed's spine. "I'm in hot water since Elijah escaped. The Council's angry and expects me to find him. I know exactly where he's going to be this afternoon, and I'm bargaining with them for that information right now. I've named my price, and they can't say no. They want him too badly. If you mess anything up, you will pay for it. I've never even met Elijah, but I will make sure he is destroyed, and you, too, if you get in my way."

The utter hatred and cruelty that filled every word shocked Reed. With his mask off, Hunter was a different person—a monster. His complete callousness left Reed hurt, stung, reeling. And the realization that he *had* led the Council to Elijah's door was terrible to him. But above all these, another thought rose in his mind. This treachery, this *baseness* was what he had ascribed to Gabe. Gabe who, he saw, had only acted out of loyalty and love for the others' safety all along. Gabe, who fought for his friends with the same tenacity that Hunter fought to destroy them. To load him with this betrayal… it was unjust, cruel, undeserved. Reed saw that plainly now.

They had reached the Hill and climbed the sloping road to the Dorms, wrapped in the conversation. Reed broke from his swirling thoughts to find they were some of the last to arrive on the Square. The crowd was enormous; the entire Hill was outside.

Why don't they go inside? he wondered. "What in the world?"

This last comment was spoken out loud as he realized the pandemonium that filled the Square. All was confusion. Five thousand teenagers swarmed over the pavement, buzzing like a hive of upset bees. Some appeared bewildered and lost; others looked angry. The walls of the Dorms echoed and doubled their babbling drone.

Reed searched the mass for a familiar face to question and found one almost at his elbow. It was Allie, and he grabbed her as she passed.

"Allie, what's going on?" he demanded. "What happened?"

She turned a teary face toward him. "I don't know! I just got back and tried the door to my dorm, but it's locked! They all are. We can't get in!"

"Locked? Did you try your key?"

"They don't work. All the lights are turned off, and even the Mushroom and rec center are shut up. We can't find the RDs anywhere!"

Reed was about to question her further when a boy pushed through the crowd and sprang up onto the high edging of a nearby flowerbed. He waved his arms for silence. "Hey!" he yelled. "Listen up!"

A gradual hush fell. "I just came from Dorm Four." His voice bounced off the brick walls so all could hear. "Michael the RD is gone, but his door was open. He left a note in his room." He pulled a piece of paper from his pocket and began to read aloud.

"If you're wondering what's going on, I'm not sure I can tell you since I'm not an economist or a lawyer. Most of you know our government was broke, living off credit to other nations. That stopped today. I don't know exactly what happened, but the limit was reached. It was time to pay up, and Big Bro couldn't. The market plummeted, banks closed, businesses went bust...it's complicated. In terms we can understand, the government has collapsed. All federal agencies and programs have fallen through and are dissolved. The Hill is shut down permanently."

A complete uproar erupted as the boy finished reading. The angry and despairing cries of disbelief from five thousand former Hill residents were deafening. Reed heard Hunter, still next to him, explode.

"How dare they!" he bellowed, "the double-crossing traitors!" With much more and much worse, he spun around, raging. "I'll make them pay for this!" His wild eyes fell on Reed. "You'll all pay! Nobody pulls something like this on me!" He darted away into the crowd and out of sight.

In the meantime, the boy who read the note was still atop his flowerbed, trying to restore order. This was difficult, to say the least, and it was several minutes before he could make himself heard. When the chaos died down, there was silence for a moment. Reed thought he heard a faint *tinkle* like breaking glass, but he paid it little attention. The boy was speaking again. "You heard what Michael said. We're dumped."

"What do we do?" cried a girl in the crowd.

The boy waved. "The Dorms are still here; who's going to stop us from living in them? They can't kick us out."

"But the water and power are both out," objected someone else. "That's no good."

"I say we go downtown," shouted another. "The Council got us into this; they should get us out!"

A widespread rumble of assent went up.

"Yeah! This is the Council's fault!"

"They should fix this for us!"

"It's their responsibility!"

Everyone began shouting. Reed shook his head. He didn't know where this was going, and he didn't know what to think about it. He needed a few moments of quiet to absorb it all and think it through.

No one else seemed to need any time. Momentum mounted, sparked by the accusation and fanned by the anger that swept across the Square. The confusion and chaos were swallowed up by the raging fire of a new sentiment; a scapegoat had been found. All the murmuring vanished, beaten down by the thundering drum of thousands of united voices. The crowd was chanting. *"The Council's fault! The Council's fault! The Council's fault!"*

Reed turned and surveyed the sea of angry faces. There were so many! What could any of them do now? Their world had fallen out from under them in one day.

He caught sight of a lone figure streaking away from the Square and away from the city. He had a vague suspicion who it was but didn't have long to reflect.

At that moment, there was a terrifying roar from the east side of the Square. Reed spun around and froze. On the side of the Square farthest from him stood Dorm Six, its narrow front facing the crowd. Reed's eyes fell on the building just in time to see its windows vaporize before the power of a massive explosion. Time slowed. Flames and smoke shot out from the bottom-story windows. The brick walls bowed outward and then, in a curtain of fire, disintegrated with an earth-shaking roar.

The deafening explosion drowned out the screams and cries that replaced the chanting. The force from the blast swept the Square and flattened the crowd before it like a battering ram. Dust mushroomed over the Hill in a choking cloud as glass, brick, concrete, wood, steel, and tile rained down thicker than hail. For what seemed an eternity—an awful eternity—the world turned upside down.

The shower of debris ceased. The rocking earth righted and stilled as the last echo of the explosion died away. There was absolute silence. Dazed, Reed rose to his feet and looked around him. A thick haze of smoke, dust, and ash hung in the air. Where Dorm Six had once stood, there was only a pile of rubble with an occasional flame licking upward. The trees near the site were blasted of their leaves and blackened on one side. All the windows of the other Dorms facing the Square had been blown out.

The other teenagers were getting up now, staring about them in silent shock. Many bled from gashes on their faces and arms. Not a word was spoken by anyone for a moment. Then a wail rose from one of the girls. "They're trying to kill us!"

Her cry was joined by others. "The Council did it! They want to murder us all!"

"They don't want us to use the Dorms again!"

"This was their plan all along!"

The boy who had read Michael's note leapt back up onto his flowerbed, gripping his forearm with a gory hand. "See what they've done?" he shouted. "They dragged us here, and now they're trying to destroy us! Are we going to stand for that?"

"No!" The angry cry echoed back as one voice.

"No, we're not!" the boy yelled. "We won't be slaughtered like cattle! We won't be duped again! We won't let them get away with it!"

The crowd responded with an unintelligible roar.

"There's only one thing they'll understand: make them pay! *Let's go get 'em!*" He flung his blood-covered arm toward the city and jumped down from his platform.

In a deafening uproar, the mob—for such it had become—broke from the Square and poured over the Hill like a raging waterfall, surging onto the road down toward the city below.

The last of the furious mass streamed away, and their roar faded into the distance. Reed was left alone on the Square. Those teens were not the same friends he had left that morning. They were ferocious, out-of-control animals. Something terrible had transformed them in a few short hours. It was betrayal, anger, and the hopeless loss of everything they loved. It was the unleashed rebellion that had been simmering since the beginning. Woe to the Chairman and the Council now!

Reed, dazed, dragged his eyes over the empty Square. Empty? Not quite. Amidst the thick litter of timbers, brick, chunks of concrete, and broken furniture, there were bodies, dozens of them. They lay where they had fallen—broken, twisted, unmoving. With a rush of horror, he realized that not everyone had escaped with only cuts and bruises.

He dropped down to the nearest form and felt for signs of life.

There were none. He moved to the next and stopped. It was Allie. She wasn't breathing. He realized then that none of them were. There was not a single cry or groan, not a movement in the entire Square. He stood up and stared about him. He knew many of them. There, off to the left, was Sam lying on his back. Poor, foolish Sam. He had loved the Dorms, but they had destroyed him in the end. Reed suddenly understood how Elijah had seen him the whole time.

Elijah! Reed had completely forgotten. He was supposed to meet him at the Gorge hours ago. One glance at the sun, hanging red through the smoke, told him it was growing late. Lucy must be there already. With a last look around him, Reed snatched up his backpack and ran out of the Square.

Down the North Stairs, across the Mushroom parking lot, through a maze of sidewalks, out onto the country road, Reed did not slow his pace until he reached the creek that marked where he was to turn off into the woods. He stopped to catch his breath and looked back the way he had come.

The Hill was still partially shrouded in a dusty haze, the Dorms jutting out of it like an ancient ruin. From the city, billows of smoke swelled up from what he guessed was downtown. Elijah had been right. Woe to anyone caught in the Council's headquarters that day!

Further to the right, another dark, swirling pillar towered into the sky. Reed knew that area well. It was the Boulevard or, rather, it had been. Apparently, the mob's wrath knew no bounds. Before nightfall, the whole city would probably go up in flames.

He took a last look at the spreading darkness, inky black in the red rays of the dying sun, then turned his back on the scene and plunged into the woods.

CHAPTER 37

⁕

R eed ran as fast as he could, tearing through the underbrush and branches of the forest. He stopped once or twice when he thought he heard faint popping noises somewhere in the distance, but his pounding heart was all that thundered in his ears. The woods were quiet.

He slowed his pace. Here, in the peaceful forest, the horror of what he had just lived through fell away, forgotten, and he could breathe, taste, smell again. He didn't feel the desperation and the rush anymore. The sunlight was golden and pure as it trickled through the trees, untainted by smoke. The quiet rustle of leaves in a late afternoon breeze was the only sound. He relaxed. Elijah had said he would not leave without him. Once he explained why he was late, the others would understand. He took a few deep breaths and began to enjoy his walk.

At last, he heard the murmur of running water. He was nearing the Gorge. A few steps later, he broke out of the trees into the familiar clearing and stopped dead.

At the foot of the gentle, green rise, two figures lay on the turf. He recognized both in an instant. One he knew by the hair and clothing. Hunter lay face down in the grass, unmoving. The other, on his side with his face averted, was Gabe. A pistol lay between them.

As he stood there, Gabe coughed and groaned. Instantly, Reed was at his side, rolled him onto his back, and raised his head in his arms.

"Gabe! Gabe, can you hear me?"

The young man snapped his eyes open. "Reed!" he gasped. "Where's Lucy?"

"I thought she was here."

"No, no, she left. She went looking..." Gabe broke off and coughed again. Reed glanced down and saw that Gabe's left hand, blood oozing between the fingers, was pressed to his upper abdomen. Reed lifted it, and his breath caught. He put the hand back. "Gabe, listen, you're going to be okay."

Gabe shook his head jerkily. "No—no, I'm not. But, Reed, you have to know. Elijah, he..."

"What? Where is he?"

Gabe, in obvious pain, squeezed his eyes shut. "He's... he's dead. The guy shot him, and he fell. He fell into the Gorge!" The sentence ended in a gasping sob.

Dead? Elijah? It couldn't be! Reed could only stare at Gabe in disbelief. "No!"

"Yes," Gabe choked out. Each word seemed to take an agonizing effort. "I came here after the explosion—was going to meet him. I heard voices and came up slowly. He..." He jerked toward Hunter's form, "he had 'Lijah backed up against the Gorge. He had a gun; I jumped him, but I was too late. One second too late! He fired just as I hit him. 'Lijah fell over the edge. He's gone!"

Reed felt like his lungs were collapsing.

Gabe went on, half-crying. "We wrestled for the gun. It went off and got me. But—but I won. Reed, I was too late!"

Reed leaned over him, thrusting aside his own feelings. "You can't blame yourself, Gabe! You couldn't help it."

Gabe rolled his head. "But what if... maybe I could have gotten here sooner or found the ringer or..." He broke off suddenly. Grabbing Reed's shoulder with his free hand, Gabe pulled himself up and fixed his eyes, intense and penetrating, on Reed's face. "Reed, tell me the absolute truth: *did you do it?*"

"No, Gabe! I swear it!" A tear trickled down Reed's cheek. "I wasn't ever the ringer! *I wasn't!* But I found out who was. And you... you took him out just now. That's him over there."

A look of utter relief washed over Gabe's face, and he sank back.

"I got him," he breathed. "I got him!"

Reed could hardly speak. "But, Gabe... Gabe, I'm so sorry!"

"No, Reed, *I'm* sorry. Don't say another word. I suspected you! I accused you, I was unkind, I was so wrong!"

"Forget it, Gabe." Reed mastered himself. "It's okay. I was suspicious. You were only doing your job."

"But—but we could have been friends... all this time," Gabe breathed softly. His voice was getting weaker.

"We still can be," Reed whispered, taking Gabe's free hand in his own. "We are."

Gabe looked into Reed's face and gripped his hand tightly. "Yes—yes, we are. But not... not for long. I'm going, Reed."

"Then go, Gabe," Reed said gently. He hardly knew where the words came from. "Go and sleep in peace... brother."

Gabe smiled slightly and let his eyes drift closed. "Brother," he said softly. "Brother."

"Goodbye, Gabe."

Reed had seen death before, but he had never seen someone actually die. Perhaps it was always like this, or perhaps it was different for Gabe. Reed never knew exactly when it happened, for it wasn't an "ending" like he would have thought. It was a passing. Reed had heard of someone's spirit departing, and that was what he saw. It was strangely sweet and awesome. Gabe sank away, slipped away, slept. Gabe was gone.

When he knew for sure that it was over, he laid Gabe's head back onto the grass and placed the hand, still gripping his own, by his side. Then he rose and walked up the slope to the point overlooking the Gorge. He stood at the edge, staring down at the dark, swirling waters below. The current was deep and smooth, flowing on—ceaselessly on and on. In his mind, Reed saw the dandelion falling, falling and spinning down to dark water, its yellow crown for an instant on the surface, and then it was gone—sucked down and gone forever. His sorrow overwhelmed him, and he fell to his knees, crying silently and uncontrollably.

How long he remained there like that he never knew. The dark water swirled on; his tears fell onto the grass and down into the current. The rest of the world ceased to be, or perhaps it simply went on and left him and that clearing behind in a still capsule in time, like water flowing around a rock.

In that moment, though he hardly knew what was happening, something in Reed ceased to exist and something else began. There, on the green cliff above the dark river in the quiet woods, a new Reed was born. In an encounter with the all-powerful, all-loving God, the old burned away, leaving a strange new gift in its place. After a whole lifetime, Reed knew peace. The prayer of Elijah was answered.

At last, Reed let his eyes drop down to the grass beside him and caught a faint gleam. There was blood on the turf, deep crimson and, in between the darkened blades, something glistened. Reed reached down and lifted it. A silver chain draped over his fingers, dangling a green leaf pendant. There was only one like it in the world. Somehow, Elijah had dropped it as he stood there, perhaps intentionally. The clasp was unbroken.

Reed held it in his hands, gazing at it. It was not a thing to be taken lightly, not a thing to be trifled with. The meaning it had for Elijah still held true—both meanings. It was a weighty thing to accept. Reed hesitated, then slipped the chain around his neck.

He rose and walked heavily back down the slope to the edge of the clearing. What now? There was Gabe to be taken care of, and Hunter, and... no, there was no Elijah. No Elijah anymore. Reed sat down on a log and buried his face in his arms.

A hand touched his shoulder. He looked up and saw Lucy, her eyes red and her face streaked with tears, standing over him. He had almost forgotten about her. "Lucy. You're here. He said you went looking for me. Elijah..."

"I know, Reed. Gabe told me before he sent me to find you." Her voice was thick with the effort to hold in what must have been raging inside. "But I wasn't here. I missed... Elijah, for one last time."

Her restraint burst like a dam before a swollen flood, and the turbulent waters poured out—trauma, shock, grief. She covered her face, and her shoulders shook with wracking sobs.

He looked down, fighting to keep his own husky voice calm. "Then you know he waited for me. I was late and now... he's gone."

"No, Reed!" She sat down beside him, her own tears still streaming but her sobs held back in an effort to comfort him. "You can't blame yourself! He wanted to wait for you. He knew the danger, but he still wanted to. He wanted you to come. He... he loved you."

Her voice softened as she said the words, and she broke off, overwhelmed by her emotions. Reed said nothing. He could not.

Lucy cried silently for a moment, her tears falling into a sorrowful dew on the fresh blades of grass. Then a new thought seemed to rouse her. Taking a breath, she spoke again. "But, Reed, even now, he's not really gone. He never will be! That's why Elijah was so special. His spirit will never die, Reed, never, because he had something that no monster with a gun can end. It outlasts everything, even death. He had... Jesus."

Reed swallowed. "I know. And now... now I do, too, thanks to him." He looked up and met her eyes squarely. "He said God would make it all clear to me and bring it together, and he was right. I believe."

"Reed, do you mean... Oh, that's wonderful!" Her face lit with joy even through her tears. "I'm so happy! And I know he would be, too."

"Yes, he would. He was the one who showed me. He prayed for me." Reed's voice broke. "Oh, Lucy! He was my... my..."

"I know," she whispered. A tear ran down her cheek. "He was mine, too."

They sat for a moment with only the faint swish of the water breaking the silence. Reed heaved a deep sigh. "So now what? What do we do?"

"Do?" She wiped her eyes. "You still have to get out of here."

"Leave?" He was surprised. "But why? The Council doesn't exist anymore."

She fixed her eyes on him. "*It* might no longer exist, but the power behind it still does. And until the day that power is gone, it will pursue you, Reed. Satan hates you, and he will try to destroy you. You have to be expecting it."

Reed frowned. "So I'm running away?"

"No! That's not what I meant. I mean you should understand that's what's going on, but you have to leave because... maybe because you're being called to go."

"Called?"

"Yes! We've all felt since the beginning that God had big plans for you. Think what you've experienced! Everybody out there wants to find true stability and hope; they need someone to show them the way. We're all called to do that. Don't you see? You can help them, Reed! You understand what they're feeling, and you know what they need."

Reed reflected for a moment. Lucy's words awakened something in him, something that had stirred once before. It grew like a flame. slowly, but strong and unquestionable. With it came a whisper in his heart, the echo of a familiar revelation.

Just like me.

It was an echo from the shooting, when he had suddenly longed to help his hurting fellow teens. He was needed. He had escaped the collapse, but others had not. They were out there everywhere—hopeless, helpless, hungering. He stood up. "I... I need to go home."

She rose as well. "Back to California?"

He nodded. "It's a long way, but... I think that's what I'm supposed to do." He turned and looked at her. "But what about you? What are you going to do now?"

She swept her eyes over the clearing. "I've got to let the others know what happened. I'll send Matt to get them. I'll need the guys' help with Gabe. We'll bury him here; it's so lovely." She wiped a tear from her cheek. "They can decide what to do with the other one."

"And after that?"

She met his eyes. "I'll go where He calls me. You have your purpose, and I have mine. I don't think I'll stay here, though. None of us will. We'll probably scatter."

Her eye fell on the pendant dangling on his chest, and she caught her breath. He followed her gaze.

"I found it in the grass," he said quietly. "He dropped it... somehow."

She reached out and touched it. "I think he'd want you to have it," she said softly. "Do you know what it means?"

"I do. That's why I put it on."

"Then wear it like he did. It's very special."

"I'll always remember him."

"So will I. But you need to go. I don't know what this place is going to be like tomorrow. You have to get out of here tonight."

Reed nodded. "But where will I go? I mean, how will I get there?"

"If God wants you there, He'll get you there. Trust Him and don't worry. There's a network of Christians all over the country. Go to them. They can help you get wherever you need to be."

"But…" he was having a hard time expressing what he was feeling. "Will I see you again?"

She smiled. "God only knows, Reed. We might not find each other again in this life, but we know we will in the next. I'll pray for you."

"Then… then goodbye, Lucy. I'll miss you." He swallowed. This was difficult. He had never realized before just how beautiful she was.

Lucy caught his hand. "Goodbye, Reed. I'll miss you, too. God be with you."

With a final, lingering look over the clearing, Reed picked up his backpack and turned into the woods. He looked back once and saw Lucy standing where he left her, her blonde hair gently tossing in the evening breeze. She waved a hand in farewell, then the trees and shadows swallowed her from view.

He turned back to the way before him and squared his shoulders. He didn't know what lay ahead, but he had a purpose, and he knew peace for the first time. He was ready to take it on. As he broke out of the trees and set his course westward, Reed lifted the chain around his neck and slipped the pendant inside his shirt. Settling into a steady pace, he took a deep breath. The sun had set, but the air was warmly soft, the hills were green, and the sky overhead was clear in the twilight. It was the beginning of high summer.

Reed could feel the pendant riding against his chest as he walked and thought of Elijah. He always would; he could never forget him—him or the days he had known him—days when everything had changed.

Far ahead, just where the last bit of fleeing day met the oncoming night, a star, silver and brilliant, glimmered in the West.